Stories *from the* Porch

Roger L. Guffey

Charleston, SC
www.PalmettoPublishing.com

Stories from the Porch

Paperback ISBN: 978-1-64990-261-0

ACKNOWLEDGEMENTS

Writing a book requires the assistance of many more people than the author. I have had the good fortune to know several folks who have been instrumental in my writing this book. I want to thank my editors, Joseph Hayse and David Miller, who patiently reread the manuscript several times to catch errors. I assume responsibility for any errors in the book. I am also grateful to Alan Moorer, Susan Wilson, Margaret Jones, and Joy Jerkatis who offered advice and encouragement while I was writing the book.

TABLE OF CONTENTS

A PENNY FOR YOUR THOUGHTS

Quadruple coronary bypass surgery had saved my mother's life in the winter of 1994 and, after a suitable recuperative respite, she resumed her life of cooking and keeping house for herself, my dad and my brother Jack and his wife Doris. Unbeknownst to us at the time, one consequence of bypass surgery is a gradual decline in mental function. Doctors think this decline is a result of being under general anesthesia while on the heart lung machine for too long. Within a few months, we began to notice little lapses that we naively dismissed as a symptom of getting older.

As a single man teaching high school in Lexington, I could go home as much as I liked. On one of these visits, Dad confided in me as we sat drinking coffee at the kitchen table.

"Johnny, I'm worried about your mother."

"Why? She seems fine to me."

"Well, you have to be here to see it. She still gets around pretty good — better than before her operation. But I'm noticing things."

"Like what?"

Dad scooted his chair closer to me, lowered his voice before continuing, "Now, I don't want to scare you, but I think she's starting to lose her mind a little. She forgets things. The other day, I noticed that she kept checking on the eggs she was boiling for dinner. She must have made ten trips to the stove to see if they was boiling. I thought the burner might be out so I went over to check on it. She had forgot to turn the stove on."

I reassured him, "I did that a couple of weeks ago. I was baking a cake for church potluck and I forgot to turn the oven on. "

"There's been other stuff. Ina Jean stopped by Friday and I don't think your mom remembered her name."

He paused. "I can't be here all day. I'm still working the logging woods. I leave at six and don't get back til four."

"Daddy, maybe you should quit. You're nearly eighty. Maybe time to hang it up."

Dad bristled, "I have worked my whole life and I ain't going to stop till I die or they make me quit. I like my job and I'm keeping them in more logs than they can handle."

"Well, I get that, but still, I don't know what else you can do. Jack is working in his shop and he can't stop to take care of her. The rest of us are still working."

"You may be right. I'll quit if she gets worse."

II

As I drove back to Lexington, I thought about how hard mom's life had been. Ora Cooper, was born to Frank and Aggie Cooper in a small log house in Tuggle Hollow fifteen miles out of Monticello, Kentucky, on August 7, 1919. Like most folks in Wayne County, the family struggled to survive by subsistence farming. Grandpa Cooper tended a small tobacco base, hunted opossums and raccoons for their pelts, and dug ginseng plants to supplement their meager income. While she was a toddler, Mom contracted smallpox and was given up as dead before she somehow found an inner spirit to wrestle at least a draw, at best a small victory, over the pestilence. Her beautiful young face would bear the pockmarks the rest of her life.

She was still a small girl when the family moved out of Tuggle Hollow to a house at Powersburg, Kentucky, that would later belong to her Uncle Stanley and Ella Mae Cooper. She walked a mile and a half to the Jennings Hollow School before dropping out after sixth grade.

When she was twelve, her parents managed to buy her a toy doll that she balanced on her knee in the sole photograph of her childhood. In the photograph, her eyes are dark and as empty as the broken panes in an abandoned house. Her hard, Spartan life had beaten any joy out of her soul.

A baby brother, Rueben, joined the family when she was sixteen but, growing weary of babysitting, she married Grady Coffey when she was seventeen in 1936. Dad was a hard worker who moved the new couple to the vast rich farmlands outside Decatur, Illinois, where they could survive during the Great Depression. They had three children before moving back to Kentucky in 1943, where Mom gave birth to their youngest four children.

By the time I arrived on the scene, clouds of fear, dread and exhaustion gripped her life and very soul. The only hint of vitality I ever saw in her joyless eyes was when she was caring for her pets she loved so dearly or when we were all home for Christmas.

In many ways, Mom lived for Christmas. Dad's sister, Aunt Ruby, taught her how to be a superior cook and she took refuge from the harsh realities of her mundane life by cooking three meals a day for her family. While my family was never as dirt poor as her life before she married, neither were we Rich Uncle Pennybags in the Monopoly Games. She and Dad somehow scrimped, saved and bargained so that each of us found some gifts under our red cedar tree every Christmas.

After the older children had married and started their own families twenty-five of us would crowd into our home and gather around a huge cherry table my dad had made from a single enormous tree he had bought from a neighbor. Mom was most in her glory when she would get up at five a.m. and begin cooking the turkey and fixings, pies, biscuits, and cakes to feed her growing family.

Mom was never one to wear costly jewelry, perfume or any dress fancier than a simple house dress, so every year we five sons had no idea of what to give her for Christmas. In retrospect, I see how cruel we were to buy her kitchen appliances: toasters, mixers, crockpots and electric knives, gifts she treasured as much as strings of pearls because she could use them to feed the family she loved so much.

Warm memories of past Christmases made me smile, but Dad's comments nagged at me. I vowed to go home more often to see for myself to see if he had reason for concern.

III

Within a few more visits, I realized that mother's mental decline was accelerating. Finally, I decided to talk to Dad about what to do. As we sat at the table drinking coffee, he confided, "Johnny, it's getting worse. Look there. You see that black ring in the rug? Last week, she was cooking dinner and went off and left a skillet of grease on the stove. It caught fire and she tried to take it outside. It burnt her hand and she dropped it on the floor there. Lucky, I was in the front room and heard the commotion. I smothered the fire and got the skillet outside. It would've burned the house down."

He sipped his coffee and continued. "Two days ago, I found she had put dirty dishes away without washing them. She forgot to feed the cats and dogs yesterday. I've started cooking because I'm afraid to leave her alone in the kitchen. I cook a lot of hamburgers on that George Foreman grill. Jack calls them the O'Grady burgers. "

He sighed heavily. "I've got no choice. I'm going to quit work next week."

"That's probably the best thing to do. What does she do all day?"

"Jack bought her some coloring books and she spends the day coloring or drawing little pictures. Plays with her dogs. Breaks green beans. She can peel potatoes with a peeler. I won't let her have a knife. Watches 'Price Is Right'. I have to watch the mail because I caught her buying a lot of stuff through the mail. Jack found some envelopes with money in them, but he took them before she could send them."

After draining his coffee cup, he added, "You know that big piggy bank setting in the front room? Last week, she dumped it onto the dining room table sorting through the piles of coins. She was trying to read the dates on some of them. Of course, even with her glasses she could barely see them. Every once in a while, she'd ask me what year was on a penny. Hell, I could barely see them. I remembered we had a magnifying glass somewhere, and I found it for her. She spent the rest of the day going through the pennies. And after all that, she just put the money back in the bank."

I sighed. "I know it's hard on you, Daddy. You know what they say. 'Once a man, twice a child.' Mom is showing signs of dementia. Or even Alzheimer's. We just have to watch her."

"Johnny, I can't take care of her. I heard there is a place up town where older people can go and stay during the day. I think they call it adult daycare. Raeburn Burke drives a bus and picks people up in the morning and then brings them back. You think they'll take her?"

"You might as well ask. All they can say is no. You want me to call for you?"

"I was hoping you'd do that for me. I ain't told the other kids."

"Well, if any of them complain, tell them the alternative is for them to take care of her."

Within a few minutes, I had made arrangements for Mom to spend her days at the Adult Daycare Center so Daddy could have the time free to work on his truck or help Jack in his cabinet shop.

IV

The other children agreed that sending Mom to the daycare home was the best thing. Realizing that our parents were getting more helpless, we all decided that we would spend Christmas with them. Daddy still insisted on buying all of us presents. On Christmas morning, he gave each of us a new comforter set, all exactly the same. As we thanked him, Mom's eyes twinkled.

"Now I want to give you my presents."

Daddy sat back in his chair. "What are you talking about? I never took you shopping."

Mom replied, "You didn't have to. Just wait here."

She went back to her bedroom and returned with seven envelopes decorated with small Christmas bows. Her face beamed with a glow of delight as she started reading the envelopes and passing them out.

"Otis, 1937. Sally, 1939. Charlie, 1941. Now hold on. Leonard, 1945, Judy 1952, Johnny, 1955, Jackie, 1958. I went through the big piggy bank and found each one of you a penny that was made in the year you were born. MERRY CHRISTMAS!"

We sat dumbfounded, struggling to keep from crying as we watched Mom in her moment of triumph. As we had feared, her mind and body had begun to succumb to the ravages of Alzheimer's. That would be the last Christmas we would all be home.

V

Dad developed chest pains that the doctor diagnosed as the symptoms of heart disease. In 2000, he came to Lexington for coronary bypass surgery. He had a pathological fear of general anesthesia, and as fate would have it, he had a stroke during the surgery that destroyed his brain above the brainstem. Since his vitals were normal, we did not know the extent of the damage until the surgeon ordered an EEG that showed no higher brain function. We agreed that he would not want to be alive in that condition and we removed life support; he died two days later.

Mom's mental and physical state continued to deteriorate; she became increasingly recalcitrant and combative, even assaulting Jack and Doris as they tried to take care of her. She had indeed entered her second childhood, showing only short flashes of mental competence until she passed away in 2004.

EPILOGUE

All the pennies Mom had given us except Jack's were "Wheat Pennies" whose obverse showed a right-side profile of Abraham Lincoln. The penny is the only American coin in which the president is facing right: that was purely the personal choice of Victor D. Brenner who designed it in 1909. Until 1956, the reverse side bore two ears of durum wheat, to commemorate the bumper crop of wheat in the United States in 1909. In 1956, the mint changed the reverse side to feature the Lincoln Memorial; a close observer can even see his statue between two of the columns.

Wheat pennies have become the most collected coin produced by the United States Mint. Some vintages are extremely rare. During World War II, the mint diverted most of the copper supply to the war effort and produced steel coins for the 1943 mintage. The government estimates that only forty 1943 copper pennies were ever minted and they are extremely valuable. When one last appeared on the numismatic market, the buyer paid over $200,000 for it.

From time to time, I find a wheat penny and squirrel it away in a special box. On Christmas Eves, I sit in my recliner holding a small golden frame that displays my 1955 copper penny Mom gave me. As the snow settles softly onto the frozen ground, I listen to Mannheim Steamroller's version of Silent Night, remembering Christmases past, and wondering what my penny is worth.

SUFFER THE LITTLE CHILDREN TO COME UNTO ME

On Sunday, June 28, 1914, Leopold Lojka, the Czech man driving the car for the Archduke Franz-Ferdinand and his wife Sophie as they toured Sarajevo, Serbia, misunderstood the directions for the tour and took a wrong turn. The royal couple had already survived assassination attempts, but fate caught up with them on that portentous date when the wrong turn placed them squarely in the sights of Gavrilo Princip, a Serbian national obsessed with ending the Austro-Hungarian rule of Bosnia and Herzegovina, who shot and killed them both. As he was only nineteen at the time, he was not eligible for the death penalty, so his captors incarcerated him in hellish conditions where he contracted skeletal tuberculosis and died in 1918.

The tragic upshot of his heinous crime was to start the First World War that engulfed Europe and the United States until November 11, 1918. How could anyone have predicted that the fallout from that single precipitous murder would have played out in a remote one room school house in the backwoods of Kentucky?

As horrible as the violence, brutality and carnage of war is, warfare typically has epidemic disease as a traveling companion and in this case, that epidemic became a pandemic, the Spanish Flu of 1918-1919 that would kill as many as 100 million people worldwide. In those days, transcontinental troop movements relied on huge passenger ships where soldiers huddled together in the stagnant miasma of poorly ventilated quarters that spread the airborne diseases with every breath. When American troops returned home after the war, they brought this grim specter of death and other deadly diseases, such as rubella, or German measles as the hill folks called them, back to the states. Once the troops disembarked from their ships and dispersed to their homes across the United States, the virulent pathogens carried in their bodies broke free of their flesh and blood hosts and infected millions of Americans from the largest cities to the edges of civilization in the Appalachian Mountains.

No one can ever be sure who brought the rubella to rural Kentucky, let alone the small community of Hidalgo twenty miles from the county seat at Monticello, but once the viruses were let loose, they sliced through their community as easily and unrelentingly as a hot knife through softened butter. In the days before immunizations and antibiotics, the cruel scythe of rubella viciously attacked the home of John and Emerine (who went by the name of Mary) Guffey leaving eight orphaned children in its wake: Marie, Lee, Melvin, William, Newt, Daniel, Phillip, and Abigail. In those days in the hinterlands of a perpetually impoverished and isolated state like Kentucky, there were no orphanages or social services to rescue and place the children into foster homes so the benevolent good Christian neighbors congregated at the Guffey home and took the hapless children under their wings and into the warmth of their hearths to rear as their own. Their ancestral farm was sold and the proceeds were divvied up equally to the families who adopted the orphans.

When Elijah and Thelma Asberry saw the three-year old twin daughters, Marie and Lee, their hearts embraced them and, fearing the long-term effects of separating twins at such an early age, agreed to adopt both girls and raise them in a God-fearing, loving Christian home, even going so far as allowing the girls to retain their family surname, Guffey.

So, on a bright spring morning, the girls moved into their new home at Windy, Kentucky, fifteen miles from Monticello. Lige Asberry, as his friends knew him, owned a small farm off of Kentucky Highway 1009, where he survived as a subsistence farmer who grew most of the crops and livestock to feed his growing family and somehow managed to raise half an acre of burley tobacco that provided a stipend of money to fund the Christmases that brought joy to all of his children: Ralph, Silas, Mary, EllaMae and perhaps some balm of Gilead to assuage the pain of the newest additions, Marie and Lee Ann.

Though Lige and Thelma could only more or less read and write and do simple ciphers, they, like so many other poor farmers who had grown weary of the harsh unforgiving yoke of subsistence farming, dared to have bigger dreams for their children, especially Marie and Lee, as if by some Providential and compensatory calculus, they had already paid their dues with the loss of their biological parents. With more than a hundred schools scattered across the county, every small community had one-room school houses within easy walking distances of up to three miles of the children's homes.

Within the confines of those white, slat-boarded schools, a single teacher supervised and taught all the children whose parents permitted them to attend in the dead times of the agricultural way of life that dictated every hour, every day, every month of every year. This teacher had to be gifted with a huge dollop of patience, empathy, humility and forgiveness as well as the academic fields of reading, writing, arithmetic and, eventually, history geography, and citizenship. From July to February, the time when farm work was largely laid by, save tobacco stripping, students pored over worn copies of McGuffey Readers and the King James Bible, learned to read simple passages that taught some good Christian virtues like love, charity, humility and salvation of the eternal souls. For an hour or so each day, the students learned to count, add, subtract, multiply and divide two digit, and, sometimes, multi-digit numbers, as well as how many pecks in a bushel of corn, how many acres in a field and a plethora of other unit conversions deemed necessary to survive in their world.

The number of children in each grade dwindled slowly from first grade to eighth grade because most of the young boys abandoned their schooling to devote themselves to farming, lumber mills, and sharecropping. The girls got married and started families as early as age fourteen. Perhaps, Lige and Thelma came to believe that the twins entrusted to them deserved loftier goals than farming and baby making. No doubt that belief was bolstered by the proximity of Windy High School, one of only three high schools in the county; the others at Mill Springs to the north and Parmleysville at the extreme eastern edge of the county near the South Fork River which bordered the newly formed McCreary County.

When the twins had mastered all there was to master in their one room school, Lige and Thelma sat them down at the kitchen table and discussed their futures with them.

Lige cleared his throat and began. "Marie, Lee, you've come as far as you need to in school to build your own lives, but your mother and me want more for you. Maybe we ain't your ma and pa.... maybe that is why we want more for you, but if you want to continue your schooling, we would be happy to help. We still have your shares of the money from selling your dad's farm. You can go on to Windy High School and if you do good there, maybe you can go on to college."

He paused to purse his lips and knit his brow, "Ain't nobody around here ever been to college so we ain't no help to you but maybe you could become teachers. I know Doc Powers said it took him ten years to become a doctor and he don't hold out much hope for you girls becoming doctors but people are always needing school teachers. You both have got real good grades in school and Odell Campbell tells me that you are both smart enough to go to college so if you want to go, we'll try to help you. Now you have to decide what you want."

Both Marie and Lee were beside themselves with joy. They had loved school, learning all about the new places and things they could only dream of seeing or doing and the recommendation of their teacher, Mr. Campbell, sent their hopes and souls soaring. They squealed their excitement at the opportunity to continue their education and agreed to work for pay to get new clothes to attend the Windy High School.

In due time, they graduated from Windy High School and used their shares of their inheritances to enroll in the Eastern Kentucky State Normal School and Teacher College at Richmond. Now Richmond, Kentucky, is not by any stretch of the imagination a cosmopolitan oasis, but for the two young girls it may have well been Paris, France. Though they were only fraternal twins, they both had very small statures, four feet, eight inches, but within those small bodies were fireballs of determination, finely honed warriors who resolved to grab life by its throat, and wrest as bright a future as possible for themselves.

Both girls excelled in college and in four short years, they graduated certified to teach first grade to high school. After graduation, Marie married Guy Blevins in 1938 and taught grades one through eight at the Dry Hollow School; Lee Ann taught the same grades at Sandy Valley. Both women migrated between other one-room schools as attendance waxed and waned across the county.

In May of 1955, the superintendent of Wayne County Schools, Ira Bell, sent word to Marie at Sunnybrook School to come to his office to discuss her placement for the coming school year.

In and of itself, this was not unusual as teachers were regularly shifted between communities; in some cases, teachers had to ride horses or mules to their new assignments. Automobiles were still largely luxuries unattainable on a teacher's salary. But by scrimping and saving, Marie's husband, Guy Blevins, had squirreled away enough money to buy her a car, a 1951 Ford car, so she could be spared the indignity of hitchhiking or riding a horse side-saddle to reach her school.

When she entered the outer office of Ira Bell, the superintendent of schools, his secretary Eleanor Keeton, ushered her into his office. He rose to greet her.

"Good morning, Marie. It's always a pleasure to see you. You're looking well. How's Lee?"

"She's fine. This is her seventeenth year at Sandy Valley unless she's being reassigned."

"Oh no, she's very well-known and respected there. All the kids love her so I don't see her going anywhere else for quite a while. Please sit down."

Marie nodded and took a seat in the cane-bottomed chair. Bell sat down in his leather rolling chair, pulled the chair closer to the desk and leaned over the desk to take Marie by her dainty hands.

"Now, Marie, you and Lee are both respected and are two of the finest teachers I have ever known. But something's come up and we need to address it as soon as possible.:

He drew a long breath and leaned back, "There's a lot going on in the world now, stuff that maybe you know about and maybe you don't. Well, there's this case before the United States Supreme Court that deals with public school education…has to do with the coloreds. This here case, Brown vs Board of Education of Topeka, Kansas, was argued before the Supreme Court and they decided that having separate schools for coloreds and whites was unconstitutional. Starting this year, schools have to be integrated. Teaching the colored kids in the same schools as the white kids. Now we have a perfectly good colored school, Travis School at Frazier, but we have some colored kids who live too far away to go there."

As an astute and observant teacher, Marie had learned to anticipate what to expect. "So, I guess what you're telling me is that you want me to teach in one of these schools."

Bell lowered his head and nodded slightly. "Well, there's actually only one such school. Yes, that's why I called you in. When word came down that I needed to find a teacher, I immediately thought of you. Now here's the rub."

He took a deep breath. "There's a colored family, the Stonewalls, out at Griffin who want to send their kids to school. They're refusing to let us bus their kids to the Travis School when there's a perfectly good school right there where they live. The thing is the teacher there quit when she found out she was going to have to teach the coloreds. That was not the way she put it, but we can't call them niggers anymore."

Marie nodded slightly, more out of politeness than approval. Bell continued, "So under the law, we got no choice ... we have to provide a school where colored and whites can both go. Now, as you know, most of the colored live up around Frazier...... the Cowans, the Allens, the Browns ... and they're all happy at the Travis School. There's some more coloreds,.. I think their name is Coyle around your old stomping grounds...live up on a mountain around Harmon Holler, but I don't think they're too keen on going to school anyway. I hear that the folks teach them enough to get by and it is not like they will ever amount to much anyway. Probably just be farmers... they stay pretty much to themselves."

He drew himself up straight and continued, "From what I can find out, this Stonewall family —daddy's name is Clark Stonewall — has been homeschooling their kids but they've reached their limit. There's six kids, ranging from six to fifteen....and I think there are fifty-three white kids who go to school there.

Before you turn me down, let me tell you a little bit about the job. Do you know where Griffin is?"

"I have heard of it...seems like it is way out near the South Fork River...around Parmleysville."

"I'll be blunt. It is so far back in the sticks you have to wipe the hoot owl crap off the clock to see what time it is. Pardon my French. We are talking way the hell on the other side of the world. Pardon my French again. I checked it on my odometer and it is about eighteen miles from town. Some of the roads are graveled and some are just muddy paths. It's south of Rocky Branch and you know how far out that is...on the McCreary County Line. There's quite a few kids who use swinging bridges to cross creeks to get to school. You got a car, don't you?"

"Yes, Guy bought me a Ford so I can get to work wherever I have to go. I have been over some pretty rough roads so I can probably get there okay."

"That's great...but now there's more stuff you need to know. The school has been let go for a while. I mean, some of those hill people out there never come to town more than once a year...if that. So, it's run down. I was out there last week checking on it. There ain't no front door and no desks or chairs. I've ordered a cast iron potbelly stove to be installed before school starts and I'll get some of the men out there to lay in a big supply of firewood and coal before winter gets here. I hope to have some blackboards put up by start of school and I am donating a desk and chair for you."

He must have seen Marie's eyes glaze over before he cooed, "Now, Marie, if you don't want to do this, I'll understand, but I have to find a teacher somewhere. I might strong arm some new teacher to do it but I would prefer to have an experienced teacher. My guess is that this little school will be in the national spotlight since this will be the first integrated school in Kentucky.... one of the first in the country. This is the wave of the future whether we like it or not. It may all blow over if things don't work out. I have to admit, I have my doubts about it. Now we don't have that many coloreds here and we all get along pretty well, but the experts are predicting this could get real ugly in the southern states...Mississippi, Alabama.... There's a lot riding on this, so your heart really has to be in this. You don't have to tell me now... just let me know by Wednesday."

Marie licked her lips and smiled, "Mr. Bell, I can give you my answer now. I'd love to teach those kids at Griffin. I know some of the colored folks around town and they're fine people. And the Supreme Court got it right... they're entitled to the same education as white kids."

Bell heaved a sigh of relief. "Oh, thank you, Mrs. Blevins, thank you. I was dreading that you would say no but now I can sleep again. I've not been able to sleep for several nights. Thank you. Now I'll try to get you whatever you need."

"Schools start on July 18 this year. So, can we at least get a front door put up, some stools and desks and get that stove put in so we won't be disturbed later on? Maybe you can put the word out and some parents and other teachers can help me scrounge around and find supplies."

"I expect a lot of folks won't like this and some will fight it tooth and nail, but like I said, this is the future of education. I imagine if I pitch this right some churches and businesses will donate pencils and paper and I can gather extra books from the other schools. The hardware store said they will give us water pails and dippers and a shovel for snow. George Huffaker said he would repair the windows so they can be raised to let fresh air in during the hot summers. The state department of education will pitch in quite a bit because if this thing all falls apart, it will make us all look bad. God, Marie, I cannot tell you how much I appreciate you doing this. And I know you'll give the kids the best education you can."

"Mr. Bell, I'm flattered that you thought of me and I'll do my level best to give these kids the best education they can get."

Marie and Superintendent Bell began collecting donations and promises of help to get the school ready by July. They managed to get some chairs and desks but had to be content with homemade benches and tables to make up the difference. Some churches gave copies of Bibles and Sunday School leaflets to teach reading, but students would need to share some of the McGuffey's Readers.

On the outside, Marie projected a sense of calm, but her insides were a knot of panic and turmoil. She had made several trips to the other schools around the county and talked to the teachers at the Travis School. The black teachers of the Travis School offered advice and support, assuring her that teaching colored kids was no different from teaching white kids. She lay awake all night on July 17th, terrified at what the next day might hold, wondering if she had made a mistake. She prayed for guidance several times, and, though her adrenaline was spiking when she arose the morning of July 18th, she felt calm enough to take on the day.

After packing some peanut butter and jelly sandwiches and a Thermos bottle of hot coffee, she kissed Guy goodbye.

Guy hugged her close and kissed her forehead. "You'll be fine. Them kids are going to love you. I'll be looking forward to hearing about it tonight. Be careful driving out there... some of them roads are rough. Be real careful on those one lane bridges. Love you."

Marie got into her car that slowly crept onto the blacktop of Highway 90 through town. On the east side of the town square, she turned east onto Kentucky 92 that snaked through Oil Valley, Barrier, past the flourmill at Coopersville before turning right onto the gravel road KY 1756. She felt her heart creeping up in her throat as she turned the curve that led to the Griffin School.

As her car glided to a stop, she surveyed the school grounds, Several white children were playing tag and a few of the older boys were sitting under a big white oak tree whittling to pass the time. The six Stonewall children sat near the coal pile cradling Fleischman's lard buckets that held their lunches. The oldest boy stood up and walked over to greet her.

"Mrs. Blevins, my name is Nelson Stonewall and these are my brothers and sisters. That is William, George, Cassie, Francine, Tommy and Loretta. We're so excited to be here to learn. Thank you for being our teacher."

Marie replied, I am very pleased to meet you, Nelson and all of your brothers and sisters. Let's all go on inside"

She pulled a large brass bell out of her oversized purse and began to ring it loudly to call the students inside. The kids hurried inside and jostled around to find seats. Marie laid her purse and paperwork on the desk. After introducing herself, she went around the room and had the children introduce themselves as she furiously wrote down their names.

Her heart was beating audibly while she searched her mental files to find something to do before an inspiration hit her.

"Okay, children, we are going to start off the new school year with a song that I know you all know. Jesus Loves the Little Children. So, follow along with me."

Her heart slowed as she motioned to begin the hymn:

Jesus loves the little children
All the children of the world
Black and yellow, red and white
They're all precious in His sight
Jesus loves the little children of the world

The children chimed in and followed along, filling the crude schoolroom with sounds of joy and delight that streamed out the windows onto the dusty, sparsely grassed over schoolyard.

So on July 18, 1955, Marie Blevins, became the first teacher in an integrated school in Kentucky and one of the first in the nation.

A new world, borne of war, disease, racism, fear, and hope had begun.

SWEAR NOT BY HEAVEN OR EARTH

When he heard the doorbell announcing a customer's entrance, Gary Morgan looked up from his paperwork in the office of the Whitley Funeral Home. He pushed his swivel chair back from the desk and went to the front foyer where sweet aromas of roses were wafting through the room. There a rough-looking man was meandering around eyeing the bouquets of gladioli and roses lining the room.

He stepped over to greet the man, "May I help?"

The man turned to face him. "Yes, is Mr. Whitley here?"

Gary extended his hand and said. "Hello, I'm Gary Morgan. No, he just stepped out for a few minutes. I think he went to the bank and post office. Would you like to wait?"

The man shook his hand and replied, "I'm Nick Slagle. Nice to meet you. I need to do a few things in town so I will do them and come back. When do you think he'll be back?"

"He should be back any minute. You are welcome to wait. Would you like a cup of coffee?"

"No, thank you, but I need to talk to Mr. Whitley Would you please tell him that Nick Slagle stopped by and I will be back later?"

"Sure, Mr. Slagle, but like I said he should be back any minute."

"No, I have to get some bean seeds and seed taters at the hardware store. I'll see him then."

Nick closed the door behind and walked briskly down the street toward the hardware store that always carried garden seed in the spring planting months. Gary returned to his desk and had just settled in when the bell rang again. It was Whitley Vaughan, the owner of the mortuary and funeral home returning from his errands. As he entered Gary's office, he asked, "Did anyone come in?"

"Yes, you just missed him, Nick Slagle. Said he would be right back. I tried to get him to wait, but he wouldn't."

"Oh, so Nick came in. I was expecting him any day. Could you pull his file, please?"

Gary nodded and flipped through the files until he found a thin manila folder with NICK SLAGLE on the tab. He pulled it out and opened it only to find a plain paper with IOU $2400 and a shaky signature Nick Slagle scrawled across it. He took the folder into Whitley's office.

"Here it is. Not much in it. An IOU."

"Yep, that's it. He'll be back soon to settle up."

Gary looked puzzled. "Is that the only paperwork we have?"

"That's all we need. He gave us his word he'd pay. I trust him."

"I guess I am not so trusting. My old boss in Cincinnati had a long contract form for these things. Frankly, he didn't look like he was good for it."

Whitley motioned for Gary to sit across from him at his desk. "Well, we do some things different around here.. at least we can for people we trust. I trust Nick to pay up."

Sensing Gary had questions, he continued, "Do me a favor. Get us some coffee and let me tell you about Nick."

Gary fetched two cups that he filled from a carafe of hot coffee. Whitley nodded as he took his cup. "Thank you, Gary. Now let me tell you Nick's story."

He stirred his coffee with a spoon and took a sip. "Nick was born over in Slickford… at least I think that is right but his family moved over to Hall Valley when he was little. Just hill people. I think his daddy's name was Sam Slagle. Mom was Anna Lee. They were just farmers and Sam worked in the logging woods driving the mule teams for Jim Perdew. Supposed to have been a real good driver."

Whitley paused to sip more coffee before adding, "Well, one day, they were trying to pull a big white oak out of a ravine and the chain came loose and broke Sam's leg. Set up gangrene and he died. I think Nick was still young...maybe ten or twelve. Now they had no money so they had to hire out as help…I think they got a little money from the state."

"So what could they do?" Gary asked.

"About all they could do was to work on farms. Nick hunted squirrels and rabbits and quail to eat. Hunted coons, possums and mink to sell their fur. They dug ginseng roots, may apples. Neighbors helped a lot.'

He took a long drink, "The thing is, Nick had epileptic seizures from time to time. He went squirrel hunting one day and had a seizure up the mountain somewhere and passed out. When he didn't come home, Anna Lee got worried and asked the neighbors to help find him. A bunch of men and boys scoured over the woods for several hours before they found him..... he was still groggy but okay otherwise."

Gary started to speak before Whitley cut him off, "So now Anna Lee started going squirrel hunting with him. They depended on hunting to live sometimes."

"You're kidding me."

"No, she would never let him go off into the woods alone again. She used to work hoeing tobacco crops with him...stripping tobacco and so on. By the time he was sixteen things started to look up some."

He finished his coffee and motioned to Gary to get him some more. Gary drained his own cup and refilled each cup before settling back.

"Well, as it turns out Nick wasn't really as stupid as people thought he was. He didn't get very far in school because he was busy working on farms. But he had helped some of the farmers who showed him how to work on tractors and such. Turns out he had a natural talent for it."

Gary raised his eyebrows. "So could he get a part time job or something?"

"Yeah, everybody knew how hard up they were so Willard Gossage and Fred Lykins hired him on to work as a grease monkey in their service stations. Used to be there were a lot of small country stores and gas stations scattered around the country and some of them offered some mechanic work. Nick could change oil, replace spark plugs, ... eventually got to where he was able to do just about any kind of work you needed."

Whitley started to drink his coffee but got choked as he started to laugh. " Damn, look at the mess I made. Get me some paper towels to clean this up. Dammit."

Gary rushed back with paper towels to wipe up the spilled coffee.

"So what was so funny?" he asked.

"It turns out that someone gave Nick an electric motor to tinker with and he got it running just fine. Took the fan off a motor and made a good fan for him and Anna Lee to keep their house cool. Now she pretty much stayed home. She started running punch boards."

"Punchboards?"

"Oh, I forget how young you are. Back in the day, people bought punchboard — Illegal as hell. They were made of cardboard and rows and columns of little round discs that you could punch out and win prizes. The prizes were usually just candy bars or cheap shit. Of course, the companies guaranteed better prizes were possible, but no one ever won one. Neighborhood kids played them, sometimes Anna Lee just sold them the candy. No one ever thought about turning them in to the law. What was the point?"

"Sorta sounds like the lottery today."

"Exactly. But back then the Baptists ruled the roost in these small rural communities and if they said something was gambling or whatever, it was the kiss of death. Now running a punchboard never harmed anyone but some of these self-righteous busybodies got them outlawed.

"But back to the fan story. The next thing you know, somebody gave Nick a propeller off a small plane. Nick got it in his head that it would make a better fan so he mounted it onto his electric motor and turned it on."

Whitley laughed loudly and slapped the desk. "Now Anna Lee was skinny as a rail so when he turned it on, the fan blew her out the back door and blew the wallpaper off the kitchen walls. All hell broke loose until finally some of the neighbors got it turned off. Everybody had a good laugh about it… lucky no one got killed. That fan could have sliced them up like hamburger."

Gary was still snickering as he imagined the chaos of the scene. "Pretty amazing he got it to work. How did he hold it?"

"Oh, he built a frame of some kind like he had seen at the garage. He was pretty good with his hands."

"I would think he could get a better job."

"The problem was that since he had epilepsy, he couldn't get a license. He would still have those seizures from time to time. Scared poor Anna Lee to death. They were too poor to afford a car, but Nick figured out a way around that."

Whitley leaned over his desk. "This is where it gets funny. Nick got it into his head that he didn't need a car because they could buy just about any groceries they needed at Willard's store. If they needed to go to town, they could get a neighbor to take them. That is what neighbors do. They only lived about a mile from the store … a mile ain't too far to walk. But Nick was determined to join the automobile age. He bought a Briggs and Stratton riding lawn mower with a twenty-horsepower motor. He took the blade off of it. They never had a yard worth mowing anyway. The next thing you know, here comes Nick Slagle going to Willard's store on his new mower with Anna Lee walking along behind him."

"Now I know you are pulling my leg," Gary scoffed.

"If I'm lying, I'm dying. People were laughing their asses off. Nick just shrugged it off. He had been laughed at before and lived to tell about it. After the initial shock, though, people started to admire his ingenuity. Who was he hurting? He took the blade off so he wasn't throwing rocks or things and he never went on the main roads anyway."

"I guess they had a point. It is funny, but I have to admit it was creative."

"It gets better. Nick felt bad that Anna Lee was having to walk so he bought an old toy wagon that had little racks from somebody.... Joe Kinnett, I think... found a big purplish couch cushion to put in it. Now Anna Lee didn't have to walk behind him anymore. She could ride in style. That twenty horsepower motor was strong enough to pull the cart.... Painted the racks bright red so people could see him. He got that thing to go over ten miles per hour.

"I bet that made people guffaw"

"Of course, but after a while everybody got used to it, just a part of the community. Once in a while he'd put that blade back on it and made money mowing some of the bigger yards. Riding mowers are not really practical for most people."

"Did anyone ever take a picture of this caravan?"

"Never heard of any.... Most people would say that is mean. And what would be the point?"

Gary shook his head and sighed, "It's a different world than I'm used to. He would have been locked up or arrested in Cincy."

"This ain't Cincy, Gary. We ain't the slick city jet set. People here are just trying to get by. Some of us may be ...I was going to say nutty, but let's go with eccentric. Most of us are pretty decent folks."

Flustered by his own indiscretions, Gary replied, "I don't mean to sound judgmental or ridicule him. But you have to admit this is funny to think about.

Whitley finished his coffee and leaned back. "Let me tell you about Nick. Oh sure, people made fun of him, but they never questioned his basic honesty and integrity. One day he and Anna Lee were coming back from the store, just tooling along like always. Turns out somebody had robbed a grocery store in town and the cops were chasing them down highway ninety. Thief tried to lose them by cutting across highway eight fifty-eight where Nick lived. Cops kept going down ninety. The getaway car clipped Nick and turned him over... threw Anna Lee into the ditch. Somehow, the bag of money fell out of the car, but the thief didn't stop…didn't want to get caught. I guess he thought he had killed Nick and Anna Lee and he didn't want to risk being charged with murder so he lit out like a bat out of hell."

"My God, were they alright?"

"Thank God, they just got scraped up and bruised. No broken bones, but Anna Lee had to use a cane for a while. Nick saw the bag of money. Over nine hundred dollars in it. Now knowing what I've told you about Nick what would most people do? Keep the money. Not Nick. He called the police and told them what had happened and gave the money back. Every nickel of it."

"Wow. Did he get a reward?"

"I think the store gave him a hundred dollars. That covered getting the damage to his mower and trailer fixed. Rear axle was all catawampus. Broke one rack. But in a few days, things were back to normal."

"That's a pretty wild story."

"I ain't finished. By now Nick was nigh unto thirty and decided he needed to get married. He started courting one of Pig-Eye Stinson's girls, Velma."

"Pig-eyed Stinson?"

"There's some families around here have a genetic condition everybody calls Pig-eye because their eyelids cover the top half of their eyes. Now people weren't trying to be mean by calling them that and no one ever took offense. I looked it up when the daddy died. He was

Jedediah Stinson. It's called droopy eyelid. Here's a new word for you, city slicker, ptosis. That's the medical word for it."

"Never heard of it. Is it dangerous?"

"Naw, you just look funny. I guess a plastic surgeon could fix it, but who can afford that? People just figured that's the way God made some people. Oh, I guess some kids might tease them, but a quick rap on the side of their heads stopped that. Any of that coffee left?"

Gary shook the carafe before draining it into Whitley's cup.

"Thank you kindly, We can make a new pot later. I have the Southwood family coming at three. Now where was I?"

"Nick was getting married."

"Oh, right. So he and Velma got married and she moved in with him and Anna Lee. Problem was Nick now had two women and only one wagon. So they took turns riding in the wagon. Velma would ride out to the store and Anna Lee would walk behind them and they switched places on the way back."

Gary shook his head slowly. "I have never heard of such a thing. It is a different world, down here, ain't it?"

"It is for a fact. Yes, indeed, it's different."

They sat in silence for a few minutes before Whitley said, "By now, living a hard life of being poor and not going to a doctor finally caught up with Anna Lee and she died in July of last year.... She wasn't that old... as I recall seventy-three. I picked the body up and handled the funeral arrangements. Helped Nick and Velma pick out a casket...something simple was all they could afford. Some of their neighbors felt sorry for them and donated money to cover expenses. That left that balance of $2400 on the IOU. Nick promised he'd pay me off when he had the money."

The front door bell rang again and Nick came in. Whitley and Gary came to the foyer to greet him.

"Well, hello, Nick, how are you?"

"I'm fine, Mr. Whitley. I'm here to pay off my debt. Here's the money."

He pulled a smudged wrinkled envelope out of his pants pocket and handed it to Whitley. "I think it's all there, but you might want to count it."

"That won't be necessary, Nick, I trust you. I am sorry about your Mom. Guess you still miss her.'

"Oh yeah, but it's getting better. Me and Velma just have the place to ourselves now. Sometimes we get lonely with the quiet and all but she's in a better place now."

"Yes, she is. I guess some day we all hope to be there. Do you need a receipt?"

"Yes, I would like one…just to remember Mom by. Could you write me one out?"

"Sure. Gary, would you make out a receipt for $2400? Make it out to Nick Slagle. And give him back the IOU."

Gary went back to the office and returned with the receipt and IOU. Whitley signed them and handed them to Nick.

"Here you go, Nick. Tell Velma hello. You catch a ride in?"

"Hershel Bell gave me a ride.…he had to come to town to get seed corn and hog feed. He's putting out two hundred acres of field corn this year. He told me that he has forty head of pigs he is finishing off so he needed a lot of feed. Thank you for everything, Mr. Whitley."

They shook hands and Nick left the parlor.

Gary returned to the main office and started to count the money in the envelope. Whitley asked, "What do you think you're doing? Didn't I tell you that he gave that stolen money back? To the grocery store?"

APOSTROPHE TO ALENE

PROLOGUE

PETRICHOR-noun- the earthy scent that results when a soft rain falls on dry dust. From the Greek petra meaning 'stone' and ichor, the fluid that flows in the veins of the gods in Greek mythology.

I

When Alvin Denney received his honorable discharge from the Army after the Korean War, he married Alene Stinson and bought forty acres, fifteen miles south of Monticello down a steep graveled road that ran past the Taylor's Grove Baptist Church were they faithfully attended Sunday School and church. The gently rolling hills provided excellent pastures for six Jersey cows and enough level ground to grow half an acre of burley tobacco.

An ordained deacon of the church, Alvin took it upon himself to keep an eye on the church's graveyard and be sure it was presentable for the annual Decoration Day in late May. Several times each year, he and Alene strolled through the cemetery to pay respects to their deceased son, Jesse.

As a veteran, Alvin could use benefits from the GI Bill to better himself so he decided to enroll in a correspondence course in oil painting. He had long enjoyed sketching the countryside and with the expert training from the course he became a highly respected landscape painter. He always entertained suggestions from Alene as to any improvements he should make.

"Alene, what do you think about this sky? Got any more of that coffee?"

She always made the best coffee..

"Why, of course I do. Pass me your cup. Now what do you want to know about that sky?"

Where did I put my boots? That one needs a new lace.

"Well, this is supposed to be a morning scene so I need some colors in the sky besides blue. Is this too pink?"

I need to wash out that Mason jar to put the flowers in.

"Hmm. Maybe just a little. Now I have seen some pretty bright pink sunsets, but mornings are a little softer. You need more cream?"

And half full of water…

"No, thank you. I think you are right. And that cloud is too big.… needs to be thinner."

Where did I put my cap? Is it with my cane?

"You are such a perfectionist. Everybody will know it is the Massengale farm."

She always likes pansies and johnny-jump-ups…

"Well, if I ain't happy with it, I ain't giving it to them. I do have a reputation to think about. What is today?"

"Friday"

"Ain't you the smart one. I meant what date."

I can't forget a peony and some iris.

"May fourth. Why?"

"I promised to have this done by the eighth. I had better get busy."

"It is mostly done. You got time. Besides, I need some help peeling apples so why don't you take a break and think about it?"

She always liked pink flowers …maybe a wild rose

"That is probably a good idea. I picked a half bushel last night and set them by the swing. I'll get started while you do the dishes."

"Just need to rinse out the cups. Here's the bowls and paring knives. Should I make a pie or just dry them apples?"

Oh good there are some daisies blooming.

"Maybe a small pie and dry the rest."

Alvin held the screen door open while Alene fetched the bowls and knives. He scooted the basket in front of the porch swing and they took their seats and settled in to work.

She did like our swing… especially in the cool evenings..

"Now you know, not everybody has Bart apples. I bet most young people have never heard of them but they make the best apple pies. And dried apple cakes."

I can hear her now...get them wet boots off my clean floor.

"Now there is something we have not had lately. Maybe you can make one."

"Maybe I will. Now don't throw that apple away because it has a little worm hole in it. Just cut the hole out and slice it up like the rest of them. Goodness, you would think you have never peeled apples before."

Why am I thinking about peeling apples now of all times?

"I think at our age we don't have to eat wormy apples."

"We ain't eating wormy apples, but ain't no sense in wasting them."

She never wasted anything...

They rocked gently in the swing as Alene began to hum 'In the Sweet By and By.' Alvin joined in softly, occasionally interjecting a few random words.

That was always her favorite hymn, even when I sung it.

"Decoration Day will be here soon. What? Three Sundays from now?'

"Yep, I need to call Billy Joe and tell him to mow and trim the graveyard by then."

She lived for Decoration Day... and dinner on the ground

"My, what changes have we seen in our lives. Used to be such a job using scissors to cut the fescue away from the tombstones. Course there was always some people who didn't trim their stones so the cemetery looked pretty ratty. Now with them weed eaters one man can do the whole thing by hisself. And Billy Joe does a good job. Which reminds me, did you check the donation box yet?"

She never complained about trimming around Jesse's rock.

"I found twenty dollars in it last week. I'll check again next week. I expect people will donate more the closer we get to Decoration."

Alene paused her peeling and sighed. "Alvin, do you ever think about little Jesse?"

Alvin knitted his brow and heaved a sigh of his own. "Why are you asking that?"

"I wonder how our lives would have been different if he had lived. Maybe we could have grandchildren here helping us peel these apples. Or maybe you could take a grandson fishing or coon hunting."

She always knew in her heart how much I wanted a son

"Or maybe you could dress up a granddaughter like Cinderella and show her off at the ice cream social. Wouldn't that be fun?'

I know it broke her heart to not have a little girl with an Easter bonnet and little white gloves and black patent leather shoes.

"Yes, it would."

They paused the swing to stare at the apples in their pans momentarily before resuming the rhythmic creaking motion of the swing.

"Now, dear, you know there ain't no sense in supposing things that we cain't change. God's will is going to be done."

"I ain't saying that it shouldn't be. But don't you wonder why…."

We cannot question what God does..

Alene caught her breath as small tears welled up in her eyes… "Why…."

She dropped her knife into the bowl and wrestled a small handkerchief out of her apron pocket to wipe her face.

"Remember how excited we was before Jesse was born? Didn't know if we was having a little girl or little boy and didn't want to know. That was the fun of it… We made lists of names for girls and boys and finally decided on Jesse if it was a boy and Lena if it was a girl. The church had a baby shower for us and everybody was so happy."

My God we were so happy.

Alvin sat quiet. "But it wasn't meant to be. We ain't the only ones who don't got kids."

"No, but it hurts so much. He only lived four hours... "

"Why are you bringing this up now?"

"Because it still hurts. We would have been good parents, everybody says that. I wonder if I could have loved him more if he had lived longer."

I loved our son so much...

"I don't know if we could have loved him more....I just don't know.. ... there's a lot I don't know."

Alene sighed again. "Course the church was so good to us in our time of grief. They took up money for the funeral and the tombstone. We couldn't afford one."

Farmers don't make enough to bury their own kids right.

Alvin's lips twisted into a wry smile. "They paid that man to carve out a little lamb on top of the stone. It was supposed to say 'Our little angel."

Alene nodded and smiled," But he misspelled it to say "Our little angle...nobody said anything and it really didn't matter. We all knew what it was supposed to say and it was too expensive to redo it."

I never told her that I was the one who spelled it wrong.

"We need to go to town and get a wreath before Decoration Day. Remember when everybody made their own out of crepe paper?"

I hated making them flowers... Too sissified for a man but I did it anyway ..for her.

"Now cain't even find crepe paper. And I forgot how to do them anyway. Of course I always liked the real flowers myself. "

"How can I forget that? When we was courting, I always brung you fresh flowers I picked along the roadside. Sometimes Mom would give me some old maids from her patch. She told me that a lady like you always wanted real flowers."

It must have sprinkled some this morning ....I bet the grass is slick.

Alene's eyes twinkled. "And you was always so good about bringing me fresh flowers. Remember we used to go back up there every day to put fresh flowers on Jesse's grave?"

My God I miss her so much.

"Every day for years. Every day we took the old dead ones away and put new ones in if we could find some. Sometimes it was hard to find fresh ones. So why did we stop doing that?"

Weatherman said it was going to rain today... wait, there's some drops now ....better hurry

"You just said it got too hard to find fresh ones. And at some time you just have to move on. Hard as that may be."

Alvin finished peeling and slicing his last apple. "I need to get back to work on that painting. Give me your peelings and I will get rid of them."

Alene nodded approval and said, "Now I'm going to get that pie made. No ice cream, but we have hot coffee.

This walk gets harder every day, but I have to do it because

Alvin poured himself another cup of coffee and returned to his painting.

"Now that I look at it, I do need to make it a little lighter pink."

"That is what I think. How much longer are you going to work on this?"

Need to rest and catch my breath for a minute...huh, huh, huh.., Oh God that hurts.. can't fall... spill flowers... too late gotta catch myself..

Oh I love the smell of wet spring grass and rainy dust...dust... got to hold onto the flowers...

II

Abel Stinson loved his job as a meter reader for the RECC office in Monticello. He hated sitting behind a desk so driving around the county reading meters allowed him to enjoy the outdoors and occasionally chat for a few minutes with people he knew. The weekends were free to fish or work on his four wheeler he used to travel between hunting locations.

The home office set the schedule he used to read the meters. On Mondays, he worked the southern end of the county and he always looked forward to visiting a few minutes with Alvin, a visit that had become all the more meaningful since Alene had died last January leaving Alvin alone with his paintings when he could summon the energy and motivation to work on them.

The tires of the service truck scrunched the loose gravel as he turned into the road leading down to Alvin's house. He recorded the meter reading and knocked on the door. When no one answered, he knocked louder and opened the door.

"Alvin? Are you home? Alvin, it's me Abel here to read your electric meter."

Hearing no answer, he looked into the garage; Alvin's truck was still there. Now puzzled and confused, he began to panic and paced around the house yelling "ALVIN. ALVIN DENNEY! WHERE ARE YOU?"

He got back into his truck and was driving back up the driveway past the cemetery when he saw Alvin's crumpled form lying in the cemetery near Alene's grave. Now panicked more than ever, he screeched the brakes hard, parked the car and ran to where Alvin's body lay. Sobbing loudly, he turned Alvin's body over to see if he were still alive. Storms had peppered the county all weekend and Alvin's clothes were soaking wet and clung stubbornly to his cold stiff body. Realizing that Alvin was dead, he stood up and dialed 911 on his cell phone.

"Police department. Can I help you?'

"Yes, this is Abel Stinson. I am the meter reader for the RECC and I want to report a death. Yes, ma'am. His name is Alvin Denney and I just found him in the graveyard by his wife's grave. By the looks of it, he has been here for a while because his clothes are sopping wet. I guess he could have been here all weekend. Yes, I will wait here until the ambulance and police arrive to take my statement. I need to call the home office. Thank you."

Abel hung up the phone and strolled through the graveyard, picking clovers and dandelions to replace the wilted ones Alvin had placed in the Mason jar on Alene's grave.

WHAT MEANETH THIS NOISE OF THE TUMULT?

Marvin Bryant had served with honor in France in World War I and, not wanting to leave behind a grieving widow who might be forever denied the joy of having hearth and home, he had delayed marriage until after he had returned home safely from his tour of duty "Over There" in 1919. He married his betrothed Abigail King in 1920 and together they moved to their home at Flat Springs. They bought an old-fashioned dogtrot house (really two small cabins connected by a breezeway with bedrooms in one cabin and kitchen in the other). Such designs were once popular in the southern part of the country.

When the World War I Memorial Doughboy Statute was installed in 1923, the young couple had gone to town in a farm wagon drawn by two small horses. The bronze statue, designed by E.M. Viquesney, showed a soldier carrying a rifle in one hand and a grenade in the other. It stood atop a truncated obelisk bearing a bronze plaque inscribed with the names of the ten dead and forty-five wounded in the war, one of whom was Marvin Bryant. A smaller plaque bore a quote from Theodore Roosevelt:

> "FOR WHEN THE TRUMPETS SOUND FOR ARMAGEDDON, ONLY THOSE DESERVE UNDYING PRAISE WHO STAND WHERE THE DANGER IS SOREST."

Marvin had served long enough to earn five hundred dollars from the World War Adjustment Act which remunerated veterans for their service. He had used the money to enlarge and improve his property. Since he owned the first telephone in the community, he and Abby became the answering service for everyone who did not have a phone. They would get a phone call and Marvin would walk to a neighbor's house to relay a message or tell them to call someone. Sometimes these trips often left him breathing with difficulty, a war-related disability stemming from having received a whiff of mustard gas in the trenches.

Despite earning a purple heart for being wounded in the war, Marvin rarely talked about his years in the army. The scuttlebutt was that he was a crack shot in the Army and had killed several German soldiers, but that he became so shell-shocked and lost his edge. A stoic man with a stout physique, he seldom engaged in small talk, possibly because his conversations were peppered with fits of coughing, preferring instead to save his words and opinion until an important issue came up, particularly religious issues. A firm believer in the doctrine of apostasy, he lived his faith lest he lose his salvation and be damned to hell as a backslider. A life-long Methodist at the Flat Springs Methodist Church, he served twenty years as a trustee. He also supervised the maintenance of the church graveyard.

Marvin and Abby had two adult children, Allan and Geneva, and one grandson, Allan's twelve-year old son, Ricky, who enjoyed spending time with his grandparents whenever he could because they doted on him.

One day, Ricky was chasing butterflies around Abby's flower garden when he heard her call out his name. "Hey, Ricky, Grandpa is down at the barn trying to kill his groundhog. It's a bit chilly so I bet he'd like some hot coffee. Would you run this thermos down to him, please?"

Ricky ran into the house to get the coffee. "Ok, Grandma, no problemo. Can I go watch Grandpa battle the groundhog?"

"It won't do me any good to say 'no' because I know you will anyway. Just stay out of the way and be careful."

Ricky took the thermos bottle and ran out the door and down the hill toward the barn. The road, rutted by wagon wheels, was so strewn with rocks that caused him to slow his pace. When he got to the clearing above the barn, he saw Marvin sitting on an upside down wooden crate drinking from a whiskey bottle. Ricky thought he could hear his grandpa crying softly.

His sudden appearance startled Marvin, who took a big swig out of the whiskey bottle before he tried to hide the bottle under his coat.

He stammered, "Well, Ricky, you surprised me. Now you won't tell on me, will you?"

Ricky grinned, "Don't worry, Grandpa. Your secret is safe with me. Daddy keeps a bottle of Old Granddad. He says it is strictly for medicinal purposes like the croup, but I know he takes a nip now and then. Grandma says today is groundhog day for you. Can I watch?"

"Sure, but let me get another swallow," he giggled as he took another drink.

"It's a bad habit and a hard one to break. The Bible warns against drinking, but then Jesus' first miracle was to turn water into wine. What does that tell you?"

"I don't know the Bible as good as you, so I don't have any idea."

"I don't see the harm of a little nip. I ain't driving or beating your granny up. Let's go into the barn and wait for them rascals to come out of their holes. You don't smoke do you?"

"No. Why?"

"I got a coffee can of gasoline poured out in the barn."

"Gasoline? Why?"

"You'll see."

They went into the barn and took seats on some old crates where they could just barely see out of the barn where the groundhog had dug holes along the chestnut picket fence. Ricky noticed his grandpa wipe a tear off his cheek.

"You still got that pocket knife I gave you?" Marvin asked.

"Sure. I always carry it except to school."

"Well, I found the best red cedar sticks for whittling. Here is one for you. Let's chew the fat for a while before we go after that groundhog."

"Okay, but don't you just shoot him? I hear you're a great shot."

"Maybe one time I was, but not now. I can't hit the broadside of a barn. Wait, you see that hole over there? Guess I did hit the broadside of the barn" he laughed.

Ricky couldn't help but notice that Marvin was getting a little more tipsy as he continued to sip the booze while he talked and whittled. He began to suspect that the old man was too drunk to shoot well.

"How old are you now, Ricky, about 15?"

"I'm fifteen. Got three more years in high school."

"You plan on going to college?"

"Don't know. We might not have the money."

Marvin stopped whittling to look down his stick to see if it were still round. "Well, take my advice. Work hard and get scholarships. If you don't, you'll probably get drafted for that Vietnam War."

"But Grandpa, you were in the army in World War one. You earned a purple heart."

Marvin peeked around the barn door to see if the groundhog had emerged from his burrow. Seeing no sign, he turned back to talk to Ricky.

He took a longer drink from the bottle. "We may be talking too much. Let's just sit here for a few minutes and see if he comes out."

Ricky nodded and they fell silent. The only sounds were the scratchings of knife blades shaving away wood. Finally, Ricky asked, "How come you don't talk about the war much? You were a hero."

Marvin paused and coughed. "A hero? Maybe, maybe not. A war changes a man."

"Why's that?"

"War today is a lot different than it was in the Great War— a lot different."

Ricky looked puzzled. "We got better guns — wait, look, the ground hog is sticking his head out."

Marvin laid his whittling down and watched the animal sniffing the air. He winked at Ricky and whispered, "Now we know what hole he is in. Wait right here."

He quietly picked up the coffee can of gas and walked toward the hole. The groundhog disappeared down the hole. Marvin ran over to the hole, poured gasoline into it, and stepped back. He lit a match and threw it into the burrow.

The gas exploded into flame and the ground shook with a loud roar. Ricky sat stunned and terrified by the explosion.

"Holy shit, Grandpa! Why'd you do that? That's dangerous1 You could get hurt or catch the place on fire!"

Marvin shook his head. "Haven't caused any damage yet. I don't think I've ever hurt the groundhogs, and I've been doing it for years."

"But why do that? Why don't you just shoot him?"

Marvin sat back down and resumed his whittling. "Well, Ricky, let me tell you about how I got my purple heart."

He leaned forward and rested his elbows on his knees. "Maybe you know this and maybe you don't. Have you ever heard of mustard gas?"

Ricky nodded, "I've heard of it, but I don't know much about it."

"The Germans were using it against us in the war.. Every soldier had to take training on putting on gas masks really fast. At the first sign of gas attack we were supposed to put on the masks. But by then, most of the time it was too late. Thousands of boys died from mustard gas. Horrible way to die."

"What was it anyway?"

"I think it was mostly sulfur and some chlorine. It was yellowish. That's why they called it mustard gas: it looked like mustard. But it was nasty! Sticky so it grabbed onto you and wouldn't let go. It made huge blisters that burned away the skin and wouldn't heal. It caused your lungs to bleed. The pain was unbearable and there was nothing you could do to ease it. The gas was heavier than air so it settled into the trenches where we were holed up. Most of time…"

He coughed violently and paused before continuing. "A lot of time you did not even know you were exposed. We only learned the hard way that gas masks didn't stop it. In a few hours you felt its effects. Sometimes it killed you outright. But if it didn't, you would hang on for three or four weeks of pure hell. They couldn't treat the burns and nothing gave relief from the pain."

A violent spasm shook his body and he paused again, wracked by a paroxysm of coughing. After clearing his throat, he began again, "That stuff went right through your clothes. Nothing could stop it. Stayed in the ground for months so you could be exposed if you crawled through. Killed hundreds of thousands of people, soldiers and civilians."

Ricky sat transfixed by the horror of the images Marvin described. Marvin eyed him and whispered, "Take a minute to calm down. It's bad stuff to think about."

In a few minutes, he resumed. "Anyway, one day, my troop was hiding in a trench, pinned down by machine guns. A ricochet bullet took my best friend Charlie out. Then one of them krauts lobbed a gas canister into the trench. I had watched my friends die and suffer from it and was terrified of it. I got a whiff of it—that is why I cough a lot. It damaged my lungs. I knew I had to get out of there."

Another violent coughing fit seized him and he had to pause before continuing. "I had two grenades left. I grabbed one of them and jumped out of the trench and ran toward the machine gun nest. One of them shot me through my right shoulder but I managed to lob a grenade into the nest. Killed all of them."

Suddenly, he began to sob and tears streamed down his cheeks. Ricky was stunned to see his Grandpa crying. To him, Marvin was the toughest man he had ever seen, the only war hero he knew. He sat in silence before patting Marvin on the arm. "That's okay, Grandpa, that's ok."

Marvin tried to regain his composure, but the crying had only made the coughing and choking fits worse. He finally got a respite and softly said, "But here is the bad part. In all the confusion of war, that was a troop of our own men firing on us. They called it "friendly fire" — when soldiers accidentally shoot their own. I had killed my own men."

Stunned by the revelation, Ricky objected, "But you said they threw a gas bomb into your trench."

Marvin took a deep breath. "What most people don't know is that our side used mustard gas on them, too. We probably used more than they did. We had many kinds of gas weapons —mustard gas, tear gas, chlorine, something called phosgene —terrible weapons, terrible. Sometimes the gas masks helped, sometimes they didn't. We spent every waking minute scared to death. We were even afraid to sleep in case we got bombed in the night."

A look of sad resignation passed over his face and he stared at the ground. "So I bombed my own troops but probably saved some others from being gas bombed or shot by our own troops. Do you still think I'm a hero?"

Ricky was crying loudly, his slender young frame shaking violently. "Grandpa, you'll always be a hero to me."

Marvin motioned for him to come closer and hugged him tightly to his body to comfort him. "I know, son, I know."

Ricky sat back down and Marvin continued. "Well, after the war and people saw how awful these gas weapons were, the countries met and enacted what they called the Geneva Conventions. You may have heard of them. These people decided to make rules for war things like treatment of prisoners and so on. After seeing the effects of mustard gas, they outlawed all chemical and bacterial weapons in war because they were 'inhumane.'"

Marvin stopped and shook his head. "Now think about that, Ricky. You are in a war trying your damnedest to kill your enemy any way you can but now they say some ways of killing them are inhumane. So, I guess that means there's humane ways to kill someone. What kind of sense does that make?"

"I don't know, Grandpa. I don't know."

Marvin patted his knee. "So instead of shooting groundhogs, I started doing this. I put gasoline in the hole and light it. Now, them little bastards have tunnels and holes all along that fencerow. As near as I can tell, I ain't never killed a single one this way. I don't know why I keep doing it, but I do. Drinking a few shots of whiskey seems to calm me down. I think it helps me forget some things. Guess I need to see a doctor to get my head examined."

He handed Ricky a handkerchief to wipe his face and blow his nose and used his shirt sleeve to wipe the tears off his face.

"Now, Ricky, I am asking you a favor. Don't tell anybody—not your grandma—your folks or parents—no one about this. Let them keep thinking what they're thinking. I'm only telling you to make you understand how insane wars are and try to convince you to avoid it at all costs. Promise me?"

"Yes, Grandpa, I promise. I guess I never thought about it too much. In school, we are always learning about how we are the good guys and we always beat the bad guys. A lot of the time, the books don't really talk much about how awful the suffering is on both sides."

"No, they don't. Even the movies don't get it right. We're always John Wayne protecting us from the enemy. Now don't get me wrong. Sometimes there are good sides and bad sides. The Civil War was needed to end slavery. The world wars to stop tyranny from ruling the world, but sometimes there ain't no clear good side and bad side."

He knitted his brow. "Take this here Vietnam War. I used to think it was the right thing, but now I don't know. That's why I hope you can stay out of it. Wars change a man, and not in a good way. I pray every night you don't have to be in one."

They sat silently and resumed their whittling. In a few minutes, the smell of gasoline and smoke dissipated and the fresh air cleared their heads. A few minutes later, the groundhog poked his head out of the hole, his nose sniffing the air for threats. He crept out of the hole and inched his way to the garden where he began to eat some of the early green beans. Marvin coughed again and the groundhog scurried back to the safety of his burrow.

Marvin laughed, "See what I mean? He' s scared, but he ain't hurt. I won't put him through that again— once a year is enough. He'll eat some of your grandma's vegetables but we always plant a lot of extras. Some for him, some for us. The world goes on. That ain't the same groundhog. I always see little ones running around. I guess they just move on to someone else's fencerow."

Ricky smiled at the thought of the young groundhogs frolicking in the garden as they nibbled on the plants. "Grandpa, I do have one question."

"Yes?"

"Knowing what you do now, do you think you were a good guy or a bad guy in the war?"

Marvin's face wrinkled with a sad smile as he answered, "Yes."

TEARS OF THE PENTITENT

By all accounts, Brennan Doyle, was a successful businessman who as a teenager had recognized the need for burlap sacks and baling twines in the grain and livestock feed sector of the economy. Like so many boys in the rural community of Hidalgo, he earned money by the sweat of his brow, reaping and storing rectangular bales of hay and straw for the farmers whose families were not sufficiently blessed with strong young sons to do the day-to-day burdensome labor required to make a farm profitable. Perhaps he had inherited a gene for business acumen, or more cynically, a gene for miserliness, from his paternal grandfather who had built a respectable empire operating a coopery that turned white oak timber into barrels for the bourbon distilleries in the Bluegrass region of the state.

A benevolent soul, generous to a fault, Brennan embodied the golden rule and egalitarianism and inculcated that value into his son from the earliest age. Yet despite his cheery, indeed almost saccharine, disposition, an astute observer may have sensed a lugubrious undertone lying hidden behind his mask of joviality.

Perhaps it was those unseen and unrelenting thorns of contrition piercing his very aggrieved soul that precipitated the coronary infarction that cut his prosperous life short at the unexpected age of forty, leaving behind not just a heartbroken widow and son, but a community grieving the loss of one of its most well-loved members.

But whatever the cause, nearly the entire community gathered in shifts at the Lee Funeral Home to reminisce about the man who had enriched their lives. After a solemn viewing to pay their last respects, an enclave of his Masonic brethren gathered to swap stories of his life.

Delbert Simpson started the conversation. "Well, boys, I guess Brennan is in a better place. But I gotta say we're in a sadder state now that he is gone. He was a good Christian man, God rest his soul."

Chester New shook his head in agreement. "No finer man ever lived if you ask me. I'm going to miss him something fierce."

Harlan Adkins added, "He never had an enemy in this world. And he'd give you the shirt off his back. Somehow it don't seem fair that he's gone so soon. Just the other day, he was telling me about what he was planning in the coming year."

Delbert said, "He did so much good for everybody around here. I remember when he helped my dad and me mow that big wheat field and haul it in. He was as strong as an ox. Never complained about anything."

Chester nodded approval. "I remember him saying to me one day, that a man could make a fortune in the burlap business. You might say he was a man of vision…no one else ever thought about that much. All we saw was another bushel of wheat or a bale of straw we needed to haul in. Guess that's why he got to be so rich and I'm still poor."

All the men laughed loudly. "The thing is," Harlan said, "you'd never know he was worth a wooden nickel. He never put on airs or nothing…. he was always just Brennan."

A young black man joined the group. "Howdy, fellers, it's a sad day for us all ain't it?" he asked.

"Good afternoon, George. We was just saying what an awful thing this is. Gone too soon." Delbert said.

"Anybody know how Arlene is taking this? George asked.

Chester grimaced. "Not too well. I heard the doctor had to sedate her. She was nigh out of her mind. You gotta feel sorry for her and Jackson."

"I know Jackson is grown now, nearly nineteen, but he was awfully close to his daddy. Thought the world of him." Harlan said.

Delbert replied, "And he was so proud of him being a lawyer… damned good one. Wasn't he involved with that civil rights group, the Southern, damn it, I can never remember what it is. Help me out here, fellers."

George said. "Southern Poverty Law Center. They're that group that's always fighting the racists, bigots, the Ku Klux Klan morons, and Neo Nazis. Brennan never had any use for them. You know, me and my sister Frances and my cousin Loretta were all in the same second grade class with Brennan. I never understood all this hoopla about integration of schools that caused so much trouble. Hell, we all went to integrated schools and never thought much about it."

"Thank you, George, I can never recall the exact name. I think they do a lot of …what do you call it when they do it for free….?"

Harlan replied, "Pro bono. It's Latin but I looked it up one time... means for the public good."

George snickered, "Well, that about describes Brennan to a tee, don't it? He was always doing something for somebody."

"I heard that every Christmas, he'd buy as many turkey dinners as it took to feed Cox's army and invite anybody who couldn't afford it to come and eat." said Delbert.

"You know he gave away ten scholarships every year to needy kids, mostly black kids, but a lot of white kids too. Color never mattered to Brennan. He just saw people, especially people in need."

The men stood quiet as Chester and Delbert fished out cigarettes. "Harlan, you quit smoking?" Chester asked.

"Five years ago. Them things are going to kill you guys."

"Well, Brennan never smoked but here he is…just as dead as if he did. We all gotta go sometime." Delbert said.

"You know, that was the thing about ole Brennan…never knew him to have any vices. He lived a good Christian life."

"If he ain't in heaven, I don't want to go," added Harlan. "Always willing to help people."

George said. "He sent my boy, George Junior, to engineering school and my daughter to medical school. That ain't cheap. I wonder what he was worth."

"God only knows. Brennan never discussed how much he was worth."

Delbert continued, "He was always in such a good mood. But I gotta tell you guys something. One time we went rabbit hunting together. Now I never knew Brennan to shoot any critter. I think he just went along for the company. It was middle of December. We had a little dusting of dry snow... what some people call a rabbit tracker. All of a sudden, this rabbit jumps out of the brush and lights out like a bat out of hell. I took a shot but missed...recoil nearly knocked me down. We had a good laugh.

"So, we just sat down on hickory stumps and started talking. Bragged about our kids. He asked how the dairy business was. I said okay, what with the government subsidies and all. So then he asked what kind of cows I had. I said Holstein because they produce the most milk of any breed."

He paused as he struggled to recall. "Then he said, 'That's them black and white cows, ain't they?', and I said 'yeah.' Then he said he sometimes wondered why there were so many breeds of cows."

Delbert took one last draw of his cigarette before grinding it out on the sidewalk. Harlan chided, "I hope you're going to pick that up, litterbug."

"Don't have a cow, no pun intended. So, I said I don't know — some of them give richer milk. Jersey milk is higher in butterfat — makes good ice cream."

The men smiled as they feared they had opened the door to let Delbert give a sermon on the dairy business, but they felt relieved when he continued, "Then out of the blue he said 'I guess it's for the same reason there's so many colors of mankind.' I was so shocked by that comment, I don't think I'll ever forget it. Didn't know what to say but agree. Damnedest thing."

All the men mumbled their confused surprise of the story before Harlan asked, "Wasn't Brennan from out around Hidalgo?"

"Yeah, he was," Chester replied. I think his old homestead is still out there. Don't think anyone lives there now. You know how it is with these old farms."

"Guess it will just stay abandoned. Jackson lives in Louisville. I hear he just got married. Too bad Brennan never got to be a grandpa. He'd have been a good one."

They all nodded before Harlan said, "Now, I am not speaking ill of the dead. God knows no one can speak ill of Brennan. But I've heard he was a little, what's the word, eccentric. in some of his ways."

George whispered, "I'd heard that too, but I don't know what people meant by it. Every time I saw him, he was just good ole Brennan."

Harlan continued, "Someone told me that he always went to church on Valentine's Day and made a big donation. Now I know being from Hidalgo, he wasn't no Catholic so he didn't put no stock in all them saints like Saint Valentine."

"That is peculiar. You ever see the inside of his house?" Delbert asked. "A real mansion. Full of antiques. Had a whole wall of family pictures of his mom and dad and his own family."

Harlan asked, "You ever see his lucky key? He carried it with him all the time. Sorta looked like an old-fashioned skeleton key. You know what one looks like."

Delbert said, "Come to think of it, one time he gave me his keys to unlock the trunk of his car and I noticed that weird key. I had to ask about it."

"And?"

"Said his mother gave him a little treasure chest for a birthday present when he turned ten and this was the key to that little chest. He laughed and called it the key to happiness."

"Did he show you what was in it?" Harlan asked.

"No, he was always sort of mysterious about it. I guess he left everything to Arlene and Jackson, but I would feel funny asking about it," Delbert said.

"Yeah, he left most of it to them, but he also left a lot to a bunch of charities I guess we'll never know what was in that chest."

Chester asked, "Not to change the subject, but have any of you fellers ever done a Masonic funeral? I never have. I guess the Mason handbook tells us about it but I'd like to talk to someone to be sure we're doing it right. It's the least we can do for Brennan."

Harlan said, "I know a man who has done a couple of them so I'll ask him to meet with us before the funeral Thursday. I'll call you tonight."

True to his word, Harlan telephoned all of the Mason brethren in their lodge and got copies of the Masonic service to everyone. The funeral procession ran two miles down Highway 200 to the Keene's Chapel Church. Arlene and Jackson greeted the mourners as they filed past the casket one last time. Mourners had bought so many flowers the church couldn't hold them all and many were placed in front of the church. Chester, Harlan, Delbert, George, and two more Masons, Daniel Neal and Arlie Gossage, were the pall bearers who bore the plain oak casket to its final resting place before the crowd dispersed.

In six months, Brennan's will had passed through probate. The will insured that Arlene, Jackson and his new family would be able to live comfortable lives. Curiously, he specifically bequeathed the chest to Jackson. The will left a donation to his Masonic Lodge and set up the Brennan Doyle Foundation to fund the Southern Poverty Law Center. After the will was read, the lodge met and renamed it the Brennan Doyle Lodge of Otter Creek.

A few months later, Delbert ran into Harlan and Chester at the local diner and they began to talk about the friend they had lost. After much banter, Delbert lowered his voice and said, "Now, guys, admit it, you're as curious as I am about that chest. You think Arlene or Jackson would show us what was in it?"

Although they acknowledged their curiosity, the men were clearly uncomfortable about how to go asking what was in it. Finally, Delbert said, "Well, I was pretty close to Brennan so I'll volunteer to ask about it. Does anyone know if Arlene still has it or did Jackson take it back with him?"

Harlan replied, "I don't know, but if you ask and it ain't there, we'll just have to let it go. No way do I want to pester Jackson about it."

Two weeks passed before Delbert got up the courage to visit Arlene and ask about the chest. He drove to her home and rang the doorbell. He could hear her stirring in the house before she answered the door.

"Good morning, Arlene. I thought I'd stop by and see how you are doing."

"That is mighty kind of you. Every day gets a little better. Won't you come in for some coffee?"

"That would be great, but I can't stay long. Maybe just a cup or two. Thank you."

They chatted small talk while the coffee brewed. After Arlene poured them a cup, Delbert said. "Now, Arlene, I hope you don't mind, but there's something I want to ask you. You don't have to answer if you don't want to and it's really none of my business but me and the fellers were curious about that little treasure chest Brennan had...the one with the key to happiness he always carried with him. Do you mind telling me what was in it?"

Arlene sipped her coffee before replying, "No, not at all. In fact, maybe you can shed some light on it because neither Jackson nor me can make heads or tails of it. Wait a minute while I get it. We keep it in his den."

She left the room and returned with a small ornately designed chest with the key in the lock. She set the box in front of Delbert, turned the key and lifted the lid.

Delbert stared into the box. "Do you mind if I get a closer look?"

"Help yourself. Don't drop it."

He reached into the box and carefully removed its contents: a small mirror and an aged Valentine card bearing the name Loretta printed in a child's hand writing. He looked up at Arlene with a look of utter confusion. His mouth moved as if to ask a question, but no words came out.

Arlene asked, "Do you have any idea what this means? Jackson and me have puzzled over this since Brennan died and we can find no clue."

Delbert softly laid the mirror and valentine back into the velvet lined chest, shaking his head in disbelief. "Well, I guess this is one thing Brennan took to his grave. Maybe someday we can figure it out. I need to go. You have a good day, Arlene and thanks for satisfying my curiosity."

He gave her a hug and a quick kiss on the cheek before leaving to report his findings to his friends. They were as confused as he was so they decided to lay the matter to rest.

EPILOGUE

"Time to get up Brennan. It's seven o'clock and the bus will be here soon. I know you don't want to miss today. It's Valentine's Day. Did you get them all addressed?"

"Almost, Mom. I still have one or two."

"Now you listen to me young man, like I told you last night if you send valentines to any of your classmates, you send them to all of them. You hear me?"

"But, Mom, the guys will tease me if I send everyone a card."

"Is that because you're sending them to the colored kids?"

"Well, not exactly. I don't mind sending one to George or Frances. They ain't that different from everybody else and they ain't too dark. But Loretta is really dark and has little pieces of paper in her hair. She is really poor and all the boys make fun of her."

"I don't care what the other boys do. Now you get a pretty card and sign it and put Loretta's name on it unless you want me to do it and hand deliver it to her. Because if you don't do it that is exactly what I will do."

Brennan sorted through the remaining cards before he chose one that simply said HAPPY VALENTINE'S DAY on it with a picture of a cute little bunny holding a heart. He hesitantly wrote LORETTA on the envelope and laid it on top of the others.

"You be sure she gets it. I'm going to trust you to keep your promise. If I hear otherwise, your daddy will take a belt to you. I see the bus coming, so off you go."

Brennan ran to the bus stop and scurried to the backseat where he could sit by himself. He bit his lip and took the envelope addressed to Loretta and thought about throwing it away in the trash when he got to school. Fearing someone would find it, he stuck it inside his jacket pocket and hid it underneath his mattress when he got home.

HE SENDETH RAIN ON THE RIGHTEOUS AND UNRIGHTEOUS

The phone rang loudly enough to stir Sheriff Joe Tucker from his post-prandial drowsiness and he snatched the phone from its cradle. His deputy Zach Parmley emerged from the back office to answer the phone, but demurred when he saw Joe talking.

"Sheriff's office, Joe Tucker speaking. May I help you?" he asked.

Zach could hear a muffled voice on the phone, a voice that was clearly shaken with concern. He strained unsuccessfully to make out the words before abandoning his efforts and sat down in the chair in front of the desk.

Joe listened to the caller, intermittently reassuring the caller. "Yes, Mr. Chriswell, I know you're worried. Yes, I would be too. Was anyone hit?... Was there any real damage? No, scaring the dog is not damage. Do you know where the shots were coming from? Yeah, it's hard to tell with the echoes. Okay, I'll look into it. Take care."

Zach asked, "So what's that all about?"

Joe got up from his chair and walked over to the gun cabinet. "Stanley Chriswell says somebody is shooting out his way. I'm pretty sure I know who it is. Let's see, where did I put them bullets?"

Zach asked, "So who is it?"

"I'm pretty sure it's Thelma Jones shooting at her cats."

"Why would she shoot her cats?"

Joe picked up a box of rifle shells. "There they are. I guess you're too young to know the story of the Jones family. She's not going to do any damage so let me tell you that story. There's probably a lesson to be learned. Pull up a chair."

Zach settled in as Joe began: "Several years ago, there was this family... Caleb Jones, the dad had three sons: Clayton, Howard, and Odell. Clayton moved to Texas working in the oil fields, made some good money. First wife died so he married a retired nurse, Thelma. Clayton was quite a history buff and he bought the Matt Shearer place in Hall Valley. It was called Hall Valley because Jack Hall won the whole valley in a drunken poker game. Pretty good-sized farm, maybe two fifty acres, mostly flat. He raised a lot of hay and corn and some beef cattle."

Zach asked, "So why is she shooting her cats...."

"Who's telling this story? I'm trying to make a point, so you just sit there and listen. Howard married Lizzie and they moved way the hell out to Parnell and started raising sheep. Never had any kids, not sure why. But it don't matter. They were doing pretty good."

"So, I guess you're going to tell me about Odell now."

"Odell married a woman named Edie and bought a small farm next to Henry and Dorcas Brown. They had one son Roy. He moved away from home and became an electrician in California."

"So, back to Thelma and her cats."

"Clayton and Thelma are just great people. They were delighted to find out there were six big pecan trees on the Shearer place. Pecan is the state tree of Texas. They tended those trees and soon they had enough pecans for the whole community. Thelma was as kind as a woman as you'd ever hope to meet.. Excellent cook, and always took food to people who were sick or in mourning because someone had died. One time she won a hundred dollars in a raffle at Hutchins' market and gave all of it to a poor family with five kids so they could have a good Christmas. That's the kind of person she is."

"And the cats?"

"Well, Thelma loves playing canasta with her church lady friends twice a week, but she really loves her cats. One of her neighbors told me that at one time she had forty-five cats, all barn cats to keep the mice and rats down. Still, she feeds them twice a day. She spends a fortune on Purina cat chow and every night she makes a big skillet of gravy and takes it out to the barns to feed her cats.

"About three months ago, Clayton was diagnosed with fourth-stage prostate cancer and had to start those god-awful treatments three times a week. Had to go to Lexington every other day. I told you Thelma was a nurse, so she could take care of him. But she got worried that her cats would starve. Now, Zach, feral dogs will starve but feral cats will always find a way to survive, 'specially in the country where they can catch mice and birds. But she got into her head that they would starve and she didn't want to see them suffer. So, she took a .22 rifle up to the third floor and started trying to kill the cats so they wouldn't starve. Poor old thing probably never hit any of them but sometimes a stray bullet would graze a cow or maybe ding a neighbor's car."

"Wow, that would piss me off, too. Did she ever hurt anybody?"

"Nah… she couldn't hit the broad side of a barn. I went out there and tried to explain that she had to stop the shooting, but I made sure. I took her a big box of blank .22 shells and told her to use them because they didn't go as far. She's probably running low so I'll take her another box. That's easier than trying to get her to stop. In her mind she was doing the right thing to show mercy to the cats by not letting them starve."

"So, what about the other two men?"

"Eventually, old man Henry and his wife got to where they needed help, so he starting paying Odie and Edie to come by and check on him and Dorcas, maybe fix meals for them. That seemed to work good until Dorcas died. Then it was just Henry and things changed. Henry never had any kids so he was totally dependent on Odell and Edie. A neighbor got concerned that she had not seen Henry sitting on the porch rocking for two weeks, so she went to check on him. He had nasty bruises on him and a lot of the furniture was gone. Turned out that Odell and Edie were selling the furniture off and physically abusing Henry. Neighbor called me and I went to check: she was right to be concerned. Henry wouldn't press charges so I couldn't arrest them. Henry died a few days later and it turned out they had convinced him to leave them the farm when he died."

Zach shook his head. "Crime ain't supposed to pay, but it sounds like they made out like bandits."

Joe grimaced with a sly grin. "You might think that, wouldn't you? But remember I told you they had a son, Roy. Turns out, Roy met Jim Jones in California…."

"The Jim Jones?"

"Yep. Met him, married his daughter and moved to Jonestown, Guyana, and was one of the nine hundred people who committed suicide there in 1977. Poetic justice, huh?"

"Weird. What about Howard? The sheep herder?"

"Turns out that he was a sadistic son of a bitch. Probably good thing he never had kids. I heard he used to beat up Lizzie. Game warden gave him tickets for shooting red tailed hawks because he thought they were attacking his lambs. Of course, they weren't. It was coyotes. He tried to shoot them—I think maybe killed one or two. They were too wily… get it? Wiley Coyotes?"

"Yeah, I caught that. Very funny."

"Since he can't shoot them, he starts putting out poison. Killed some of the neighbors' dogs so he had to stop that. Then he started setting traps."

"I always thought traps are cruel. I've heard of animals gnawing their own legs off to get loose."

"Oh yeah, but I told you he was a real mean son of a bitch. One day he heard a coyote yipping. He got in his new Silverado pickup and drove out to see if he had caught one. Sure enough, he had caught a big coyote. He took a rope and lassoes the poor thing and tied his mouth shut and then tied two sticks of dynamite to it and let it go: he was going to enjoy watching that poor animal being blown to smithereens. Cruel and mean as hell. Well, the sound of the fuses burning must have addled the coyote because it ran right under his new truck and wouldn't come out. Howard was trying to poke it with a stick and everything, but it wasn't budging. He got so busy trying to get the coyote to leave he wasn't paying attention to the dynamite. All of a sudden, it went off and blew that new Silverado to bits and Howard along with it. Took the coroner a while to find all the pieces."

Zach sat back in his chair. "Pretty ironic, ain't it?"

"Well, sometimes things work out. Karma is a bitch with a long memory and a voracious appetite. Howard could have shot those coyotes if he had kept at it. No reason for the dynamite. Odell could have been a good Christian and taken good care of Henry instead of beating on him and stealing from him. He probably would have got Henry's farm anyway."

"So now we see Thelma trying to shoot her cats to spare them from starving because she is busy night and day trying to take care of her husband who ain't long for this world. Now, I could go out there and arrest her or give her a bunch of fines but who would take care of Clayton and they're spending their money on cancer treatments. So, what's the point? It dawned on me that the best way to solve the problem is to keep Thelma supplied with blank shells. Like I said, her eyes are so bad she can't tell the difference. And you know that having to kill her cats was breaking her heart. If she thinks she is shooting them and missing them it must be God is watching out for them and she could live with that. I don't think she ever killed the first cat. Once she started missing feeding them, the cats just wandered off to new homes or learned to live in the wild."

Zach sat silent for a few minutes while Joe collected the boxes of blank shells and strapped his pistol on. He patted Zach on the back as he left.

"So the reason I told you that long-winded story was to make a point. There's the laws of man and then there's God's justice. They ain't necessarily the same thing."

"I guess like everyone says, 'Life isn't fair.'"

Joe opened the door and turned back to address him. "No, sometimes life ain't fair but I think I can live with it as long as it's just."

NOTHING BUT THE TRUTH

Silas Phipps and Shelby Massengale were enjoying each other's company over a cup of coffee and a game of checkers on the porch of the Farmer's Supply in Monticello when Elmore Hobbs joined them. He eyed the game suspiciously over his horn-rimmed glasses as he pulled an empty nail keg over to sit on.

"Well, Shelby, it looks like he got you in a trap. No matter what you do, you're going to lose a man next move."

Shelby sniffed and replied cryptically, "Got him right where I want him, Elmore, right where I want him. What brings you to town today?"

Elmore sipped his coffee, "The old lady needed some groceries and pillowcase ticking for new pillows. I left her at Dr. Roberts to have her blood pressure and sugar checked. The nurse said to come back in an hour so I thought I'd come down here and get some half-runner seeds and a new tobacco knife. So you think you have him, Shelby?"

Shelby's eye twinkled mischievously. "Watch this move I call right knee to corner of board." He leaned forward striking the board with his knee and scattering checkers all over the porch floor.

Silas erupted, "Damn you, Shelby Massengale. Just damn you. I had you and you know it!"

Shelby leaned back and snickered. "Tell it to the marines. Yeah, you had me. Still I had a good laugh. Say, Elmore, have you seen your neighbor Jacob Daniels lately? What kind of tales has he been telling you?"

"I ain't seen him for a week or so. The old lady said she had heard some commotion like an ambulance coming out of the holler where he lives. I asked around but nobody knew anything. His wife Alice ain't been home and don't answer the phone. It's no telling. You know Jacob. He is the biggest liar in the world and everybody knows it and don't seem to mind. You know he is a sharpshooter."

Shelby laughed, "Oh, yeah, he brags about that all the time. Did you ever go to a turkey shoot with him?"

Elmore replied, "Turkey shoot? I haven't been to one for ten or twelve years. Why did we quit having them? Yeah, I saw him shoot a few times. Thought he had won every time even after we showed him he hadn't."

Silas added, "I went to a turkey shoot one time where he did win. Two or three shoots. He filled that little white card with over a dozen pellets with his twelve gauge Remington."

Elmore said, " Now that you mention it, I do remember him on a winning streak. He won several shoots. Won a ham, two turkeys and fifty dollars, and then just quit. Never did know why."

Shelby said, "I'll tell you why. People got suspicious and accused him of choking his shotgun down to get a tighter spread. He denied it, of course, and showed everybody the gun. He was right. Until someone asked if that was the same gun he shot with?'

Elmore said, "Never occurred to me to check that. He quit coming to the shoots. Never was sure if his feelings were hurt, he didn't want to be caught cheating or was just mad as hell. He never seemed to stop his lying."

Shelby slapped his knee and laughed. "Did he ever tell you about the rabid skunk he shot in his garden?"

The other men nodded.

Shelby laughed again. "Well, let me tell you the truth. His Alice was doing the dishes one day when she saw a skunk toddling along on the edge of the garden. Now, she was afraid that a skunk out in the day time might be rabid so she yelled for Jacob who was piddling around with his tractor engine. He saw the skunk, ran into the house, grabbed the twelve gauge and loaded it in the kitchen. Alice yelled 'Don't load that thing in here!'

"Jacob told her to be quiet as he stepped out of the door when the damned gun went off. If he had been in the house, he would have blown a hole in the ceiling. He had to go get another shell, and the old skunk was still just toddling along. Jacob ran over and stood right in front of the skunk, drew a bead on him and pulled the trigger. He was too close for the shot to spread, so all he did was bloody the skunk's nose. He had to beat it to death with a piece of a two by four. Now, don't tell him you know the truth. I told Alice I wouldn't tell anyone, but I guess I lied."

They all laughed before Elmore motioned that he had something to contribute.

"I know you have seen that big telephone pole in his front yard. One year a red-headed woodpecker made a nest in it…nearly pecked all the way through the pole. They raised little woodpeckers it for two or three years and then bluebirds started using it. Now you know Jacob loves his bluebirds. He makes them little bluebird boxes and hangs them on fences all over the county. Well, one day some starlings moved in, they're hole nesters too. They attacked the bluebirds and yanked them out of the hole. Well, that really pissed Jacob off and to hear him tell it, he blew them starlings to bits."

The others shrugged as if to say so what.

Elmore twittered. "Oh, he shot the starlings all right —off the telephone wire. Next thing they know, their phones aren't working. They called Ma Bell and the repairman came. He had to dig the shot out of the cable, and the damned starling was still laying there. On the ground."

They all laughed so hard they cried and gasped for breath.

After they regained their composure, they sat in silence for several minutes. Silas broke the silence. "What's strange is that anyone who knows him very long will tell you that he didn't always tell such outrageous lies. When we were in grade school, I don't recall him telling such bold-faced lies. I'm sure he may have fibbed to his parents —who hasn't —but somewhere along the way something happened to him."

Elmore agreed. "One day, several of us were sitting at the diner and this out- of - towner came in and Jacob started talking to him.

The guy's car had broken down and he was having dinner and coffee while they fixed it. Next thing you know, Jacob was telling him some of the godawfullest lies you ever heard. He told the man he once saw a black snake that was trapped in a barn wall because it had swallowed an egg on one side of the wall, crawled through a hole and swallowed another egg and was trapped. I could tell that the man did not believe him but he never let on."

Shelby said, "He told my grandson he won a purple heart in Vietnam. Hell, he was never in the army. He failed the physical for some reason."

Silas snickered, "He told the people at Beaver Lodge he caught a ten pound smallmouth bass but he dropped it trying to measure it and it got away."

Elmore smirked, "He told me one time that he could drive a nail with a .22 rifle from forty feet. I told him he couldn't see a nail head from forty feet, but he wouldn't let it go."

Shelby took a deep breath. "Two years ago, he said he killed a fifteen point buck up at Slickford. I forget what excuse he had for not showing it off."

Silas added, "Remember when he had knee replacement surgery two years ago? He had worn his knees out so much he was bowlegged. When they replaced his knees he gained almost two inches in height. Now he says that is why he can't hit the broad side of a barn when he shoots his gun."

Elmore went on, "He told me he saw a bear up around his house. There ain't been bears here for years. Next thing you know he had seen a mountain lion. It never ends."

Silas laughed, "What's next —he saw Santa Claus and the Easter Bunny? Or Bigfoot?"

They continued to swap stories of Jacob's tall tales until Barry Harper, the owner of the feed store joined them.

Elmore said, "We're just seeing what's the biggest lie Jacob Daniels has ever told. So far we don't have a winner."

Barry looked uncomfortable. "I guess you guys ain't heard that he had a stroke a few days ago and died. Caught everybody off guard because he seemed fit as a fiddle. They did an autopsy and found out that he had a massive brain tumor in the—let me get this right—pre-frontal cerebral cortex. Probably been there since he was a teenager, but it finally got so big it killed him."

The men fell silent, ashamed of their mocking of Jacob.

Barry continued. "Turns out that this particular kind of tumor causes something called confabulation. People with it tell lies but think they are telling the truth. They really believe they're telling the truth. They have a hard time remembering things so they just make stuff up to fill in the gaps. The older you get the worse it gets. So to Jacob, all those things he told were not lies. He really believed they were real."

Elmore asked quietly, "How's Alice holding up?"

Barry replied, "She ain't. She's been in the hospital under sedation since he died. All they had was each other. Really hard on her."

Shelby stroked his jaw and chin. "You know, when I think about it, he did seem to be getting worse about his lying. Like you said, Silas, I don't recall him lying when we were kids, or even as teenagers. I guess that tumor was there but wasn't big enough to cause a problem. I feel bad about making fun of him."

Barry said softly, "I'm sure we all feel bad about it. Everybody knew not to take Jacob too seriously since he was known to stretch the truth. I did a little research on all this. I found the case of a man named Phineas Gage. You fellers ever hear of him?"

None of them had so he continued. "Gage was working on a railroad. He was tamping black powder into a hole to blast rock out when the powder ignited and blew a steel rod up through his face under his cheekbone and out the top of his head. It destroyed a big part of the prefrontal cortex. The amazing thing is that he lived for twelve years after the accident but his whole personality changed. Before the accident, he was very popular and well-liked but a few weeks after the accident he turned into a real son of a bitch who swore like a sailor and treated everyone like shit. That was the first time anyone connected brain damage to personality. In Jacob's case the effect of the tumor was this confabulation stuff—lying but not realizing that he was lying. Without the autopsy, we would never had known about this. We would just think he was a liar."

Elmore sighed, "Just goes to show you. You never know, do you?"

THE LORD SHALL REWARD THE DOERS OF EVIL

Regis Clark pulled into the lot of the Wayne County Sheriff's Office and walked briskly into the building where Paul Southwood sat scribbling out the finishing touches on an arrest report.

Regis hailed him, "Good morning, Paul. How's it hanging?"

Paul answered, "Hanging too much, Regis. Needs to be more willing to stand up."

"I hear you, buddy. Guess we're getting old. You got a minute?"

"For you, sure. What's up?"

Regis sighed, "Our favorite bunch of crooks is at it again."

"Oh, shit, what did the Huddlestons do this time?"

"Where do I begin? Hallace Buttram came in yesterday madder than a wet hen. Said they drove by his house and shot his favorite rooster in his front yard, picked it up and went on like it was nobody's business."

"I think I can see where this is going."

"Probably. So, I get in the car and drive up to Bald Rock where they live. You know their damned house straddles three counties, Wayne and Clinton in Kentucky and Pickett in Tennessee. Well they saw me coming and ran to a room in another county, then stood there and mocked me that I was out of their jurisdiction. Because I was from Clinton County. Then they gave me the finger and laughed."

"Sounds about right. Do you know who shot the rooster?"

"Hallace said he thought it was Lester but they all look alike so he wasn't sure. Don't make any difference anyway."

"Yeah, I got to wonder why they all look alike, but I can't tell them apart either. God knows I've tried to arrest them from time to time but they pull that same trick. Not just you and me. Last week, the sheriff from Pickett County, Virgil York was in complaining. One of them found a pig of his rooting around in the woods, stole it and butchered it. Virgil went there to ask about it and they ran back to Wayne County rooms. Nothing he could do."

Regis shrugged, "You gotta admire them for coming up with this plan of putting their house in three counties. Who would think to do that?"

Paul added, "Crooks. Up around Bald Rock, just about everybody has had run-ins with the law. They just figured a way around it. You want a cup of coffee? All I have is black and sugar, no cream."

Regis replied, "Black is fine. According to my grandpa, that area has always been rough and lawless. He told me that he went to the last public hanging in Wayne County. Some cousin of their kinfolks. Seems like his name was Granville Prewitt, but he was a cousin of them Huddlestons. Said there was nearly five thousand people in town that day just to see the hanging. Little kids in trees and on their daddies' shoulders. Quite a spectacle."

"Now they were not the only bad ones up there, but they were probably the worst. There was the Andersons, Ayers, Bells, Hubbards. A lot of bad blood going back to the Civil War. Some on the Union side and some on the Confederate. Here you go."

He handed Regis the cup and continued. "Now this was not like that Hatfield and McCoy feud. These were just mean sons of bitches."

Paul sipped his coffee. "Oh, I know that. Their reputations precede them, as the saying goes. Riley Frost told me he knows damned well they stole his pigs when they were running in the woods. Ain't that what started the Hatfield and McCoy Feud, a stolen pig?"

"They say that but I heard a lot of that bad blood went back to the War too. But like I said this wasn't no feud, just meanness. My granddaddy told me he saw one of them boys —seems like his name was Cletus — shoot his neighbor's dog from his horse in his front yard and rode on like it was nobody's business. I mean, who's going to say anything when they just as soon as shoot you?"

Paul nodded. "My granddaddy knew about them. He said they were sitting on the porch one day and one of their big roosters was scratching in the grass. These bastards rode by in a wagon, shot the rooster and picked it up and went on home like nothing happened. Hell, I wouldn't say anything either."

Just as he finished, the door opened and Sheriff Bill York from Pickett County came in. "Well, Hells bells, what is this, a sheriff's convention? How come I wasn't invited?"

Regis laughed, "Well if you stayed in your office any instead of gallivanting around, we might have. We were just talking about your favorite family."

York grimaced. "Them damned Huddlestons. That's why I'm here. Gracie Barnett filed a report that they had stole some chickens. You know the drill. I go up there to arrest them and they run to another part of the house where I have no jurisdiction. Nothing I could do."

Paul interjected, "We were just going over some of their misdeeds in the last several years."

York pulled up a chair." Got any more of that coffee, Regis? I'd like a cup if you please. Oh, yeah, their crimes are legendary."

Regis got a cup and poured him a cup of coffee. "Anyone know how many murders they have committed? I lost count of the ones they were accused of. Weren't they arrested for the murder of Leonard Pyles. What? Thirty years ago?"

Paul replied, "My daddy, Robert, was sheriff then and they were arrested but they had to let them go. No evidence and no witnesses. That's when they built that house on the county and state lines."

Bill went on. "Whoever it was shot Leonard from ambush when he was coming back in from milking his cows. Made an orphan of his little girl.

Regis said, "That bunch was into everything. Homer Hancock had planted a lot of ginseng plants in the woods behind his barn. Goes out there one day and it was all gone. He's convinced some of them did it. They only lived over the mountain from him so it would have been easy. No proof, so nothing to do."

Paul stood up. "You fellers wait right here. I want to show you something."

He went over to a tall gray metal cabinet and opened the door. After pushing things aside, he retrieved an odd-looking shoe and returned to his seat. He set the shoe on the desk.

He said, "The last sheriff here, Sheriff Bates got this as a souvenir. Back in the days of Prohibition, the Huddlestons got involved with bootlegging and running stills. They found a good-sized rock house and set up a still in it. Now, they may be crooked as hell but they weren't stupid. They realized that the G men might track them so they built these. Here take a look."

Bill picked it up. "Well, I'll be damned. Would you look at that?"

Regis asked, "Can I see it? Well, damn. They whittled out something that looks like a cow track and nailed it to an old boot. Anybody looking at tracks would just see a bunch of cow tracks. How did you come by this?"

Paul took the shoe back. "Well, one day the G men picked up Sheriff Bates and they went up there. Followed the smoke to the still. One of them— Ephraim I think—was running the still. He heard them coming and lit out through the woods. Course, he couldn't run too good in these things, so he kicks them off and goes on barefoot. They destroyed the still, but you know damned well they had more stashed away all over that mountain."

Bill added, "They're a wily bunch. I'm pretty sure they're still running a still. Last year, I went up there deer hunting and came up on a clearing that shouldn't be there. I didn't see any place trees had fallen. So, I started poking around. Turns out that someone had cut seven big trees flush with the ground and laid big flat sandstones on top of them. If anyone in a plane flew over, all they would see is an open place with rocks. No evidence the tree had been cut recently."

Regis shook his finger. "You may remember this one. Some city slicker from Louisville stopped by my office to see if it was okay to hunt up there. I told him it was legal and all but advised him to not go there. Well, like some damned idiot, he ignored me and went on. Parked his truck outside the Chestnut Grove store and went off through the woods. No one ever saw him again, but two weeks later Ray Huddleston was showing off a brand-new deer rifle. We all knew he had killed that feller and stole the gun. But, again, no proof."

Paul nodded. "Bates told me that he knew they killed Charlie Kroger and left him lying in the road outside the Sandy Valley post office."

Bill laughed, "And it wasn't just the men… them Huddleston women was damned mean too. I heard this a few years ago. Old man Roy kept coming home drunk as a skunk almost every night. One night he staggers in drunk as hell and tells his wife Addie he wanted some scrambled eggs. Now she had had enough of his drinking so she went out to the chicken house and found some rotten eggs and fried 'em up and served them to him. How she stood the smell is beyond me. He puked his brains out all night, but that broke him from coming home drunk."

They all roared with laughter to the point of tears. Regis wiped his face and said, "Let me tell you this one. They were always getting into knockdown drag out fights and such. Melvin beat up his wife, Lucinda, one night. Not bad, but she did have some bruises. She was scared he'd kill her so she hid a shotgun out in the woodpile where he couldn't find it. I had to go up there for some complaint. I think maybe they were stealing chickens from the Peercys. I knocked on the door and Lucinda came to the door black and blue all over. I asked what had happened. She managed to say she wasn't pistol whipped, she was shotgun whipped. I asked her if she wanted me to arrest Melvin but she shook her head and pointed to his new Ford pickup where she had sunk a double bitted ax into the hood."

The other men looked incredulous. "So, she ought to know he'd beat her again," Paul said.

Regis motioned with his hands. "Of course, she did. That didn't stop her. Two weeks later someone called the sheriff's office that it looked like there had been a car wreck. They had seen the bed of a truck sticking out of the water in Otter Creek. Sheriff got a tractor and winch to pull the truck out and sure enough there was that big ax hole in the hood so they knew where it came from. They towed it back home and Lucinda answered the door. She said it was theirs and then added 'I wonder if any vehicles float.'"

His body shivered. "Turns out she should have asked if bodies float. They found Melvin's body in the creek a few days later. Coroner said he had been conked on the head with something and thrown in to drown. His widow didn't grieve too much."

The men fell silent before Regis continued, "Fellers, I have an idea. Let me get hold of some lawyers and judges and ask their legal opinions on something. Can you meet me here next Monday?"

Both Paul and Bill agreed before they left to go back to their own counties.

II

The three sheriffs reconvened in Regis's office the following Monday at two in the afternoon. Regis brewed a new pot of coffee and they all settled in around his desk.

He said, "I'm expecting someone, so let's just wait till he gets here."

They made small talk until a middle-aged man in a three-piece suit joined them.

Regis said, "Fellers, this here is the commonwealth attorney, William Broadus from Frankfort. Mr. Broadus, this is Sheriff Paul Southwood from Wayne County and Sheriff Bill Bates from Pickett County, Tennessee. I want you here to make sure we are following the law. I've outlined the problem we are all facing—have faced for year— the problem of jurisdiction with the Huddleston family at Bald Rock. I've gotten the legal opinion of Judge Fremont in Wayne County, Judge Hoover from Clinton County and Judge Parris from Pickett County and they all agree my plan is legal."

Mr. Broadus said, "Yes, I spoke with all of those judges and studied the case law and I think is it a perfectly legal and defensible plan."

Paul asked, "What plan are we talking about? I ain't heard any plan."

Regis scooted his chair closer to his desk. "Here's my plan. We all know that every time we go up there to arrest one of those assholes, they run to a different part of the house where we don't have jurisdiction. What if we all showed up at the same time?"

Paul and Bill were visibly stunned. Regis continued, "They'd have no place to hide so we could finally arrest them. All we need is a complainant and a crime and I have one. Billy Hardwick saw Ernie Huddleston stealing his chickens last Friday night about ten. After I told him my plan, he was all too happy to file the crime report. They had stole from him before."

Paul sighed audibly and raised his hand to his head. "Why ain't we thought of this before?"

Regis replied, "I think we just couldn't see the forest for the trees. We were so busy concentrating on crimes in our counties, we just ignored the others. But now we have all we need. You need to go back home, get your deputies, some flashlights and lanterns and your shotguns and meet back here around seven. I figure if we wait until dark .... say around ten... we can surround the house without them knowing it. Gentlemen, I think we will be shed of the Huddlestons very soon."

Paul and Bill left the office while Broadus shook Regis's hand. "Sheriff Clark, I think we're going to end a crime wave tonight," he said before leaving.

The sheriffs and their deputies convened as planned at seven. Regis had drawn out a map of the area around the house and had marked where the doors were on each side. By nine, the darkness had settled in and the caravan of law enforcement began to wind its way along the highway to Bald Rock.

When they got within a mile of the Huddleston house, they turned their headlights off and each posse sneaked through the woods to surround the house. When they were in place, they signaled Regis with two short flashes of their flashlights. Quietly, he slipped into the clearing outside the door to the house, held up a bullhorn, and yelled, "This is Sheriff Clark with a warrant for your arrest. Sheriff Bates and Sheriff Southwood are with me. We have the house surrounded. Come out with your hands up...no guns."

Tension filled the air as sounds of cursing and furniture moving could be heard in the house. Abruptly, a voice yelled back, "This here is Lester...Lester Huddleston. You can't arrest us because you are out of your jurisdiction. So, you can go to hell, Clark, goddamned you."

Clark aimed the bullhorn at the house. "Lester, maybe you didn't hear me. The other sheriffs are here so it don't matter which door you try to run through, we have you surrounded and your ass is ours. Now we can do this easy or we can do it hard. What's it going to be?"

An eerie pall settled in before Lester yelled back, "Like I said you can go to hell. If you want us, come and get us."

At that point, the sounds of gunfire filled the air, forcing Clark and his deputies to take cover behind their police car. He could hear guns firing from the other sides of the house and flying bullets shattered headlights and police car sirens. One stray bullet punctured the right front tire which exploded. Clark held up his bullhorn and yelled, "Okay, men, open fire."

A cacophony of gunfire and whizzing bullets filled the air amid the sounds of window panes being shattered. The cabin suddenly went dark when the inhabitants realized that the interior lights were making them targets. The gunfire abated and a silence settled in over the cabin.

"You can shoot in here as much as you want, you goddamned son of a bitch. We ain't coming out," Lester yelled.

"If that's the way you want it, Lester, that's the way you'll get it but for the love of God send the women and children out."

A feminine voice cursed, "You can all go to hell. We ain't budging. You'll have to kill us first."

Regis had counted on this happening so he and the other sheriffs had brought some bottles filled with kerosene with cloth wicks.

"Last chance, Lester."

"Fuck all of you."

Regis signaled the other sheriffs and each had a deputy light the wick, run up to the house, and throw it into the house. The interior of the house exploded into fireballs that spewed flames out the windows. The inhabitants began yelling and cursing as they poured out of the house firing their guns wildly hoping to hit someone, anyone.

Regis yelled into the bull horn. "Open fire."

A hailstorm of bullets and shotgun pellets rained down on the house from all directions for the next minute before the firing stopped. The posses cautiously approached the burning cabin where they could see eight bodies torn to pieces by the ambuscade. Regis saw one woman's body move and he ran over to see if she were still alive. To his horror, she was dead but her body had shielded a year-old baby boy from the onslaught. He was crying loudly, but had not sustained any wounds.

"My God," Regis cried as he scooped the boy up. "I have a little boy here. He don't seem to be hurt. Anybody else see anybody still alive?"

After a few fearful seconds, the others yelled back, "No, they're all dead here. Don't see any more children. Thank God, he's okay. That's a miracle."

The other men joined Regis in front of the house where he sat trying to calm the screaming terrified baby in the fierce glow of the house as it slowly burned down. Some of the men were crying and all were visibly shaken, utterly dumbfounded as each one struggled in vain to find some words to say.

Regis hugged the baby close and stood watching the reflections of the fire dancing furiously in his youthful perceptive eyes.

THE FAITH OF A GRAIN OF MUSTARD SEED

The light summer drizzle subsided as Eric Caldwell turned off Highway 92 onto Kentucky 167 and headed toward Mount. Pisgah on the western edge of Daniel Boone National Forest in the Appalachian Mountains of eastern Kentucky. As he drove along the narrow winding road, he saw a rainbow appear in the bright May morning. He smiled because he imagined that it ended just over the mountains where he was going.

The forest became denser and the topography much steeper before he topped the hill and headed into a wide valley carved out over thousands of years by the Big South Fork River. The farms lying in the valley were large so there were few houses scattered along the highway, but he did see Bailey's Country Store by the road and slowly pulled his Range Rover beside the gas pump in the graveled parking lot. A group of local men were enjoying the spring morning, passing time by whittling or playing rummy on the porch of the store and he hailed them as he walked toward the store.

"Good morning, fellows. I'm a little lost and was hoping you could help me. I'm looking for Mount Pisgah."

One of the men stopped whittling and replied, "You ain't lost, mister. This is Mount Pisgah. You looking for anybody particular?"

Eric stepped over to face the man. "I'm not looking for a person. My name is Eric Caldwell from the American Chestnut Restoration Project at the University of Kentucky. We are trying to bring back the American Chestnut tree and we had heard there might be some survivors of the chestnut blight in the deep forests around here."

The whittler stood up and said, "I'm Wendell Hurt. Glad to meet you. If you are looking for chestnut trees you're about a hundred years too late."

Eric nodded as he stepped onto the porch. "I know the chances are not good but we have found some groves of old chestnut trees in Michigan and New England We found an eighty year old tree in Adair County a few years ago, and there are a few more in Tennessee, Alabama, and Georgia. We thought that there might be some more in this part of the Daniel Boone National Forest since it includes some of those areas. Say, do you have a coke or something to drink? I'm very thirsty."

Hurt motioned toward the door. "There's some cans in the coolers in the back. They cost a dollar. Help yourself."

Eric went to the coolers and brought a coke to the cash register to pay for it. Hurt waved him off, “It’s on the house if you’ll tell us about what you’re doing. Come on outside and meet the guys.”

They stepped onto the porch and joined the men playing rummy. Hurt said, “Fellers, this here is Eric Caldwell from UK. He is searching for American chestnut trees.”

He pointed to the men and introduced them. “That’s Bobby Chriswell, Arthur Coffey, Jay Bertram, Willie Doss, and Billy Cooper.”

Eric shook their hands and took a seat with the others. “I have to ask if any of you have ever come across any chestnut trees around here.”

Bobby shook his head. “Can’t say that I have since I really don’t know what they look like. There’s lots of beech, oaks, hickories and walnuts.”

Arthur shrugged. “I have seen a couple of chestnut trees people have planted but they are those damned Chinese chestnuts. None of us were around before the blight killed the big chestnut trees off.”

Eric sipped his Coke and eyed the men. “So I guess you are all about the same age, seventy-something?”

The men nodded. “Yeah, so by the time we got old enough to remember anything, the trees were gone. I heard my daddy and granddaddy talk about them.”

Eric leaned forward. “I would love to hear what they had to say. Sometimes these local anecdotes provide useful information.”

Willie replied, “You probably know more than we do. What can you tell us about the blight?”

Eric drank his coke and sat the empty can on the porch. “Here’s what we know. The blight was first noticed in New York Zoological Park in 1904. Apparently, the fungus was growing on some trees imported from China. The quarantine laws were pretty lax back then. The park's arborist, Hermann Merkel, noticed that one of the big chestnut trees was dying, but he didn't know why since several nearby trees were okay. But the next thing he knew all the trees were dying all over the city. He and others isolated some kind of fungus resembling a common one that did not kill trees."

Eric waved his hand. "No one thought this was the cause so they tried to see if the disease was spread by insects or other animals. Of course, they weren't . In about six years, the blight had spread to ten more states. Back then we did not know much about genetics and evolution so the most common way of dealing with the disease once it infected a tree was to cut down all the nearby trees. But the spores of the blight were spreading by wind all over the country, so this didn't work. In retrospect, it was probably the worst thing we could have done.."

Jay wrinkled his brow. "That seemed like the safest thing to do."

Eric clasped his hands before replying. "Like I said, we were pretty ignorant of genetics then and very little was known about evolutionary mechanisms. Now we know that it was a huge mistake to cut all those trees because there was a very good chance that some of those trees had some genetic resistance to the blight and their seeds would still produce good trees."

Bobby raised his hand. "So it's like the seed companies producing new kinds of seed that are disease resistant."

Eric said, "Exactly. But the seed companies are crossing the best varieties on purpose. All that genetic variability is locked up in the gene pool so the natural selection would have had the same result. In fact, we are sure of that based on sheer numbers. Our best estimates now that when the blight hit, there were over four billon chestnut trees in North America. One in every four trees was a chestnut. One early naturalist reported that a squirrel could get on a branch of a chestnut tree in Maine and go all the way to Georgia and never leave chestnut trees. And almost all of them were gone by 1930."

Willie raised his hand. "I do remember one time my daddy showed me a young chestnut tree growing out of a stump, but it died."

Eric nodded, "The roots of the old tree are still alive in the soil and a lot of them put up new shoots but those shoots die before producing nuts."

Arthur took a deep breath. "You know fellers, I bet old man Ollie and Betty Young might remember them. Hell, they are both over eighty."

Wendell agreed, "You're right. He is pretty spry for his age. Arthur, why don't you take Mr. Caldwell up to meet him? Do you have time, Mr. Caldwell?"

"Absolutely, he is the kind of person I want to meet. Is it very far to his house?"

Arthur shook his head. "Not really and it's a good road there now. We can go in your truck or I can drive."

Eric stood up. "I'll drive and you can ride shotgun to guide me. Can we go now?"

"Sure, let's go. Wendell, we should be back before dark so I'll just leave my truck parked over there."

The two men got into the Range Rover and headed up the road to Harmon Hollow to Young's home. He and his grandson were sitting on the porch playing checkers when the men arrived and got out of their truck.

Arthur shouted, "Ollie, how would you like some company?"

Ollie yelled back, "Always looking for company. Come on up. Who's that with you?"

As the men mounted the stairs to the porch, Arthur replied, "This is Eric Caldwell from UK. He's looking for chestnut trees."

Ollie chuckled, "He is a little late. Have a chair. Nice to meet you, Mr. Caldwell. This here is my grandson Barry Young. Betty, come out here for a minute."

His wife Betty came out of the house wiping her hands on her apron. "What do you want? I'm doing the dishes."

Ollie replied, "We've got company. Mr. Caldwell, this is my wife Betty. We've been married sixty three years but I still love her."

Betty slapped him on the back playfully. "Wish I could say the same."

Everyone laughed and Betty went back inside.

Arthur said, "He says there might be some survivors around here because they have found some in Tennessee. My goodness, Barry, you've grown a lot since I saw you last year. How old are you now?"

Barry grinned, "I'm 15. Good to see you again Mr. Coffey."

"So this is what, nine years you have been coming here for a couple of weeks? You'll probably outgrow it soon."

"I don't know about that. I love spending time with Grandpa and hearing his stories."

Ollie said, "Yeah, I love having him around. Mr. Caldwell what can I do for you?"

Erie replied, "I am on a team at UK that is working to restore the chestnut trees. I always like to hear first-hand accounts of people who remember them. Do you remember them very well?"

Ollie looked away and answered, "I remember some things, but I remember what my dad and granddad told me about them more. I was born in 1920 so most of the trees were gone by then but there were still a few around. Granddaddy used to tell how they let the hogs run wild through the woods so they could eat the chestnuts and acorns. Free food and it improved the taste of the pork meat. Now I don't recall that personally."

He paused to lean forward. "Granddaddy remembered when there were still passenger pigeons around. He said they loved the chestnuts. The nuts were not very big so they could swallow them whole. He said a big flock of them would light in a tree and eat damned near all of the chestnuts off the tree and the ground."

Eric nodded. "Yes, we know the passenger pigeons loved them. I'm trained in evolutionary ecology and I often wonder how the world would be different if they were still here. The chestnut trees numbered close to four billion and the pigeons over two billion. They were clearly the dominant species and they were clearly dependent on each other. So what happens when you take out the dominant species in an ecosystem?"

Ollie grimaced, "Nothing good. The woods are full of them damned old maple trees and their seeds don't feed the wildlife much."

"That is exactly what we have found out. Losing both the chestnuts and pigeons has basically created a whole new ecosystem. The maple seeds spread so easily they choke out many other trees like oaks and beeches."

"Yep. But the chestnut trees were more than just nuts. The lumber didn't rot and was easy to work. If you want I can show you some chestnut rail fences that are over a hundred years old and still solid as a jug. Tell you what. Barry, fetch my walking stick and we'll show these men that fence."

Barry jumped up and brought Ollie his gnarled walking stick. Ollie took the stick and said, "Thank you, son. Ok, if you fellers will follow me."

He stepped off the porch and ambled toward a large barn and led them inside. Ollie walked over to a wall and stroked it. "This here is chestnut wood my daddy put up about 1900. It's still sound. Let me show you the fence behind the barn."

The men exited the rear entrance to the barn where a split rail fence surrounded a small garden plot. Ollie tapped a rail with his stick. 'Granddaddy put this up around 1870. There's been some rot but not much considering. Have you seen much of the lumber, Mr. Caldwell?"

"Yes, we have extensive samples of the wood. We also have a good supply of fresh sprouts that provide us with the DNA we need for our work. The old roots sometimes put up new shoots, but the sprouts die before they can produce nuts. The blight lives a long time in the soil."

Ollie replied, "I know what you're saying. I've seen it many times. So what are you fellers doing?"

"Without being too technical, we're cross breeding native chestnuts with Chinese chestnuts over several generations. Currently, we have produced trees that have fifteen sixteenths of their genetic makeup from American chestnut. That last sixteenth appears to give them disease resistance to the blight."

Ollie perked up his ears. "Have any of these trees produced nuts? How do they compare to the real thing?"

"Yes, we have had some success. The nuts are much bigger than the old chestnuts and are easier to shell out."

Ollie laughed, "A man could starve trying to live on chestnuts. Thing were those trees produced millions of them every year so you would just gather them by the handfuls. But all kinds of animals depended on them. The populations of wild turkeys crashed after the chestnuts died off. We are finally getting some decent populations of wild turkeys now."

Ollie bit his lower lip "How would you like to see an old chestnut stump?"

Eric's face beamed, "I would love it. Is it close by?"

Ollie smiled, "Follow me. Barry, would you lead the way?"

"Sure Grandpa. You guys just follow me."

Barry led them to a worn path; the men chatted while following along a meandering trail to an old hollowed-out stump about four feet high standing alone in a clearing. A single cane bottomed chair was leaning about the trunk. Ollie went over and set the chair up and sat down beside a pile of wood shavings.

He took a deep breath. "This here is the only real chestnut tree I can remember. It was almost a hundred feet tall and as you can see, it was almost six feet in diameter. The tree made a cool shade where we could play all day. Too bad we could not climb it. The first limb was forty feet up. I remember when daddy cut the tree like it was yesterday. He and granddaddy cried like babies. They cut it down on May 3, 1926. I was six years old. I still come out here and sit and whittle for a while, thinking about if I will ever see the chestnuts again. Follow me."

He rose from the chair and walked to the edge of the clearing where several saplings emerged from the ground. "There's some of them sprouts you were talking about, Mr. Caldwell. They look healthy now but they always die when they get just a little bigger. Barry, show him what we are doing."

Barry motioned for the men to follow him to a small glade. Ollie pointed at the places where the soil had been disturbed. Every year on May 3, me and Barry plant three more chestnut seeds here away from the old tree stump so we don't confuse them with the new sprouts."

Eric straightened up. "You mean you have actual chestnuts? How did you get them?"

Ollie answered glumly. "Daddy saw the signs of blight the last year the tree had nuts on it. I helped him gather up a couple of bushels of the nuts we planned to replant. I've about used them all up. But every year, Barry and me come out and plant some more nuts."

Eric said, "I hate to be the bearer of bad news, but it's not likely the seeds will still germinate. That said, do you have any to spare that I can take back to our labs? I'm sure the DNA is still viable and we might be able to use it."

Ollie poked at the ground with his stick. "I have a few left and you're welcome to them. I won't be planting them much longer anyway. Barry said he would keep planting them but we don't have many left. I keep the seeds in the back of the house to keep the varmints out of them. Barry, lead us back home."

The men slowly made their way back to the house where Barry brought the basket of the eleven remaining chestnuts out to show Eric. Eric's face lit up. "Wow. This is quite a find. How many can you spare?"

Ollie eyed the basket and said, "I can give you five of them. That will leave six to do two more plantings. Help yourself."

Eric put five of the chestnuts in his pockets. "Thank you, Mr. Young. Let me give you my card that has my contact information on it. Phone and email."

Ollie sniffed. "Email? Better give it to Barry because I don't do email.'

Eric handed the card to Barry who stuck it into his shirt pocket.

"If you don't mind, I'll take these back to the lab. I can recruit some undergraduates to come back here in the fall to do a grid search. We might get lucky."

Ollie sighed. "That'll be fine, Mr. Caldwell. Have a safe trip home."

II

Spring dove-tailed into summer and Barry had to return home to off season football practice. The day before he left, he and Ollie returned to the glade where they had planted the chestnuts. When they reached the clearing, Ollie yelled, "Son of a bitch! They came up!" He hurried over to see the three young shoots of the chestnut tree swaying gently in the light breeze.

"And he thought the seeds wouldn't come up. But then neither did I after all these years. Son, maybe you will see the chestnuts come back a little in your life. I wish I could see them but I doubt I will. Promise me you'll plant the rest of the seeds next year. Just go ahead and plant them all. Thank the lord I have lived to see this."

By the time Barry had left for the summer, word spread throughout the community of the miraculous rebirth of the chestnuts and many of the old-timers made pilgrimages to admire the tender young seedlings. Ollie spent much of the time sitting in the chair near the old chestnut stump whittling on a cedar stick. Occasionally, he went over to survey the seedlings and pull any weeds that had come up near them.

One day he did not show up for lunch so Betty went looking for him. She found him slumped over in his chair with his pocketknife and cedar stick lying in his lap. Horrified, Betty shook him to rouse him, but she was too late. She collapsed in tears near his chair and sat crying for several minutes before returning home to call their son Ryan.

When he answered, she said in a soft voice, "I just found Ollie dead in his chair. Can you please come as soon as you can?"

Ryan caught his breath as he sobbed, "Oh no. I'll be there as soon as I can, Mom. Don't do anything. Just try to stay calm."

He drove up twenty minutes later and comforted Betty. "It's okay, Mom. I'm here. Where did you find him?"

Betty wiped her nose. "He is in his chair out where he planted those chestnuts. I did not know who to call besides you."

Ryan kissed her forehead. "I'll call the sheriff and have him call the coroner and arrange for an ambulance. Do you feel like showing me where he is?"

She nodded and led him to where Ollie was still in his chair. They cried and hugged each other before returning home to wait on the sheriff.

By the next morning, they had settled down enough to start planning the visitation and funeral. Ryan drove them to the undertaker's office and scheduled the visitation and funeral for Friday afternoon. A big crowd attended the services and swapped stories of the times they had spent with Ollie. After the burial, Ryan insisted that Betty come stay with him for a few days until she was able to return home.

Summer slipped away into fall and one October morning, Eric Caldwell and his crew of researchers arrived to do a grid search for any chestnuts. When Betty met him at the door, he said, "Ms. Young, you may remember me from last spring. Eric Caldwell from UK. I am so sorry to hear of your husband's passing. I was looking forward to talking with him some more."

Betty answered, "Yes, I remember you and thank you for the condolences. Ollie really enjoyed talking with you about the chestnut trees he loved so much.'

Eric replied, "I could see they meant a lot to him. By the way, I sent five of those hybrid seeds to your grandson a few days after we were here last summer. Do you know if they came up?'

Betty smiled a Mona Lisa smile and answered, "Oh, I guess that explains some things. I can show you where those chestnut sprouts are, but if you don't mind, I would still like to believe in miracles a little bit longer, Mr. Caldwell."

NO GOOD DEED

The people of the mountains depended on chickens, hogs and possibly some rabbits and squirrels to supply them with meat in their diet. Hogs were basically safe from predators, but chickens were always on the shopping lists of foxes, bobcats, and raccoons. Every rural family had flocks of chickens to supply eggs and meat and a few sold eggs to neighbors or grocery stores in town so they were a valuable commodity that required constant vigilance.

With three children and a wife to feed, Walter Burnett kept a flock of about a hundred chickens of many different kinds that provided enough eggs to sell and the occasional chicken dinner, but with that many chickens he did not always notice if a chicken or two went missing. But when one of his two Minorcas disappeared, he began to count them every day and found that he was losing a hen every day or two.

Walter and his oldest son Marty started investigating the fields and woodlands around their farm and soon found patches of feathers that left no doubt that a fox was catching the chickens.

When they found the first kill site, Walter pointed to the feathers and said, "Marty, do you see that? There's a fox killing our chickens."

Marty stared at the feathers. "How do you know it ain't a chicken hawk?"

"Too many feathers. A hawk will grab a hen and fly off with it. And see how the feathers make a trail through the woods? If we don't kill it, it will clean us out. Probably a red fox."

Marty asked, "Can we just keep the chickens penned up?"

"No, they need to be out to eat because I don't want to buy feed for them during the summer. I bet he is killing our neighbors' chickens, too Let's go back home and call them."

After they got home, Walter called his neighbors. As he expected, the Coopers, the Sextons and the Fraziers had lost some chickens. They suspected a fox but had not had time to hunt for it.

Walter hung up the phone. "Marty, here's a chance to earn some money and do some good. They said they'd pay you two dollars apiece if you kill the fox. And you can sell the hide too. You're a pretty good shot with a rifle. Are you interested in hunting this fox?"

"Absolutely. Do I need to get a special license?"

"No, farmers are allowed to protect their livestock. We can't shoot hawks, but foxes are fair game. I think there's a half box of rifle shells for the twenty-two. You probably couldn't get close enough to use a shotgun. That rifle ain't got a lot of power so you'd have to hit it in the right spot…heart or head. I guess the first thing is to find out when it's catching them. Get the rifle and get up in the barn loft so you can see the whole place."

Marty could barely contain his excitement. He had hunted squirrels, rabbits and a few bobwhites, but this would be the first time hunting bigger game. He ran to the house and retrieved the rifle and a box of shells from the gun rack before climbing the ladder to take up a position in the barn loft. He pulled up a bale of hay and scanned the fields. He saw Walter setting a tin can on a fence post about twenty yards away.

"Hey, Marty, see if you can hit this pop can," he yelled.

Marty raised the rifle and steadied it against his right shoulder. After a deep breath, he squeezed the trigger and the can jumped off the post.

"Great shot. Let's see if you can hit one farther out."

Walter walked along the fence until he was about sixty yards away. He waved to Marty to shoot.

Marty took long to aim, but he hit the can again.

Walter came back to the barn. "You'll have to get pretty close to kill him with that rifle. Just stay up there for a little while and see if he shows up."

Marty nodded and settled in to wait, but after an hour he grew bored and left the barn.

"Dad, I don't think he is coming today. He's probably after someone else's chickens."

Walter agreed. "Them damned chickens are too stupid to stay close to the house and that's when he's getting them. Maybe we can sorta listen to see if they raise a ruckus."

The next day, Marty was watering the family's two pigs when he heard the chickens cackling loudly. He dropped the bucket and raced to the edge of the field where he could see the chickens walking around nervously. Realizing that he did not have time to run to get the rifle, he stood quietly to see what was scaring the chickens.

To his surprise, a skinny red fox burst out of the surrounding woodlands and stood looking hungrily through the wire fence, completely ignoring Marty. Marty had never seen a fox this close and he froze for a moment before waving his arms wildly and yelling "SHOO!" The fox turned and slunk back into the woods.

Marty dreaded telling his dad about the failure to catch the fox, but Walter simply said, "You need to carry your gun or have it close by. I'm a little concerned for a fox to be that bold. They are bad to carry rabies. It ain't just about the chickens anymore."

He sipped his coffee. "I'll put the word out to the neighbors and maybe one of them will get him. Still, just be on the lookout. Wait.... you hear that?"

Walter got up from the table and led Marty out to the porch. Suddenly, a high-pitched bark pierced the warm June evening. Walter whispered, "That's a call to his mate. Foxes have many kinds of barks and howls. Sometimes they sound like a woman screaming or a baby crying, it almost sounds human. They mate for life so I bet they have some pups. I'll put the word out."

Two days later, Bobby Sexton called and Marty answered the phone. "Hello, is that you Marty? I may have some good news. I found a fox killed in the road this morning... a male. I guess the vixen is still out there."

Despite the best efforts of the farmers, the foxes continued to steal chickens over the next two weeks. Marty spent a few hours each day patrolling the farm, gradually enlarging the area he covered to include the margins of the woodlands. After the third theft, he noticed that the feathers of the fox's victims followed the same path over the wooded ridge to the next valley.

Marty told Walter, "I'm going to see if I can track the fox from them feathers. I'll be careful."

Walter replied, "Don't go too far beyond where you know and get lost. You might get lucky. You need to be back in a couple of hours."

Marty nodded and started off through the woods. The trail of feathers gradually waned so that it became just guesswork by the time he had reached the top of the ridge. He remembered there were some shallow caves on the other side of the ridge and he followed an old logging road to the point where a trail veered off down the other side. Shortly, he found the cave but seeing no sign of anything living in it, he continued meandering through the woods until he reached the edge of the wheat field in the valley. The walking had tired him out so he found a comfortable spot under a beech tree and sat down to rest.

Bird songs filled the air and he passed the time trying to identify the birds. Suddenly, the birds stopped singing so he perked up his ears and scanned the area. He saw a movement out of the corner of his eye and a fox appeared at the edge of a small knoll. The fox saw him and suddenly just plopped itself down to stare at him.

Marty slowly raised his gun to take aim at the fox, but three young fox pups suddenly joined the fox, nipping and playing at each other. He lowered his gun to just sit quietly and watch the pups play with each other and the adult. The little yips and yelps as they gamboled atop the knoll made him smile.

He thought about what his dad had told him and realized that this was probably the mother fox who was the mate of the male killed in the road. Realizing that killing her would condemn the pups to starve to death, he felt tears welling in his eyes. He sighed and laid the rifle on the ground. The foxes continued to play around their mother who sat motionless staring at Marty. After a few minutes, she turned away and led the pups back into the woods.

Marty thought about what to do. He decided not to tell his dad about the encounter lest he be called weak or stupid for not shooting the fox who was raiding their chicken yards.

When he reached home, Walter was waiting for him near the chicken house.

"Well, did you have any luck? I don't see any foxes."

Fearing Walter would detect his deception, he avoided eye contact as he answered, "No, I followed the feathers as far as I could but the trail petered out just over the ridge. I tried to find their den but had no luck. Maybe I will have better luck tomorrow."

Walter shrugged. "Well, you tried and it probably won't matter anyway. Denzel Cooper killed a fox carrying one of his hens.... she was obviously nursing pups as her teats were wet. Sad to say, but without either a mother or father those pups will probably starve or get caught by an owl or a dog. No way to know where the den is so not much we can do."

Marty felt the blood rush to his face and a hot flush coursed through his body before he answered weakly, "Okay, Dad, I guess that solves the problem."

He ate his supper in silence before retreating to the porch swing that swayed gently back and forth, its chains creaking softly, muting his sobs as he listened to the kits' faint plaintive cries dying in the night.

FOLLOW YOUR NOSE

I could not see or hear for two weeks when I was born in the spring. My nose flooded me with all the information I needed to survive. The first thing I smelled was my mother's warm body. I smelled the milk from her nipples as I settled in for my first meal.

There's Mom and Dad now. I think I'll say hello. Hi, Mom. Hi, Dad.

Gradually, I picked up the aromas of my five brothers and sisters and the flood of odors from my surroundings.

I miss playing with my littermates.

After my ears and eyes opened, I saw tall things my mother called humans. They are our masters. They called me a golden retriever.

One of them cradled me in his arms and scratched my ears. His name was Jimmy and he had a young sweet aroma. He named me Duke.

Maybe Jimmy will come out and walk with me. Oh, look, there goes a bunny. They smell like new grass.

As I grew stronger, I loved playing with my brothers and sisters. Soon we went out into the yard. My nose was overcome by thousands of new smells.

I smell bacon frying. I guess Margie is cooking breakfast. Maybe Jimmy will bring me a piece.

The grass in our pen was soft and had a sweet aroma. The wind carried the smells of the outside world: the house of our masters, the flowers and freshly-tilled soil in the garden, all kinds of trees and plants.

The apple trees are blooming.

I love the smell of their pretty blooms.

I could tell the other animals by their smells, including one my master called a cat named Prissy.

There's Prissy now and she has new kittens to show off. Kittens are so much fun. I like to watch them bounce around sideways. Good morning, Prissy. Have you seen Jimmy?

She was smaller than I am and she had a different attitude about things. When she walked by me, I tried to introduce myself. She just hissed at me and swatted my nose with her paw. It surprised me, but it didn't hurt. Mom said that is just the way cats are. They don't mean me any harm.

I love her smell and the smell of her kittens. I watch them play-fighting her in the yard. I can't play with her when she has the kittens with her.

All the other humans had different aromas I could use to identify them. Margie, the mother of the family, always smelled like roses. Jimmy's father Jeff always had the odor of the outdoors.

Good. Margie is calling for me to come into the house. Today she smells like bacon. There's Jeff eating breakfast. He smells like a grown man who works hard and sweats. He always gives me a piece of bacon. I love the smells of the kitchen. I guess Jimmy is still asleep.

.Jimmy would spend hours playing with us puppies. He took us for walks around the farm where we were born. We met my father Rex, the cows, Jersey and Beulah, the chickens and ducks, and the horse Beauty.

Jeff is opening the door to let me out. There were some deer in the yard last night. The ducks and geese walked across the yard to go to the creek. I hate the smell of their poop. I need to find Jimmy.

Every day I smelled new odors. My nose got much better in sorting out the smells flooding my brain.

My masters made sure we had a lot of food and water and we all grew quickly. Jimmy always wanted to play with me. He often took me for walks around the fields. One day, he took me to the creek where we played in the water all afternoon.

I think I will go to the creek to see what was there last night. The ducks and geese are floating by. I love the smell of the water in the creek. I bet Jimmy is there.

One afternoon, Jimmy took me to the backyard and showed me something he called a ball. He let me smell it. Then threw it across the yard. He motioned for me to get it. He said "FETCH!" I chased after the ball and picked it up with my mouth and brought it back to him.

Where did he leave the ball last night? Sometimes Jimmy hides it from me.

Jimmy patted me on the head and threw the ball again. We spent most of the afternoon playing FETCH. I was tired but very happy with all the attention I got. I realized that I wanted to be with Jimmy wherever he went.

I wonder where he could have put the ball..

One day, Jimmy let me out of the pen and led me through the forest near the house. My head reeled with so many new smells.

After a few days, I learned they were rabbits, squirrels, deer, skunks, raccoons and possums.

Let's see what came to the creek last night. Raccoons, a deer, a fox and her cubs, two possums. No Jimmy.

The rabbits were too quick for me to catch and the squirrels ran up the trees and chattered at me from their perch.

I love to chase the squirrels. I think they are teasing me so I don't try too hard.

There was a strong nasty smell that day that made me sick. Jimmy told me that was a skunk. He told me to avoid skunks. We saw an ugly possum toddling along the fence row. When we tried to touch him, he hissed at us like Prissy. When I tried to play, he fainted and lay there like he was dead. I was afraid I had killed him. Jimmy told me he was just pretending to be dead so I would leave him alone.

There was a mother possum and her babies drinking here last night. I can always tell their tracks with that weird toe sticking out of the side. She had a bunch of babies. Time to go back to the yard to see if Jimmy is there.

Over the next few weeks, people came by to see the puppies. One by one, they chose my brothers and sisters to take home with them. Jimmy told me that I was his puppy. He would not let anyone else have me. Soon I was the only young puppy around. Jimmy and I had the whole world to ourselves.

Where could he be? Has he gone to school already? I didn't see the bus or smell the gas fumes.

Jimmy had to do something called chores. He gathered eggs, drove the cows to the barn and chopped weeds out of the garden. Every day, his smell changed as he grew. I could always recognize his aroma.

Now his smell has changed when he sweat from doing chores. But I can still smell him when I first met him.

By now, Prissy had a litter of what Jimmy called kittens. They were tiny versions of Prissy. They hissed and arched their backs. Prissy was very protective of them. After a while she led them over to meet me. One of them grabbed my tail and another one crawled onto my back. Something told me to be gentle with them and not hurt them. Before long we were all having a grand time chasing each other. After the kittens were tired, Prissy picked them up by their necks and carried them to the back porch.

Maybe Jimmy is checking on Prissy and her kittens. They were heading toward the barn. The smells of the barn are overpowering. The cows, the horse, the hay. It is hard to sort them out. I don't see Jimmy there.

One day, he took me out to the barn and began to dig redworms for something he called bait. The worms were moist and slimy. They wriggled between Jimmy's fingers as he dropped them into a tin can. I liked their earthy smell, but their wriggling tickled my nose. Jimmy got a long cane pole. Together we walked down the creek to a deep hole where he stuck a hook through a worm. The hook was tied to a string that was tied on the pole.

Maybe he went fishing down at the creek at the deep pool. I will run down there. Jimmy loves to fish.

He threw the hook and worm out into the deep pool and waited for a few minutes. There was a little round ball tied to the string bobbed up and down. Jimmy pulled the pole up. A strange animal was flopping on the end of the line. He showed me the animal and said "FISH". He took it off the hook and put another worm on the hook. I did not like the smell of the fish, especially because it messed up Jimmy's smell.

I am at the deep pool, but I don't find Jimmy.

He caught ten fish before we went back to the house. He took a knife and cleaned the fish for Margie to cook for dinner. Prissy and her kittens nibbled at the parts of the fish Jimmy did not want. The kittens were so funny hissing, growling and swatting at each other.

Maybe he is working in the garden. He likes to do that before it gets too hot.

Early one morning, Jimmy took me to what he called the garden where he started scraping the ground with a hoe. I watched as he moved along each row, chopping the weeds from around the plants. After he had finished, we went back to the house. He sat in the porch swing and invited me to join him. I hopped into the swing. The rocking motion made me sleepy. I dozed off until the aroma of Margie's cooking lunch woke me up.

I wonder if Jimmy is in the porch swing. He has been there a lot the last few days.

I am hungry. I have not eaten anything this morning. Jimmy keeps my food bowl full of dry food. He always gives me Alpo for supper.

One day, Jimmy and Jeff took me to a strange place they called the vet. My nose was on fire with all the smells of other dogs and cats in the building. I saw little puppies and kittens, a rabbit and two birds. Jeff lifted me onto a table where the vet examined me and stuck some needles in me. They really did not even hurt. We went back home where Jimmy played FETCH with me for a long time. He was throwing the ball farther now. I had to run faster to get it. Sometimes, he would pretend to throw the ball. I would run out looking for it before coming back to his side where he teased me with the ball.

I need to find where Jimmy hid that ball. I have looked everywhere. I bet he is playing a joke on me.

Jimmy was growing bigger. I could smell changes in his body odor. I caught a whiff of a new smell on his body that I did not recognize. I didn't like it, but it soon passed. For a long time, he was gone all day to something he called 'School'. He would get on a big thing he called a bus and disappear for most of the day. After school, he would come back and change into his work clothes to do his chores.

Maybe he is driving the cows toward the upper pastures. I will run that way to catch them.

I really liked going up the narrow road to the pastures to drive Jersey and Beulah back to the barn where Jeff would milk them. Sometimes, Jeff would ask Jimmy to try to milk them. His hands were not big enough or strong enough to make the milk flow. Prissy and her kittens would rub against Jeff's legs. Sometimes he would squirt milk into their faces and watch them lick it off each other.

I could tell the weather was getting colder. One morning, I woke up and found that the whole farm was covered in something very white. Jimmy took me for a short walk. I could feel that this stuff he called 'Snow' was cold and made me want to play. The snow was a lot of fun, but I had a hard time finding the ball when Jimmy threw it.

I wish we had snow now, but Jimmy told me it only comes when it is cold. He has taught me so much.

When we were through playing in the snow, he took me into the house so I could warm myself in front of the fire. The smell of burning wood and the smoke threw my sense of smell off. When Jimmy knelt down to comb me, I smelled that bad smell again.

Every day on the farm I smelled something new to go with the odors I already knew. Jeff and Margie found new homes for Prissy's kittens. She soon had another litter to replace them. Sometimes, Prissy would catch a mouse and lay it in front of the door. Margie would scream for Jimmy to throw it away. I could tell it hurt Prissy's feelings, but she kept bringing them in.

As Jimmy grew bigger over the years, his body odor changed. He smelled the same, but different. That strange smell was growing stronger but I still did not know what it was. The new smell made me agitated and anxious. But he was still Jimmy and we still enjoyed our life on the farm. Jeff taught him to drive the tractor so he could plough the fields or haul in the bales of hay.

I love the smell of fresh-cut hay. It reminds me of playing in the meadows with Jimmy. Maybe Jimmy is there.

I watched Jeff and Jimmy store the hay in the barn. They fed the cows and horse the hay when snow was on the ground.

One day after a hard day of work, after Jimmy took a shower, he sat in the swing and called me to join him. Any time he took a bath, the soap he used had a pungent aroma that burned my nose. I still noticed the strange aroma I had smelled before. I did not like it.

Maybe he is taking a shower to get ready for school. But it is too late for the bus.

This time the odor was stronger and it did not smell exactly like Jimmy. His voice was growing deeper and fine hair appeared on this face. He had grown taller and leaner. We still had plenty of time to play even as he did more work on the farm.

The odd smell kept growing stronger and stronger. One day, Jimmy did not feel like playing FETCH. I spent the afternoon lying beside him in the swing.

I wonder where he could be today. Sometimes he likes to play hide and seek. I bet he is still hiding in the house.

Woof, woof, woof. Margie always lets me in when I bark. That's weird. Usually, Jeff is out working on the farm and Margie is cleaning house. Now they are both just sitting and crying at the table. I can smell their tears.

Jimmy kept the ball in his room. I will look for it there.

He has made his bed. There is the ball on his night stand. I can just reach it.

Maybe if I show Margie and Jeff the ball they will tell me where Jimmy is.

Woof, woof, woof. Here's the ball. Where is Jimmy?

I need him to play FETCH!

Woof, woof, woof. Tell Jimmy to come out and play with me. We have not played FETCH for a long time. Tell Jimmy to come out and throw the ball for me. I love bringing the ball to Jimmy. I can't find him. Where is Jimmy?

A GOOD NAME IS RATHER TO BE CHOSEN THAN GREAT RICHES

The Mid-American Traveling Carnival and Petting Zoo had toured many small towns throughout the South and Midwest for years and had maintained a good reputation, as far as the reputations of carnivals go, with only minor run-ins with local law enforcement agencies. A few malcontents had accused them of running unfair games that took advantage of the dreams of children, but most of the unsophisticated people on their circuit just enjoyed going to the carnival to break up the mundane daily grind that locked them into joyless ruts.

The carnies themselves hailed from a variety of backgrounds from older teenagers who ran away from home to what they assumed would be an adventurous life to older men and women who were otherwise unemployable or unwilling to undergo retraining to get better jobs. They often were in poor health because their diet consisted mostly of corndogs, funnel cakes or kielbasa washed down with Mountain Dew or cheap booze they secreted away from disapproving eyes and inspections. The carnies formed a kind of family who watched out for each other in the face of the harassment by local sheriffs bent on shutting them down for some obscure municipal ordinance; they had a sense of camaraderie that made the following yarn so difficult to fathom.

The carnival had just pulled into Monticello, Kentucky, and had attracted a large crowd on its first two nights despite some perfunctory walk-throughs by the local police. The third day opened auspiciously when the bearded lady Josephine McComb, discovered the body of one of the carnies face down in the dirt outside the trailer he called home. After trying frantically to revive him, she yelled out for help. Several people came to her aid.

Walter Poore, the main clown of the carnival was the first to reach her. Breathlessly, he asked, "What's going on, Josey?"

She pointed to the body, "I found this dead man lying there."

Walter eyed the body before turning him over. "Yeah, he is dead all right. Don't see any wounds."

He snickered, "Maybe one of them falling stars got him last night."

Josephine asked, "What are you talking about?"

"I saw a tv show the other day that we are going to get a major meteorite shower in mid –April but I guess there could be a few early ones. Hey, I'm yanking your chain."

By now three other carnies had assembled near the body. George Mackey, the circus strong man, asked "Does anyone know him?"

Bernie Goff, who ran the pick-a-duck and ring toss games replied. "Well, I have seen him around but I never knew his name. Anybody know him?"

Linda Lawson, the tattooed lady, shook her head, "I've seen him around but never got his name. Someone should get the boss here so he can call the cops."

Walter nodded and raced off to alert the head of the carnival, Paul Greenfield, who ran back to the scene with him.

Paul knelt down and peered at the man's face quizzically. He said, "I've seen him around but don't recall his name. Anybody know him?"

A chorus of voices agreed they did not as Paul stood up. "Let me check the files in my office. He must be on the payroll. Don't touch him anymore until I've called the police. We probably should not have touched him any at all. I'm sure they will want to take statements so go ahead and get some breakfast and come back here."

Paul trotted back to his office and rummaged through his personnel files but all he could find were files for the people he already knew. There were no extra files. After going through more filing cabinets and finding nothing, he called the sheriff.

The office administrative assistant answered the phone. "Sheriff's office, how may I help you?"

"Yes, this Paul Greenfield out at the carnival. We found a dead body this morning. Can you send out the coroner and ambulance and a deputy? I have to get this taken care of before we open this afternoon."

"Sure, I'll have Brian Keller come out and bring the coroner and ambulance. They should be there in fifteen minutes. Keep people away from the scene."

Paul returned to corral the crowd that was growing larger.

"Sheriff and coroner on the way. I can't find any record of him. Does anyone recognize him? Does anyone know where he is from?"

By now the entire entourage of carnival workers had heard of the situation and gathered around the body.

Rudy Walton, the operator of the petting zoo, shrugged. "Well, I've seen him around. I never knew his name. I just called him Buddy and he always answered me. Sometimes he fed and watered the animals for me. One time I asked where he was from and he said 'Electra'. Didn't say what state and I didn't ask. Maybe I should have."

Mike Getz, who ran the carousel, added, "I always called him Mack. He had helped me maintain the carousel, oiling the gear box, washing down the horses. I never gave him much thought. I can't even remember when he started working here."

Bruce Sexton, who ran the shooting gallery, agreed. "I never knew his name other than Buddy or Mac or Hey you. He was just sort of a fixture. Let's see… I'm trying to remember when I first noticed him. I'm pretty sure he was with us at the Lancaster County Fair two weeks ago."

Shelia Morgan, the fortune teller, added, "Yeah, he was there but I think I saw him at Burnside last month. Like you say, he didn't stand out. But he was always willing to do whatever needed to be done. I don't think I ever knew his name. I just talked to him directly — no need to call him by name. He was always very pleasant. I'm trying to remember if I ever smelled booze on his breath, but can't say I did."

The coroner and deputy had arrived. Deputy Brian Keller, said loudly, "I need everyone to please step away from the body. Please let me and Coroner Walker in."

The crowd parted to allow them access to the body. Walker knelt down and began to examine the body. He fished a small tape recorder out of his jacket pocket. "This is Friday, April 2, 2010, Coroner Samuel Walker, reporting from the Carnival at the fairgrounds in Monticello, Kentucky. Preliminary examination shows no signs of foul play, no cuts, no bruises, no tears in clothing. No evidence of alcohol. Need to collect some blood for toxicology. Body is maybe six feet tall, weight, maybe one hundred eighty pounds. Dark brown hair and scruffy beard. No visible tattoos or body piercings. Rigor mortis has set in. Time of death possibly midnight. Taking body to morgue for more investigation."

He clicked the tape recorder off before stuffing it into his pocket. He motioned for the deputy and George Mackey to help load the body. The crowd milled around for a few minutes before returning to their duties to begin the day's work..

II

The ambulance wound its way back to the city morgue where Walker's assistants unloaded the body and carried it into the operating room. Walker searched through the body's clothes. He found forty-five cents and a small penknife in the right front pocket. There was a badly worn leather wallet containing a five dollar bill and a folded slip of paper bearing a set of numbers: 4-2-10 was on one side, and on the other side of the paper 4-5-10. 36.73942 and -84.95371. Walker studied the paper but could make no sense of the inscriptions. He carefully removed the clothing from the body and began to examine it more closely before clicking the tape recorder again.

"Coroner Walker continuing autopsy of unknown body recovered from Mid-American Traveling Carnival and Petting Zoo in Monticello, Kentucky fairgrounds. Age, probably mid-thirties. No obvious trauma, no scars, no discolorations. Actual height, 6 feet one inch and weight, one hundred ninety one pounds. Preliminary tests show no evidence of alcohol or drugs. Still no definite identification. We don't know any next of kin and no signs of foul play or drugs really no reason for extensive dissection. For now, COD, natural causes. Need to re- interview possible witnesses."

After gently crossing the corpse's arms across the chest, he wheeled the gurney over to the cold storage lockers and slid it into the compartment before returning to his office to call the sheriff.

"Hello, this you, Mitchell? Great. Brian came out to the carnival and helped me retrieve the body. I've completed the examination for now. MY best guess is COD, possibly heart attack. I am going to list as 'natural causes.' Any luck on who he is?"

"So far, no luck. Some smart ass, I think the clown Walter, jokingly said maybe he was hit by a meteorite. Apparently, he had heard that there was going to be a meteorite shower later this month and thought maybe he was hit by an early one, but he was just bullshitting people."

"With no signs of foul play or drugs why would you want me to open the body up? Oh, I did find a piece of paper with some numbers on it. I guess you need it for your records. Can you come by and get it?"

"Lot of time and expense for no good reason. I'm going back to the carnival in a little while to try to find out who he was. I'll let you know."

III

After stopping by the coroner's office to get the paper, Sheriff Mitchell Shelton drove his cruiser to the carnival that was bustling with crowds of excited children trying to win prizes or take turns on the rides. He found Paul and they went into the main office.

"So, Mr. Greenfield, have you made any headway in finding out who this guy was?"

Greenfield shook his head. "Not one clue. Almost everyone remembers seeing him around for the last several weeks — maybe three months. Different people had different names for him and he always answered to whatever they called him. Spent a lot his time by himself. Never talked about himself or where he was from. He never complained about the food or the work. Seemed to have a way of working with animals who were injured or sick. He never had much to say to anyone. Josephine did say that she thought she saw him praying one day when we were in Lancaster. Other than that we have hit a brick wall."

Shelton became visibly irritated. "You mean to tell me you don't know his name? No payroll records?"

"I pay a lot of my people in cash. To be honest, some of these folks have shady pasts and prefer that. My guess is some of them probably never file taxes. I don't do much research unless I have a reason. Never had a reason or any problems. I am confused as you are. Did you find anything on the body?"

Shelton Walker pulled the paper out of his pocket. "Just this paper but it makes no sense. Any ideas?"

Greenfield took the paper, eying it carefully. "Hmm. Well, that 4-2-10 could be yesterday's date. But why put the date next Monday on the other side? Them other numbers, no clue. So what do you want to do with the body?"

He handed the paper back to Shelton. "That's a good question. I don't want to cremate him in case someone shows up. I am going to make a press release and get some media coverage. We don't have a potter's field. Let me ask around. Maybe I can find some good man who wants to give him a Christian burial. I'll keep you in the loop."

"Well, we're pulling out tomorrow so I'll just have to leave the body with you. I'll give you our itinerary for the next six months in case you make any headway."

IV

The circus left town the next day, after dropping off its itinerary to the sheriff's office. Shelton and Walker composed a detailed account of the body's description and posted it to television and radio stations. Mitchell had put out some lines of inquiries to find a proper burial site. Stanley Harmon called them to say that Taylor's Grove Baptist Church had recently enlarged its cemetery plot and offered to bury the body there if someone would provide a coffin.

Shelton contacted Greenfield about the cost of the coffin and he said that he could cover the cost of an inexpensive coffin, a cheap suit and burial. He contracted a backhoe operator to dig a grave at the cemetery and the body was interred on Monday, April 5. Stanley Harmon had found a smooth limestone rock that could serve as a tombstone, a tombstone that bore no identifying marks at all.

Shelton and Walker stood by the grave, each man not sure what to say before Shelton spoke softly. "Someone said he may have been from some place called Electra. I did a little research and found a small town in Texas named Electra....maybe two thousand people.

I faxed the sheriff there a photo of his face and description in hopes that someone would recognize him. So far no luck."

He pulled the paper out of his pocket and smiled when he read the second date. "Now, I know you're going to think I'm nuts —well, that is a separate issue — but I did a google search on Electra and it turns out there is a blue white giant star by that name in the constellation Taurus about four hundred light years away. Hell, he might as well be from there as anywhere for all we know. Texas, Taurus, Neverland or Alice in Wonderland. Does it really matter?"

He took a deep breath and continued, "I couldn't sleep last night, so I went out to the porch for a while. Someone told me that the clown had suggested this man was killed by a meteorite and sure enough I saw some shooting stars last night. Some people believe that seeing a shooting star means another soul has gone to heaven. Others think your wishes will come true if you wish on a falling star. I wonder if this poor bastard made a wish on the night he died."

Walker shrugged his shoulders. "This is going to sound strange but I couldn't sleep either last night. I got up around three to take a leak and went outside to check on things. I saw a couple of shooting stars, too. My grandma always told me that I could make my wishes come true if I wished on a falling star. And you know, without thinking, I wished I knew this poor bastard's name so I could contact his family. Well, I guess that was just another stupid superstition because here we are burying him and still don't know his name. Probably never will."

He looked back at the featureless stone marking the grave before continuing, "You know I guess in a hundred years from now, it won't make any difference if there is a name on that stone or not. I mean look around. You see all these tombstones with names on them and they don't mean a damn thing to any of us. This life is all we have for sure and we had damned better be sure to live life to its fullest cause there ain't no do-overs. Find someone to love, maybe have some kids, live a good life so people will have fond memories of us and speak well of us after we are gone. That's all that matters. Otherwise, we ain't no better than this poor soul. Damn, that is depressing. Sorry I brought it up."

Shelton patted him on the back. "I guess people think about those things when they are dealing with death of loved ones. I guess we can feel that way anytime anyone dies — even if we don't know them. Maybe that is why people believe in heaven and an afterlife. They can't just accept that this is all there is. They can't conceive of a world without them in it. I say whatever gets them through the night. As for me, —well, I …"

His didn't bother to finish his sentence as his voice trailed off into an awkward silence. Walker just nodded. "I hear, you, Mitchell, I hear you. What's done is done and the guy got a decent burial. I guess that's all we can ask for in the final analysis. Cheer up. Tomorrow's another day. See you later."

They got into their cars and drove out of the cemetery to return to their boring everyday lives.

V

The mysterious death of a completely unidentifiable body was the most exciting thing to happen in the community in a long time, but it became just a memory after the circus left when the death notice yielded no leads.

Six months later, a handsome man in his mid-twenties came to Shelton's office and introduced himself.

"Sheriff Walker, my name is Robert Beale. I just found out about your mysterious body. I can't be sure, but it may be my Uncle Gabriel Stein. How to say this: he had some serious mental health issues and suffered from delusions and sporadic bouts of amnesia. Sometimes he does not even remember his own name. The last time we had heard from him, he was somewhere in Texas working with a circus but we never knew where."

Shelton shook his hand. "Glad to meet you, Mr. Beale. I hope you can clear this up. But why come forward now?"

Beale took a deep breath. "As it turns out, Gabriel may have had a substantial life insurance policy if we can indeed verify it is his body. Again, I am pretty sure that your body is my uncle, but the insurance company is asking for DNA confirmation before they pay out. I was hoping we could exhume the body to get a sample to test."

Shelton rubbed his lower jaw before continuing, "Under the circumstances, we should be able to do that if you are willing to cover the costs. Give me a week to arrange it. How can I contact you?"

Beale scribbled his name and phone number on a post-it note and handed it to Shelton. "If you could call me the day before the exhumation takes place so I can be here?"

"Sure. This looks like a Louisville number."

"It is. Thank you so much for your time and assistance."

The following week, Shelton called Beale and arranged to meet him at the office. When he came into the office, Shelton offered to drive him out to the cemetery.

"That is very kind, Sheriff Shelton, but there is no need. I can use the Garmin trip planner. All I have to do is type in location"

"Taylor's Grove Baptist Church, Monticello, Kentucky."

"Okay, I will meet you there."

He and Shelton got into their cars and drove to the cemetery where they met the coroner Walker who had already given the order to exhume the body. The dirty slightly corroded coffin was resting beside the open grave.

Walker pulled a jar of Vicks Vapo-rub. "A word of advice, gentlemen. If you don't want to hurl your lunch, place a smear of this Vapo-rub under your nose to mask the smell of decomposition. It will take me a few minutes to collect the samples."

The men smiled and nodded their approval. Shelton replied, "Thanks Mitchell. I've done this before, Mr. Beale. Take my word for it; you need to do this."

All the men applied the pungent salve to their upper lips. Walker used a small crowbar to pry the lid loose all the way around the coffin. He took a deep breath and slowly raised the coffin lid until it was perpendicular to the coffin body.

The men all gasped when they looked into the coffin that contained only a decaying cheap suit.

Shelton raised his arms. "What in the hell has happened here? Where did the body go? Any sign of grave robbers?"

Walker shook his head in utter consternation. "Absolutely not. This is the first time the sun has shone on this coffin's interior."

Beale's face showed his incredulous disappointment. "So what is going on here? You told me you had a body."

Shelton and Walker stood dumbfounded, unable to speak.

By now, Beale's voice betrayed a welling up of anger. " Did you find anything on his body?"

Shelton replied, "All we could find was this piece of paper with these weird numbers on it. I brought it with me from the office in case you have any idea what it means."

He handed the paper to Beale whose face contorted into a scowl as he walked back to his car. Shelton and Walker watched as he sat in the driver seat reading the paper again.

"Son of a bitch. Well, someone tell me what the hell is going on? You guys come over here and look at this."

Shelton and Walker joined Beale beside the open car door. Their mouths fell agape when he held the paper beside the Garmin GPS display that showed 36.73942 N -84.95371 W.

THE FOXES HAVE HOLES AND THE BIRDS HAVE NESTS

Jason Morton started his rock and mineral collection when he was twelve and nurtured his hobby so passionately into his adulthood that everyone who knew him kept an eye out for unusual specimens that might intrigue him. Unsurprisingly, he earned his doctorate degree in mineralogy and geology. As curator of the collections of his university, he amassed cabinet after cabinet of so many extremely rare specimens, including meteorites and fossils, that his colleagues referred to him as "Encyclopedia Morton".

As a tenured member of the university, he and his partner, associate professor of English Allan Townes, lived as a married couple. Their wedding had been attended by the entire departmental faculty, who presented them with a vacation to Antarctica where Jason hoped to find more samples of meteorites, possibly even ones that contained mineral amalgamations from extraterrestrial sources.

When Jason opened the envelope with the tickets, he gushed, "Thank you all from the bottom of my heart. Alan and I will be sure to get some great photos of penguins on our trip. This is a dream come true: the chance to find some meteorites is a geologist's holy grail."

After he and Allan shared a kiss and a round of applause, the party disbanded and the newlyweds went home to begin planning their trip to Antarctica. It was scheduled for the months between October to March. As the spring semester wore on, Jason noticed that he was running a low-grade fever, often accompanied with a scratchy throat. Allan became alarmed when he found a rash on Jason's torso and a slight swelling in the lymph nodes of his right arm.

Allan said, "Jason, I'm concerned and I think you should be too. We need to go to the doctor and get tested. Even if the tests come back positive, nothing will change between us. I married you because I love you in sickness and in health. We need to be honest here."

Jason took a deep breath, "Yes, we do, and if I'm HIV positive I do not want to put you at risk. Will you go with me for the test?"

Allan hugged and kissed him, "Of course, we are a couple committed to each other. Do you want to make the appointment, or should I?"

Jason replied, "I'll call tomorrow morning."

The next day, Jason called their doctor and made an appointment for the following Wednesday. With a sense of trepidation, they met their family doctor, Dr. Eric Matthews, who drew blood samples from their arms and packaged them to ship to the laboratory for testing.

Dr. Matthews asked them to sit down. "Jason, Allan, I will be honest with you. You should probably abstain from sex until we get the results, in case only Jason is affected. Please understand that I am not going to pass judgment on either of you. If you are positive, you were probably infected years ago because, as you know, the incubation period can be months or years. Let's hope that we are all wrong, but we must be safe, not sorry. The tests should be back in two weeks…maybe less. I'll call you when I get them back. Try not to stress out if you can help it."

Jason and Allan thanked him and left the office. On the way home, Jason asked Allan, "So what happens if I am HIV positive and you are not?"

Allan patted his arm, "Then we just have to practice safe sex or curtail it. I can live with that."

Jason smiled weakly and tried to calm the inner turmoil that was twisting his very soul.

II

Dr. Matthews called ten days later and asked them both to come in for the results. The two men were anxious as they took seats in the office. Dr. Matthews began, "Well, I have good news and bad news. Jason, you are HIV positive but Allan is not. I don't have to lecture you about your intimate life. You know the rules. But, Jason, do not despair. Treatment has come a long way and the long-term prognosis is very good. With medication, dietary adjustments and constant vigilance, there is no reason that you cannot have many years of a happy life together. I want to schedule monthly visits to check how your body's immune system is doing."

Jason and Allan nodded and sighed that the uncertainty was over. "Thank you, Dr. Matthews. We appreciate all you have done for us, and for your support. Please call if you need to talk to us."

Over the next few weeks, Dr. Matthews prescribed a cocktail of antiviral medications to arrest the progress of the infection. Jason and Allan had planned to leave for their month-long trip to Antarctica in late November. Luckily, Jason's health had not deteriorated at all and he looked to be a picture of health. Dr. Matthews called them two weeks before they left for vacation and asked them to come in.

A sense of dread racked Jason as they drove to the office. Dr. Matthews ushered them into his office and reassured them that there was no need to worry.

"Jason, I came across a very interesting article in the journals. Now humor me. How much do you know about your family tree?"

"Only for three generations. Is that enough?"

"No, I am thinking much further back than that. Maybe as far back as medieval England."

Jason wrinkled his face with astonishment. "Are you kidding me? I have no clue. Why?"

Matthews motioned with his hands to sit patiently while he flipped through the Journal of the American Medical Association before he folded the magazine back and handed it to Jason.

"Some researchers have stumbled onto something interesting. I'm sure you have heard of the Black Death, the bubonic plague. Killed over half of the population of Europe in five years. It waxes and wanes, particularly in England because it is isolated. There was an outbreak in England in 1665 in a little village called Eyam and a surprising proportion of the village survived the plague and recovered completely. Using genetic and DNA testing, these researchers have found that a particular gene they named CCR5 delta 32 was extremely common in the villagers who survived the plague. As one of my profs once said, 'Genetics is a crap shoot, because we are all little genetic experiments.' This gene endowed these people with a fortified immune response that allowed them to fend off the effects of the plague pathogen, *Yersinia pestis*. Are you both with me so far?"

Although they were clearly confused, they nodded slowly. "With you so far, but ..."

"Okay, here is where it gets interesting. These researchers were able to construct a direct line of descent of people whose ancestors lived in that village. They were able to track that gene through all those generations to the present. Now here is the point. Descendants of those people who carried that gene have been able to stem the deleterious effects of the HIV virus because the gene that granted them some immunity to the plague also shields them from the effects of HIV. Jason, I want to take some DNA samples and see if you have hit the jackpot and have that gene. Are you okay with that?"

Jason was beside himself, "What the hell are you waiting on? What do I have to do? Blood sample?"

"I want to submit blood samples as well as epithelial cells from your cheeks with swabs. Roll up your sleeves."

Jason laughed nervously as he rolled up his sleeve and watched as the syringe filled with blood. Matthews swabbed his cheeks with a cotton swab and placed it into a tube of preservatives."

"All we have to do is wait. I checked with the lab and it can take as long as two months, maybe longer to get the results. You and Allan can go on your vacation. The results should be back by the time you return. Have a great time. Good luck with the meteorite hunt."

III

Jason and Allan flew to Argentina where they caught a cruise ship to the harbor where they disembarked and made their way to the expeditionary settlements. The weather patterns fluctuated dramatically from day to day but there were enough relatively pleasant days for Jason and Allan to prospect for mineral specimens and meteorites. Jason's health showed no signs of illness and his and Allan's spirits were buoyed by the hope Matthews had given them. The unpredictable weather limited the range of their collection trips but together they gathered over a hundred samples. Jason's Geiger counter indicated some of them had low level radioactivity. By the time their vacation time was up, they had returned to their happy days before the medical tests.

Dr. Matthews had left a message on their answering machine asking them to make an appointment as soon as they got back. After unpacking, Jason called the office. The receptionist answered the phone, "Dr. Matthews' office, May I help you?"

"Yes, this is Jason Morton. Is Dr. Matthews in?"

"Yes, I'll transfer you. Hold please."

Matthews answered, "Jason, welcome back. Guess what? The researchers have determined that you are a descendant of someone in that village because you have that CCR5 gene. This is great news!"

Jason shouted, "Thank you God. Thank you!"

Matthews tried to calm him down. "Now, understand, that you may or may not benefit from the gene but there is hope. Let's keep our fingers crossed. Can you come in for your monthly checkup tomorrow?"

"Sure thing, Doc. See you tomorrow. Is two o'clock okay?"

"That'll be fine. See you then."

The next day, Matthews examined Jason carefully and drew blood samples.

"Did you and Allan have a good time? Get some good rocks? Any meteorites?"

"We had a great time. Got some great minerals. I am pretty sure that a couple of them are meteorites. I need to do elemental assays. One of them is slightly radioactive. That could be interesting. So, results in two weeks?"

Matthews nodded and Jason left to go back to his lab. He had booked time on the electron microscope to determine the composition of the radioactive sample. The sample resembled the Hypatia stone with high levels of carbon, aluminum, iridium, copper and iron; it also emitted low level x ray radiation. After he had completed the scan, he placed the sample in a lead foil lined container to block the radiation from contaminating the lab and went home.

Two weeks later, Matthews called and exclaimed, "Jason, can you come by my office today?"

"Sure, but what's up? Good news or bad?"

"Just drop by asap."

Jason called Allan to tell him he would be late for dinner and drove to Matthews' office. Matthews was waiting for him in the outer office.

"Come on back, I want to show you something."

Matthews laid some papers from the lab in front of him.

"I can't explain it, but the results were so surprising the lab checked them twice. The HIV titer of your blood has decreased by seventy-five percent and your T cells are aggressively attacking the virus. I have no idea what is going on, but this is great news."

Jason felt a rush of ecstasy wash over him. "Should we get another sample to be sure?"

"Already ahead of you. Roll up your sleeve."

Matthews drew a sample and Jason went home for dinner where he shared the good news with Allan.

Allan grabbed him and they danced around the room. Jason cautioned him about Matthews' warning. 'Keep in mind that this might be an artifact of the testing, an accident of sampling or just a temporary improvement. We'll know more when the next results come back. In the meantime, keep on doing what you are doing.'

Buoyed by the incredible news, Jason continued his analysis of the specimens they had gathered, focusing on the unusual radioactive piece. After doing a complete chemical and molecular structure analysis, he pored over the literature of minerals with similar composition before he reached an astounding conclusion: the sample was indeed a meteorite, but his analysis convinced him that it came from a source outside the solar system.

Jason shared the results of his discovery with the departments of geology, chemistry, and biology in a lecture he titled "Where no one has gone before: a meteorite from the Great Beyond." The audience listened intently with some faculty applauding his work, but with others dismissing the results as questionable at best. The consensus was that he re-assay the sample and perform some more rigorous, but obscure analysis to confirm his conjecture. As a man of science, Jason expected some people would be skeptical and he agreed to the suggested testing although he rejected any request for samples for other labs until his analysis was complete.

A week after the seminar, Matthews left a message for Jason and Allan to stop by for the latest test results. Unlike previous trips to the doctor that they had made with trepidation, they were very hopeful about this trip.

Matthews met them in the outer office and led them to his examining room. He invited them to have a seat and laid a lab folder on the table as he sat down on his stool. Without saying a word, he slid the report toward them before beginning his discussion.

"Jason, I am at a loss as to how this happened, but I had the lab recheck their results twice to confirm them and there is no doubt. You have no trace of the HIV virus in your body anywhere. You may be the first person who has survived HIV by completely obliterating the virus from your system. Congratulations."

Jason and Allan sat dumbfounded before shouting, "Hallelujah! Thank the Lord." All three men laughed and danced a few steps before Matthews quieted them down.

"I have done some preliminary research, but I would like to keep this quiet for a while. There are HIPA concerns and I am not sure we want to announce it until we have some idea of what happened. Can you think of anything different you have done over the last few months?"

"Not really, other than our trip to Antarctica. Could that weird gene I have somehow have mutated to supercharge my immune system so that it actually destroyed the virus?"

"It's a possibility, but we need to do some more tests. I would like some more blood samples so I can try some things of my own. Is that acceptable?"

"Doc, right now, I would give you the moon if you asked for it. Take all the blood you need!"

After Matthews had collected five tubes of blood, Jason and Allan went to celebrate at the most prestigious restaurant in the city. During dinner, Allan said, "You know, honey, we are really lucky.... I'm not sure it is all luck. We need to be more thankful because God has truly blessed us. How would you feel about attending church somewhere? I know we have discussed this before and rejected the idea because of our previous experiences. In this day and age , though we can surely find an open accepting congregation."

Jason smiled and replied, "I guess we are already an old married couple who know each other well. I have been thinking the same thing. There's a geologist at work who goes to Deep Springs Presbyterian Church and he has in fact invited me to join him some Sunday. He says it is open and affirming and has a gay couple who are members. Let's surprise him this Sunday and go."

IV

They attended the church the next Sunday and over the next weeks, they decided to join. The church held a reception every quarter to celebrate new members and Allan agreed to say a few words of introduction. After the usual greetings, Allan laughed. "I just told Jason last week all we need is a station wagon and we could be the Ozzie and Harriet —make that Ozzie and Harry of the community."

The party erupted with waves of laughter before the crowd dispersed.

However, dark clouds were building on the horizon. The pendulum of public opinion in the community had taken a distinctly more conservative swing. As an ultra-conservative evangelical movement that condemned gay rights swept through the nation, some of the more traditional churches began to lobby against gay rights in general and same sex marriage in particular. Even after ACLU lawyers appeared on television and radio talk shows and reminded them that with the Supreme Court ruling in the landmark Obergefell vs Hodges case in 2015, same sex marriage became acceptable under the law of the land. Local opinion or disapproval could not change that, although several of these evangelical churches collected money to put up billboards with messages condemning gay marriage.

Social media spread messages decrying homosexuality as sinful and same sex marriages as blasphemous.

'God created Adam and Eve, not Adam and Steve.'

'You can be gay, you can be a Christian, but you cannot be a gay Christian.'

Jason and Allan had heard all of this before and just shrugged it off, but when some extremists started a petition to get the university to fire gay faculty, they became concerned. Luckily, they were both tenured with long records of excellence in teaching and research so the university refused any attempts to dismiss them. Both men were furious that some major donors threatened cutting off donations for the university as well as research programs. Some parents refused to allow their children to enroll in classes the two men taught. Nonetheless, the university remained adamant in its commitment to academic freedom and tolerance, maintaining support for all gays and lesbians on its staff.

As tensions mounted in the community, Jason and Allan kept a low profile to quell any unrest. Two months after the first billboards were put up, Dr. Matthews called them and asked them to come into his office.

He could barely contain himself when he met them.

"Jason, I have done scores of tests with your blood and the results are beyond incredible. The antibodies in your blood not only attack HIV viruses, but also malignant cells. We may be able to use them to cure cancer if we can maintain a pure cell line that can replace itself in perpetuity without losing its effectiveness. Have either of you heard of Henrietta Lacks?"

Both men said they had not.

Matthews continued. “Henrietta Lacks was a poor black sharecropper’s wife who developed ovarian cancer in 1951. Her doctors collected biopsies of her tumor and they discovered something phenomenal. Most cells have some internal mechanism that keeps track of the number of times the cells divide and, after a certain number of divisions, the cells die. But her cells did not die. They were the very first immortal cell line that could divide repeatedly without mutation or weakening the cell virility.”

Jason and Allan looked at each other quizzically. “What does that mean to us?”

“Mrs. Lack’s cells have been used for almost all cellular experiments on diseases because the cells were always clones, exact duplicates, that could be replicated as much as needed. They became known as HeLa cells, obviously named for her, and have been the foundation on which almost all research on cancer and some other diseases like polio have been based. Frankly, without the HeLa cells, the survivor rate for cancer treatments would be much, much lower.

“But here is the tragedy. Even though these cells have been used worldwide since their initial discovery in 1951, her descendants did not even know of their existence until about 1975. Think about that. How many hundreds of billions of dollars have been generated through research and treatment using her cells while her family never made a cent from their use. That is unconscionable. Neither Henrietta nor her family gave anyone permission to use the cells, because back then, researchers did not need a patient’s approval to use their cells. Once the family found out about this they sought to gain control of the use of the cells as well as to receive financial remuneration for their use. I think it was in 1996. Atlanta declared October 11 ‘Henrietta Lacks Day’ and in 2010, Johns Hopkins Institute established the Henrietta

Lacks Memorial Lecture Series. And she has been granted honorary doctorates from some schools."

"So why are you telling us this?" asked Jason.

Matthews leaned forward. "Because if we can determine that these antibodies you are producing have widespread utility and effectiveness, we do not want you to be taken advantage of. Under the new HIPA Guidelines, your right to privacy is shielded from public eyes and will be until you grant permission for their use. Gentlemen, this news is beyond incredible. *If* we can make it work. You need to think this through very carefully as to what you want to do, and I am bound by law to keep your confidentiality. In the meantime, I will keep doing some research that may require more blood from time to time. I wish we could figure out how this happened, but let's not look a gift horse in the mouth."

Jason and Allan thanked him and went home to contemplate their next move. They decided to just keep their secret strictly between them and Dr. Matthews.

V

After Jason and Allan discussed the ramifications of embarking on trying to develop the cell line, they decided to delay any action that would put them into the spotlight because they knew the rising tide of antigay sentiment would be focused on them and neither of them wanted the extra stress. Jason called Matthews and told him of their decision and he agreed with their reasoning.

Before he hung up the phone, Matthews asked again, "Jason, have you thought of anything different that you did that might affect your body in any way? I'm going to keep doing some research with the understanding that it's all very hush-hush for now. Anything come to mind?"

Jason replied, "I've been thinking about that since the last time you asked. All I can think of is our trip to Antarctica. I did find the unusual meteorite that I'm pretty sure is from deep space. It has a very low level of radioactivity but nothing that would be a threat since I have not been exposed to it for any extended time. I keep it in a lead-lined box locked away in the lab. I did check with a radiologist, and he agreed it was no risk unless I handled it a lot and even then, there is not much risk."

Matthews said, "I agree. Well, keep thinking."

Jason and Allan tried to ignore the incessant anti-gay harangues of the evangelical extremists, but the stress began to take its toll. The university refused to pressure them to resign and the support group of friends and family bolstered their resolve to stay above the fray.

A few weeks later, Matthews called them again.

"Jason, can you come back in this week? Don't worry; there is no bad news, unless you have some."

"Sure, Dr. Matthews. How about tomorrow at eleven?"

"That is fine. See you then."

Despite Matthews' reassurance, Jason was apprehensive about the visit. Matthews showed him to his office. "Well, Jason, as it turns out, my theory was wrong. The cell line died after about sixty times, pretty much the average for most cells. We won't be millionaires. On another front, my wife Peggy and I are having a twenty-fifth anniversary celebration next Wednesday. Can you and Allan come/ We can celebrate your recovery as well."

"We would be delighted. We can bring a bottle of wine."

Jason and Allan arrived along with several other guests. Matthews introduced them to everyone else as being one of his best success stories without going into details. Most of the guests already knew the couple and assured them of their support for their marriage. Some made donations to the university when they heard that some donations had dried up. The party broke up around midnight and the men left.

Although three students dropped Jason's introductory mineralogy class to protest his marriage, the semester proved uneventful and his theory of the deep space origin of the unusual meteorite enjoyed increased acceptance. Allan published his second book on voodoo and folk religion in the Southern United States. Both men received grants to supplement their work and they were interviewed by the Chronicle of Higher Education.

Four months after the Matthews celebration, the doctor called Jason.

"Jason, this is Dr. Matthews. I was wondering if you could come back in to discuss something that has come up. You don't have to bring Allan. Say tomorrow after the office closes?"

"Sure, is there any reason you don't want Allan to come?"

"Well, for now, just you."

Matthews met Jason in the outer office and led him to his inner office.

"Have a seat. First thing, you have to agree that you don't discuss this with anyone, not even Allan — at least for now. Agreed?"

Jason sat back in his chair. "Well, I guess. But why the cloak and dagger stuff?"

"Fine. I am not sure how to start this. Remember our party a few months ago?"

"Sure, it was a great time and we met a lot of good people."

"Due to the doctor-patient laws, I cannot reveal particulars and I am not even sure I am in a legally defensible position now: that is why

I need your silence. I purposefully invited ten of my patients who have cancer and made sure each of them met you. Now every one of them is cancer-free."

"What?"

"You heard me. Completely cancer free. The other guests were just a control group. I can't explain it, Jason, but somehow when you shook their hands or had other physical contact, you bolstered their immune response so they could destroy the cancer cells. I still can't believe it."

Jason sat stupefied. "I don't —"

"Me neither. I am at a complete loss. The best thing I can think of is that in some way that weird meteorite's radiation transformed your immune system so that its efficacy can be transferred physically, but your cells are not immortal. You can see why I do not want this to get out. Everybody would say I am nuts! The AMA might even strip my license. We have to keep this strictly between us."

"That goes without saying. I don't want people invading my privacy hoping I can cure them. Is this going to wear off, or will it last until I die?"

"I'm not sure. But through God's will, Providence, karma, or sheer luck, you have the ability to cure people of AIDS and cancer so let's take advantage of that. What I want you to do is just go through your everyday life, but try to make physical contact with as many people as you can. Shake hands, pat them on the back. Some of those people will almost certainly have cancer and, if I am right, you will cure them and neither they nor their doctors will be able to explain it."

A sly smile crossed Jason's face. "This is so ironic. Two years ago, I thought I had received a death sentence and now not only am I well, but I can save other people. It is pretty damned amazing! Sure, I'll do what you ask, and I won't tell Allan. Let's hope this works out for everyone."

VI

Over the next several months, Jason lived his life as if nothing were changed. Little by little, stories of cancer patients who were miraculously healed began to leak out, but no one could explain why or how. Jason and Matthews met occasionally to discuss the cures, still amazed at the turn of events.

As these reports of cured patients reached the Center for Disease Control, the agency became so intrigued they sent doctors to the town to gather as much data as they could to explain their recovery. The doctors and statisticians interviewed cured patients and pored endlessly over the data, but none of them could find any convincing connections. They had different doctors who had used different treatment protocols and they all lived in many different parts of the area. The CDC released their findings without making any definitive statement.

The evangelical extremists did not exhibit that restraint. Once the stories of the cures became widely known, the fundamentalist preachers hailed them as proof that God was rewarding their harassment of gays and same sex marriage by the miraculously healing of people who had literally been facing death itself. They redoubled their attacks on gays and lesbians and erected more billboards condemning same sex marriage.

In the absence of any reasonable alternative theories, people began to believe the hyped up condemnation of gays. From time to time, Jason and Allan received hate mails, crank phone calls, and threats of violence. Finally, they had to call the police. The university assigned a security detail outside their offices after they had received a particularly profane violent threat. As their stress grew, they began to quarrel over silly things. They developed headaches and attacks of insomnia and nausea. Eventually, they sought a counselor to help them develop strategies to cope with their anxieties and restore normalcy to their lives.

Once they were able to focus on their situation objectively and dispassionately, they considered moving to another region or even another country. Their investments and royalties from their books had begun to add up, and they could afford to sell their house, retire early and start over elsewhere. The counselor agreed that if that was a feasible alternative, they should take it.

Jason finally broke his vow of silence to Dr. Matthews and confided in Allan, who was suitably incredulous. He agreed to maintain the secret and suggested they meet with Dr. Matthews to get his opinion. The doctor sat silently as they told him of the hell their lives had become, but tears of frustration welled up in his eyes.

"Well, guys, I can't say as I blame you. Life is too short to have to put up with this kind of harassment. Maybe moving away is the best solution, but I strongly suggest not telling anyone where you go. You may even want to assume new identities, but I don't know how to go about doing that. I do know an FBI agent I worked with on a drug case. Maybe he could talk to someone in witness relocation program. I'll give him a call and get back to you."

Both men were fluent in French and had enjoyed the country when they had gone there on vacation. They contacted the state department and the French consulate who arranged for them to meet with real estate agents in a video conference in France. The agents found several homes and small estates they would like and the two flew over to begin the process of buying the house and becoming ex-patriates.

When the semester ended, Jason met with Dr. Matthews and asked him if he would oversee their affairs to close out their lives here until their house sold. Matthews listened to their plans and arranged for them to meet the FBI agent, Mark Richland who listened to their plight of harassment and agreed that relocation was the best option.

"Well, guys, after what you've been through, I can't blame you for leaving the country. Europe long ago abandoned its obsession with religion and you'll fit into the secular society there well. I can arrange for the three of us to meet with a former colleague who lives there before you move. At least you deserve to have a peaceful life together."

VII

Jason and Allan sold their house and downsized their chattel to facilitate the move to France. They gave Dr. Matthews their new address and contact information and they extended an open invitation for him and his wife to come visit any time they liked.

Matthews was heartbroken to see them leave, but did ask for Jason's approval to tell the community the truth after they had moved. He agreed as long as Matthews did not reveal any details of their new lives.

Matthews agreed. "Of course, I will take your secret to my grave. I am so angry that these haters have persecuted you so badly you have to leave. Peggy and I have decided to move as well just so we will not be bothered by people trying to track you down. I'll give you a copy of what I'll say to people for you to approve before you leave."

Jason and Allan agreed and the three of them embraced, sobbing softly.

When the SOLD sign appeared in their yard, the evangelicals held a rally celebrating their success of hounding the couple out of town and the people of the community accepted their explanation. Church attendance and membership soared and right wing tele-evangelists made guest appearances that were broadcast over the whole region.

Once Jason and Allan had settled into their new home, Matthews contacted the local television stations and arranged for them to play a videotaped message on air. He placed an ad in the local newspaper and bought public service announcement time to announce when the message would be broadcast.

Matthews had seethed for months since his friends had moved, and the continual crowing of the evangelicals proclaiming God's condemnation on homosexuality angered him so badly that he schemed to find the perfect revenge. He innocently contracted with the television stations to broadcast his message on April 1.

After a brief introduction, Matthews began to speak.

"Ladies and gentlemen, good evening, you probably already know me but in case you do not, I am Dr. Eric Matthews, a family doctor for over twenty-five years and I have to address an issue that has arisen in our community. Jason Morton and Allan Townes were two of my patients before they were harassed so badly they had to leave town. Those of you who are delighted that these two fine men who had served the university and the community for over twenty years are hypocrites and bigots. You should be ashamed to call yourselves Christians dismissing the two fine men as 'filthy perverts who will burn in hell'.

"I have scheduled this announcement for April Fool's Day for good reasons. First, I am painfully aware that the frauds and false prophets who twist the Holy Scriptures to justify their hateful agendas and fleece their gullible sheep have convinced you that the miraculous cures of the people who had cancer are proof that God hates gays and endorses the spiteful homophobia that you have all too readily embraced.

"In fact, nothing could be farther from the truth. As I was bound by doctor patient privilege, I could not divulge details about my treatment of these men, but since they have left the community, and with their permission, I can set the record straight. A few years ago, Jason and Allan took a vacation to Antarctica where Jason found a really unusual rock that turned out to be a meteorite. However, it was not just any meteorite. Jason's analysis determined that the meteorite originated in deep space from far outside our solar system and was very slightly radioactive.

"Jason was HIV positive when he discovered the meteorite but to my, and his, complete shock, somehow the meteorite cured him of his HIV. Over the next few months, Jason graciously donated several blood samples so I could continue my research. During that time, I discovered that not only did it cure cancer, but that its healing properties could be transmitted by simply having Jason touch someone. So, you see, these cures were not religiously-based miracles touted by liars and thieves, but by the very man whom you tried to claim Almighty God hated and condemned. In the months since Jason and Allan left, I have discovered five new cases of cancer, one of which is a stage four melanoma that has no medical cure. That person's days are numbered. As you sow, so shall you reap.

"Finally, as a man of science and a staunch adherent to the Golden Rule, I have decided that I too will be closing my practice here and moving to a new home. I can't tolerate the hate that ignores that Jesus Christ told us to love one another.

"To conclude, you have all been played for fools by these charlatans and, in your hatred, you have rejected the one man who could save you. I leave you with the words of someone wiser than I.

'We are punished by our sins, not for them.'"

THE CHURCH AT EPHESUS

Chestnut Grove lay in one corner of a narrow hollow dotted by houses, barns and churches that its inhabitants had built to support their simple agrarian and pious lifestyles. A few families still dwelled in the hollows that snaked their way up the mountains surrounding the shoestring valley, but most of the homesteads in these remote areas had long since been abandoned as the younger generation left to seek their fortunes in careers other than farming. Shrubby undergrowth and blackberry brambles overran the fields and creek banks so that reclamation would be an expensive and time-consuming venture. Most of the people came to accept this as a kind of buffer against the over-development of nearby abandoned farmland that had damaged much of their arable land and many took a kind of pride in their refusal to compromise their way of life for financial gain.

Growing small acreages of burley tobacco and subsistence farming occupied much of the year, but a few men worked at local sawmills and some of the women carpooled to work in the shirt factory at Albany. In the summer, the townspeople harvested buckets of blackberries and raspberries from the abandoned fields and fence rows of these old homestead and berry-picking time generated a carnival-like atmosphere. Whole families would brave the heat and chiggers and briar pricks in pursuit of the juiciest berries. Occasionally, someone would yell "Snake", a cry that evoked some primeval fear and that section of briars would be abandoned.

In Fall, the people reaped their corn, cooked their molasses from the sugar cane, and cut and hung the tobacco crop so it could cure for stripping. Once the cold weather had settled in and the tobacco leaves had attained the right moisture content to allow it to be handled without falling apart, the people helped each other strip its leaves and tie them into "hands" of tobacco, sorted by color. Local men with large trucks hauled the tobacco off to the auction houses in Lexington or Louisville. The money was always on time to prepare for Christmas. After the first frost folks went through the woodlands gathering hickory nuts, walnuts and butternuts to use in desserts made for the holidays. In winter, people cut small red cedar trees from the fencerows to use as Christmas trees and endured the tedium of the winter cold until the spring returned and the cycle of planting, tending and harvesting was repeated.

The greatest social events of the year were in the summer when the revivals sprang up at the various small churches to occupy the hot humid nights. For the most part, work tending the crops was over and with the crops laid by, people had spare time to spend in other pursuits. Few people traveled for vacation. Hot weather ruined the prospects for fishing and since there was no legal hunting season then, people turned to more socializing with their neighbors in the small churches that peppered the region.

The biggest such revival was sponsored by the Ephesus Baptist Church which usually drew a few dozen people during the weeknight gatherings and a bit more on the weekends. Visitors from other nearby communities drifted into the revivals, particularly if there was special singing scheduled. Occasionally, a few souls were saved to earn a ticket to posthumous and glorified rest, a ritual brought to full fruition in one of the small streams where people gathered to witness the full immersion baptism that emulated the death, burial and resurrection of their Lord Jesus Christ who died for their prodigious and unending sins. Bare-footed children as young as ten were goaded, even coerced, into answering the altar call to renounce their sins and accept the sacrifice Jesus had offered. Loud sobs of gratitude and shouts of "Praise the Lord" rang out like joyous bells announcing the salvation of the children who were quite ignorant of theology, but were willing to partake of the spirit to please their elders or to garner attention for their piety.

The church's preacher, Wheeler Stinson, enjoyed a bit of a reputation as a hellfire and damnation prophet who would lead the lost sheep to paradise. His day job was being the county clerk in Monticello and though he had never been trained in any formal theological seminary, he preached because he felt "The Call to Ministry" and supplemented his clerk income with the meagre donations in the offering plates that were passed to collect funds to pay the clergy salaries and operating expenses of the church. Swept up in unrelenting spiritual ardor, preacher and parishioners alike prayed loudly for miracles of healing for people with various ailments or other calamities afflicting the members of the community. However, despite lachrymose lamentations of penance and unshakeable faith, no one had actually seen any evidence of miracles.

So, life in Chestnut Grove plodded along at the same leisurely pace as it had for years. Its simple people had simple dreams: of family, home, work and God, all realized amply by the land and the people they lived with in the community. The attendance at Ephesus Baptist Church slowly waned and the plates' collections dwindled as religious fervor faded.

Then Dr. Nick Harry moved into the community.

II

The county seat, Monticello, came alive one bright June morning when a sleek black Mercedes pulled up in front of the courthouse and a dapper looking gentleman emerged to survey the town before striding purposefully into the courthouse. Carrying two briefcases, he approached the front desk of the clerk's office where Wheeler, the clerk, rose to greet him.

"Good day, sir. May I help you?"

The man set one of his briefcases on the desk and popped open the locks as he replied, "Yes, my name is James Wilding and I represent Dr. Nicholas Harry. He's interested in buying a piece of property, the Ben Lowe place. Could you find the deed and the appraised value of the farm, please?"

Wheeler stood transfixed by Wilding's gleaming smile and mellow voice before stammering, "The Ben Lowe place? Sure, I know the place, just live a couple miles from it as the crow flies, farther if the crow has to drive. That place has been abandoned for years. I think the bank owns the title to it after the last owner died. Sad thing really, last surviving member of the family, no will, so the bank owns it. Wait right here."

He ambled back to the filing cabinets where, after two false starts, he managed to produce a yellow folder marked DEFAULT. He returned to the desk and handed the folder to Wilding. "Looks like the appraised value is only twenty thousand dollars. Two hundred acres more or less. Not much good farmland up there. Do you have any idea where it is?"

Wilding smiled, "Why yes, Dr. Harry told me exactly where it is, so today I am just here to begin the purchase process. Do you have someone here to witness documents? Dr. Harry and I have already drawn up the necessary papers and cleared the title in the capital. Could you see if anyone at the bank is available to sign these forms and collect the purchase price?"

He swung the other briefcase onto the table and popped open the lid to reveal rows of neatly-banded hundred dollar bills. Wheeler swallowed hard at the sight of more money than he had ever seen before.

"I believe that Fred Cowan himself will come over if I tell what I got setting here in front of me!"

He dialed the number and asked the secretary to speak to Fred Cowan, the President of the bank.

"Fred? This is Wheeler. I have a gentleman named James Wilding here with a suitcase of money wanting to buy the Ben Lowe place. I know it went into default. How long have you held the deed to that place? Three years? Well, it looks like all the paper work he has here is in good order and he has the appraised value here in cash. Why don't you come over and bring a witness and a lawyer and you can be shed of that property? Says he is buying it for somebody named Harry, Nick Harry. Yeah, he knows where it is. Okay, we'll see you in a few minutes."

Shortly, Cowan and his attorneys appeared and exchanged a few pleasantries.

Wheeler had watched all the legal proceedings with a puzzled look. As he looked over the documents and signed the line for the clerk's signature he asked, "So exactly who is this Dr. Harry? I hate to be indelicate, but how do we know he can afford to buy the place? He is not from around here."

Wilding nodded. "Oh, I would be surprised if you didn't ask. No, he is from Chicago and has a Ph.D. in herpetology — studies reptiles and amphibians. He has grown tired of the rat race and plans to retire someday away from the city. Still plans to do some research work and write more books."

"Wait a minute, Mr. Wilding. Can you wait for a spell while I count the money? Not that I don't trust you but I don't want to cheat you either," Cowan said.

"Not a problem. It should not take long to count. I can wait."

Cowan deftly flipped through the bundles of cash to be sure there was ten thousand dollars in each briefcase.

"Well, Mr. Wilding, everything seems to be in order. Here is the deed and transfer paperwork. Dr. Harry is now the owner of the old Ben Lowe place, but I have to admit I am glad to get rid of it. If you don't mind me asking, what does he plan to do with it?"

Wilding smiled, "Use it mostly as a vacation haven. He has already chosen a house plan and employed a contractor so you should expect some crews shortly to begin construction. Well, gentlemen, I have enjoyed meeting you and, speaking for Dr. Harry, thank you for all of your help."

Fred and Wheeler accompanied him to his car and watched him drive off.

Wheeler stroked his chin and mumbled, "Fred, there is something strange about all of this. I think I need to learn more about Dr. Harry."

III

Within a few weeks of the deed transfer, large trucks laden with lumber, blocks and bulldozers began to wind their way up Burnett Hollow to the Lowe place to begin the clearing of land and home site for Dr. Harry, a man of obvious wealth but rare public appearances. Wilding moved into a rented home in the valley and spent ten-hour days supervising the construction and landscaping of what was surely to be a mansion of kingly dimensions. Day by day, the people below could see the mansion rise out of the ground below Ben's Cliff, a vantage point from which the whole valley could be seen. The crews completed the house in a little over seven months and it stood at the end of a long winding road, awaiting the first visit of its owner.

Wheeler had watched the traffic flow and construction with a wary eye. A week after the construction began, he called Fred at the bank.

"Fred? This is Wheeler. Do you have time to meet for coffee? You do? Great. See you at the diner in five."

Fred had already taken a seat in a booth and ordered black coffee for them by the time Wheeler arrived. Fred could tell something was troubling him. "So, what's on your mind, Wheeler?'

Wheeler leaned in across the table and replied in a whispered voice, "Well, I'll tell you. I have been checking up on our Dr. Nicholas Harry."

Fred shrugged and wrinkled up his face. "So, what's to check other than he must be richer than chickenshit to plop down that much cash?"

Wheeler glanced around the diner nervously. "I did some computer searches on him. Now you would think that as a scientist I could find some mention of him somewhere. Sure enough, turns out that he is an expert on venomous snakes."

"Not too much about him though. So, I contacted the county records office in Chicago and asked them to check if they had any record of him. They found one name. A Mr. Nicholas Harry who lived on the west side in 1898. So, it cannot be the same man unless he is 120 years old.'

"Maybe he is just a very private man and wants to be left alone. So, what are you getting at, Wheeler?"

"I am not sure, but you have to admit it is all very odd. I will be very interested in meeting Dr. Harry when he gets here."

IV

Two weeks after the crews had left the mansion, a black Mercedes pulled into a parking place in front of the courthouse and a thin handsome man got out of the back seat. A couple of townspeople gathered to see the fancy car and its occupant who waved greetings to everyone as he entered the courthouse. Wheeler was at his usual post and he stood abruptly to greet Dr. Harry.

The man extended his hand, "Nick Harry. I assume you are Mr. Stinson."

"Yes. Good morning, Dr. Harry. I am sure I am speaking for the whole town when I say how glad we are to meet you. I'm Wheeler Stinson."

"Just the man I was looking for," Harry replied. "I want to thank you for expediting the transfers and deeds so I could get my home built. I really appreciate all you did."

"Have you actually been up to the house yet? It looks mighty fine from here."

"We are going there now, but I wanted to thank you personally. Wilding is driving me up to look things over. I should be moving in soon.

He got back into the car that drove up the road to the mansion. In a few hours, the car returned and Wilding blew the horn lightly to summon Wheeler to the curb.

Wheeler approached the car as Harry lowered the window so he could see Wheeler clearly. "Mr. Wheeler, I built this house for a vacation home basically, so I will not be living there all the time. Wilding will be in and out to maintain it but if he isn't here, be sure the gate across the road is locked. I notice that there are several fruit trees and berry bushes up there and you are welcome to harvest as much as you want. The house is locked up and has a security system wired to the police mostly to keep kids out, you know. Here."

He handed Wheeler a five-hundred-dollar bill as he added, "This is for your trouble and help."

Harry got back in his car and dashed away leaving an astonished Wheeler slack-jawed and puzzled.

V

The mansion sat unoccupied over the winter months, but Wheeler occasionally saw Wilding driving his jeep up the road. Some light snows blanketed the area occasionally and a warm spring produced what the old people called a blackberry winter on the mountain where the disturbed areas around the mansion glowed with billows of white blooms. Wheeler had asked Wilding about picking blackberries on the mountain if there were any and Wilding agreed that any of the townspeople could pick there as long as they avoided the house area.

Country folks always enjoyed fresh made jelly and jams though they knew these treats came at a price. Chiggers would invade the most private places on bodies and fingers would swell from a briar stuck in the flesh. People knew that rattlesnakes and copperheads often sought shelter from the sun under the briars and brush so no one ever picked alone.

"Evadean! Hurry up! I want to get up to the old Lowe place before it gets too hot," Wheeler yelled as he sat in his pickup, strumming his fingers on the wheel.

"I'm coming as fast as I can!" came the reply from his wife as she jostled along with four lard buckets clanging along in tow. "Hold your horses!"

"Well, you know them's the best berries every year and the birds get them pretty quick."

"A person can only do so much, Wheeler. I had to finish the dishes. Been easier if you had helped."

Wheeler made a face and they continued their bantering all the way up the newly graveled road to the Ben Lowe place. He parked the truck under a big walnut tree and they set out to the fields east of the mansion.

"Hey, while we're here why don't we sneak a peek at the new house?" Wheeler asked.

"I don't know. He said we could pick all the berries we wanted, but told us to not go snooping around."

Wheeler sniffed, "And who is going to know but you and me?"

Evadean furrowed her brow and exasperatedly agreed by shrugging and nodding.

Together they set off along the road to the mansion twenty feet or so from the still empty house. An iron rail fence encircled the large yard surrounding the house. Wilding had paid a local teenager to maintain the lawn, but he had fallen behind schedule so the grass was more than ankle high. The gate was locked with a large padlock, but Wheeler carefully climbed over the fence and turned to help Evadean over.

"No, thank you. I am not going to risk getting stuck with that fence and besides I don't like this spying business."

"Suit yourself. Wait here while I look around."

He glanced around the grounds quickly before creeping up to the large mansion. He mounted the stone steps to the spacious front porch with skinny clematis vines clinging to a trellis on either end. The front door was a massive slab of what appeared to be mahogany with a small clear glass half-moon adornment at the top. He stepped over to one of the windows, shaded his eyes with his hands and strained to see past the shiny black window panes only to find that he was staring at his own reflection.

"Hmm. Looks like he has that black film on the windows to keep people from looking in. I wonder if all the windows are like this."

He stepped off the porch and indicated to Evadean that he was going around the house before methodically checking each first-floor window in vain. Harry had taken great pains to keep prying eyes out of his personal space. Frustrated by his failure, Wheeler returned to the fence and told Evadean what he had found.

"Damnedest thing I've ever seen. He's got all the windows covered with something black so you can't see in. Makes me wonder what he's got in there he doesn't want people to see."

"Makes me think he knew how nosy some people are and he was just thinking ahead. As rich as he appears to be, he may have a houseful of antiques that he knows will tempt thieves if they can see them. Look, it's going to get too hot to pick berries soon so let's get back to what we came here for."

"Yeah, you may be right. But now that you mention it, did anyone ever actually see Harry move into the house?"

"You're letting your imagination run away with you. Let's go."

They walked back to the truck where they each grabbed a gallon milk jug filled with ice water to carry with them as they picked berries. Each took a big gulp of water before veering off in separate directions on either side of the house.

"Now Evadean, don't get too far away from me or you'll get lost like last year."

"Guess I'll never live that down. I'm going this way."

"Holler every fifteen minutes so I know where you are. You know the drill."

"Yep, watch for snakes."

He soon found a clump of briars bent low with big plump berries and gingerly rolled them off the stems into his hand. Several briars grew in this small copse of bushes that partially shaded them from the summer sun that was already causing Wheeler to sweat. He set his bucket down to wipe his brow and rest a moment.

"Evadean! You okay?"

"I'm fine. How about you?"

"Hot! Good berries though. Talk to you in a few."

He had become so involved with his attempts to reach the large juiciest wads of blackberries that he had not seen the three-foot rattlesnake lying under them. He lost his balance and fell into the briars, hitting the snake on its head. In an instant, the snake struck him on his hand. A weak cry of "Oh shit" escaped his mouth before his paralyzing fear and panic collapsed him onto the ground near enough to the snake for it to bite him on the leg.

VI

By the time Evadean found him, Wheeler had turned pale and clammy, his shallow breathing barely keeping him alive. She yelled frantically for help as she tried to drag him toward the truck, but no one answered. Finally, driven by adrenaline and terror she managed to wrestle his limp body into the truck bed and rush as fast as she could down the washed-out road to the main highway where she tore to the hospital.

She raced into the emergency room yelling at the top of her lungs, "Wheeler's been snake bit! Somebody help me get him in here!"

Two orderlies rushed out to the truck and carried the unconscious Wheeler into the emergency room.

"Do you know what kind of snake it was?" a doctor asked.

"No, but probably a rattler in that berry patch at Ben Lowe's place."

"We have to be sure to give him the right antivenin. He's been bitten twice. Two puncture wounds, each bite fairly deep. 'Bout has to be a rattler with wounds that deep. He's in bad shape. My advice is to try the rattler antivenin."

Evadean, sobbing and confused, nodded agreement and watched as they injected Wheeler with several shots of antivenin before hanging an IV drip with the same medicine. Slowly, Wheeler's pulse and breathing became more measured and his heartbeat more regular. In a few hours, he roused enough to ask, "Am I still alive?"

Evadean stroked his hair back and gently patted his arm. "Yeah, you're still here, barely. Rattlesnake bit you. Twice. It was touch and go there for a while. Doc says you will be in here for a few days so get used to it."

Wheeler moaned softly before slumping back to sleep. The doctor released him in eight days after instructing Evadean how to care for his swollen discolored hand and leg.

"We can loan you a wheelchair to use for the next few weeks. He'll have to stay off that leg for a while. Now, I'm going to warn you that antivenin we gave him is higher than hell. right at two thousand dollars a shot. We had to give him three shots. Let's hope his insurance will cover it."

"Guess I really am a wheeler now, ain't I," Wheeler joked as he rolled the chair out beside the car. "Damn, that's six thousand dollars plus the hospital bill. What happens if I don't have insurance?"

The doctor made a face. "We'll cross that bridge once the final bill is tallied. Right now, just concentrate on getting well. If you feel that you are not doing well, get back to the hospital as quick as you can. But it's been eight days, so any residual effects of the venom should have dissipated by now. Call me tomorrow and tell me how you're doing."

Evadean pursed her lips, "Thanks for everything, Doc. Guess I can keep him for a while longer."

VII

Recuperation and rehabilitation for rattlesnake bites are laborious processes that provide good opportunities to enthrall the neighbors with horror stories of agonizing pain and near-death experiences. Everyone agreed that he was still alive only by the grace of God.

Wheeler retreated to a reclusive position under the pear tree in the back yard where he studiously pored over his worn King James Bible. His brush with death had made him keenly aware of the ephemeral nature of life and his need to live a more righteous life.

A week after his discharge from the hospital, Dr. Harry's black Mercedes pulled into his driveway. Wilding stayed behind the wheel while Harry got out of the back seat and hailed Wheeler from the car. "Mr., Wheeler, are you up to having company? I would like to talk to you and see how you are doing.'

Wheeler stood up and motioned for Harry to join him. "Hey, Dr. Harry, it is very kind of you to visit. Come on over. Would you mind grabbing a chair off the porch?"

"Why, sure. How are you feeling?"

"I'm still weak and exhausted. Got this strange tingly feeling all over my body. I am glad you dropped by because I want to ask you some questions. You're a snake expert ain't you?"

Harry smiled, "I don't know about an expert but I do know quite a bit. I would like to ask you questions as well. What can I do for you?"

Wheeler pursed his lips. "Now don't take offense, but the hospital said you had paid the bill off. I really appreciate your generosity, but you didn't have to do that."

"It seemed like the thing to do if I wanted to become a part of the community. I understand you were bitten near my house. But don't worry. I am not pressing trespassing charges. I did tell Wilding to give permission to pick berries there. I just hate that this happened."

"How long will it take to get over all this? Have you known other snake bite victims?"

"Quite a few. In fact, I have been bitten by many different kinds of snakes. Some are worse than others. Luckily, here in the states, we don't have very many poisonous species: rattlesnakes, copperheads, cottonmouths, coral snakes. Most bites are rattlesnakes. Been bitten three times myself. Good thing you were in good health and not too old."

"I don't feel too lucky. I am still hurting like hell."

"Oh, I understand. The pain can be excruciating, but most dangerous for older people, kids or immunocompromised. Maybe one in a thousand is fatal. Cold comfort when you are hurting. Can you tell me what you felt like after the bite?"

Wheeler replied, "I have a hard time remembering. It seems like I was floating in a bright white light. I think I saw some figures moving around. Heard someone talking…can't recall what they said. It is all still fuzzy."

Harry scooted his chair closer. "Sounds a lot like what I felt… almost like what they say heaven is like. After the first time I was bitten, I lost all fear of snakes. Isn't that bizarre?"

"I hadn't thought about it that much. Maybe you're right. Thought for sure I was going to die… I guess the fact that I didn't means something."

"You know, some people who have been bitten have visions… really feel a closer connection to …"

"To God? I can sorta see that. And you're right…I don't seem to be afraid anymore."

"I hear there are some people handle snakes in their churches. Have you ever heard of that or known anyone like that?"

Wheeler shifted his weight. "Not personally. I have heard of them doing that. Never had much interest in trying it."

"Me neither, but some people quote the verse in Mark's gospel about taking up serpents."

"Yeah, I have read that…but never thought to take it literally."

"I guess you never heard of how it all got started. Started in East Tennessee by Holiness Church by a man named George Went Hensley. Married four times and often drunk as a skunk. Died of a rattler bite in 1955, but people still defend him as a prophet.'

Harry paused before continuing, "I hear that people who go to those churches donate a lot of money because they think handling snakes is a sure sign of their faith being rewarded."

"But does everyone handle the snakes?"

"Oh no, just people who feel their faith is strong enough to survive a bite. No kids. Usually only women. "

"But don't some people get bit and die?"

"Sure, people get bit and some die, but believe that is because their faith isn't strong enough."

Harry leaned in and whispered, "I'll tell you a secret. I did a little research on this and some of the more unscrupulous people cheat."

"Cheat? How?"

Harry grinned ever so subtly. "There's a couple of ways. First, a lot of them use copperheads, not rattlers. Copperhead bites are not fatal most of the time. Over the years there have been a few deaths but everyone who died was bitten by a rattler."

"Now that you mention it, I know some people who have been bit by copperheads and never died .... just real sick and sore."

"But here is the real sneaky part they use with rattlers and sometimes copperheads. Some people milk all the poison out of them before they handle them. And some people pull their fangs out so they can't bite. That is what those Indian snake charmers do with their cobras. The fangs eventually grow back so you have to pull them again. Who's going to know? Do you know of anyone who is going to look that closely at a snake's mouth?"

"Probably not many."

Harry smiled again. "People believe what they want to believe and most of the time you can't make them stop believing it. Especially when it comes to religion. If you think about it, this could be a perfect scam. If they get bit and survive, that's proof of their strong faith and they add to their donations. You have stacked the deck so people are not likely to die. On the rare occasion that they do die all you have to do is to say their faith wasn't strong enough. Let me show you something."

Harry reached into his jacket pocket and pulled out a newspaper clipping about a snake handling church and its charismatic preacher, Preacher Billy Joe Putney.

"See how famous he is? He was bitten once early on so now he convinces others to handle the snakes while he preaches. He only handles one snake and I would bet money that snake has no venom or fangs. And look at this."

He pointed to a picture of a simple wooden church. "That's his church he runs. Look at what he drives."

Harry produced another picture of Putney driving a silver Cadillac. "Now if I went to church there I might get suspicious but they don't. They just think he is entitled to that Caddy because he is such a great preacher."

"Really?"

"Really. These are not worldly people. If anyone asks questions, all he has to do is to quote some obscure scripture and they calm down. Do you know much about Shakespeare?"

"No, why?"

"In the Merchant of Venice, he says 'Even the devil can cite Scripture for his purpose'. Now how many of your congregation know much about Shakespeare other than Romeo and Juliet — possibly Hamlet?"

"I don't know. It sounds shady to me."

Harry winced. "Maybe, but is it any shadier that this so-called "Prosperity Gospel" that is so popular now? These are rich well-educated people who buy into the idea that God wants them to be rich. You know what Mencken said."

"No, who is he?"

"He was a famous American writer who said 'It is the natural tendency of the ignorant to believe what is not true. Now I am sure that your congregation is not ignorant… just secure in their beliefs. Mencken also said 'Faith may be defined as an illogical belief in the occurrence of the improbable.' Isn't that what the faithful think it is all about anyway?"

"I guess maybe it is. But I don't see my faith like that."

Harry made a face. "Of course, not... and I am not telling you what to do or what to believe. But it seems to me that a really good preacher would do anything to help people strengthen their faith and show the world how strong their faith is. So many people today don't put much stock in religion these days. I'm just saying."

Wheeler sighed and nodded.

"People need signs. They look for connections between things that have no connection at all —apophenia is the word for it. Superstition is a good example of it. Things like using woolly worms to predict the weather. Humans are particularly prone to seeing faces. People see Mary's face in toast and frost patterns on window glass. I know you have heard of the Man in the Moon. Even ancient people imagined they saw a face there. Remember that face they found on Mars a few years ago? Scientists say it was just a pile of rocks but you cannot convince some people of that."

"And people are really stubborn about religious images. I had a student one time bring me a picture of his x-ray of his cranium that he thought showed Jesus' image in it and he claimed that gave him the reassurance that he was going to be okay. Nothing I could say or do was going to convince him otherwise. I finally gave up. What was the harm?"

Harry could see he was piquing Wheeler's curiosity.

"Now you have heard about near death experiences. Didn't you just tell me that you had one when you were bitten? Turns out that a lot of people have the same sort of memories when they have traumatic experiences ...and they always sound a lot alike. People got it into their heads that they had gone to heaven and been brought back to life. I bet you have people in your church that believe you had one. It seems to me you could build on that."

Harry stood up and shook Wheeler's hand. "Well, something to think about. Glad you are getting better. I will check on you from time to time."

"Thanks for stopping by. And thanks again for paying the hospital bills. I don't know how I can ever repay you."

"Don't worry about it. Glad to help. I may need a favor someday. You never know."

Harry got back into the car and waved out of the window before he rolled it back up and Wilding drove the car away.

"So how did it go?" he asked Harry.

Harry leaned back in the seat and exhaled. "Like shooting fish in a barrel. The seeds are sown — just got to wait for them to grow —and they will grow. I got people to burn witches in Salem, didn't I? Like shooting fish in a barrel."

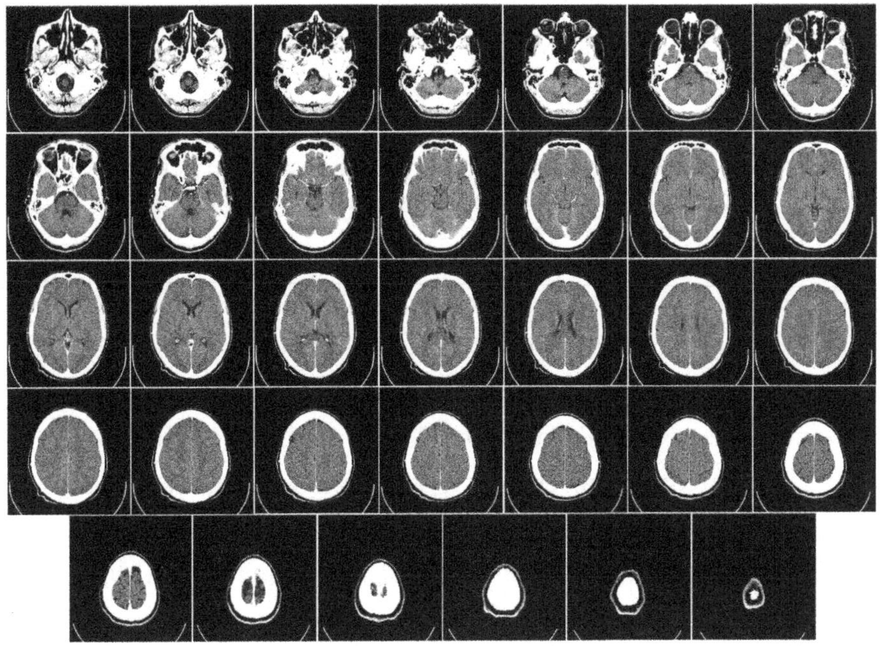

THEY HAVE MOUTHS BUT DO NOT SPEAK

No one knew for sure why Jeremiah Kane fixated on Batman at a such an early age; not even his parents could remember a time when he was not enthralled with the comic book hero. Perhaps he had seen some dark shape that resembled a Rorschach ink blot or maybe he fell at an inopportune locus along the autism spectrum that fed his obsession, but in the end the genesis of his identification with the Dark Knight did not matter. Like his idol, Jeremiah excelled in school and worked to stay as physically fit as he could. His parents, Marla and Bob, enjoyed watching their son in his small Bat suit running through the house chanting the music from the old Batman television show and fed his compulsion by customizing his tricycle to look like some kind of Bat vehicle like those he saw on his favorite show.

His parents were amused by the antics he copied from the campy old television show where has-been celebrities past the perigees of their careers played some absurd criminal masterminds. Unbeknownst to his parents, their prepubescent Caped Crusader abandoned the television hero and adopted the Dark Knight of a man so obsessed with guilt and grief that he patrolled lonely roof tops from which to swoop down and beat the hell out of criminals.

When the newest Batman movie debuted, the entire family attended the premiere, even though Jeremiah, at fifteen, was old enough to go to the movies by himself. Maybe his parents realized that they were seeing their baby was inching closer to adulthood and they wanted to enjoy the last vestiges of those innocent days. On one fateful night, they were attacked by a criminal Batman would battle.

As they left the theatre and were walking to their car, an unkempt slovenly man accosted them brandishing a pistol and demanded, "Give me your wallet and purse, and that pearl necklace if you want to keep on living!"

Bob had learned from the police that the best thing to do was to comply with the robber's demands because financial losses can be recouped while lives cannot. The robber pointed his gun at Jeremiah to deter him from any desperate heroics, but the would-be hero lunged at him and tried to pull him down. In the fracas that followed the rattled crook shot all three people before running down a dark alley. A passersby who had heard the shots and called 911 strove to contain the damage until the ambulances arrived.

"Shooting on Baxter Street, possible fatalities, suspect gone."

Officer John Michaels grabbed the radio in his cruiser. "Car 34, Officer Michaels en route to scene. Over."

He tore at breakneck speed weaving in and out of traffic with sirens blaring and lights flashing and slid his cruiser to a stop. When he jumped out to see if there were any survivors, a man greeted him, "Officer, my name is Harry Baldwin. We managed to control the bleeding, but he needs an ambulance stat."

"Thank you, Mr. Baldwin, the ambulance is on the way. There it is now. Please step back."

The EMTS rushed to where the bodies lay oozing blood. Marla and Bob were already dead, but an EMT found signs of life in Jeremiah's crumpled body.

Between life and death, Jeremiah could barely hear the EMTS' panicked cries. "Okay, bleeding stopped. Ten cc's of adrenaline, stat! Beginning CPR and ECT to revive...getting a pulse...weak...slow... BP still falling ... epinephrine into heart...pulse steady...stronger... BP rising...plateauing...I think we got him...to hospital....

"Officer Michaels reporting in. Two dead from gun shots, one teenager critical, on way to hospital. Finishing reports of any witnesses. Only rough description of shooter — white man, about six feet, in old clothes with green khaki jacket."

The ambulance flew down the street to St. Mary's Hospital where emergency surgery removed the bullets and cauterized the bleeding so that the five units of whole blood would not be wasted. After the operation, Jeremiah was stabilized and he lapsed into a hallucinatory state. He could not hear the doctors worrying about his erratic EEG even while they congratulated themselves with saving his life. After three days in the surgical ICU, Jeremiah was wheeled into a room to complete his recovery over the next eight months.

II

Fifteen years later, now Detective John Michaels was working the late shift 911 center. When a call came in, he replied quickly, "Police 911, what is your emergency?"

A guttural voice intoned, "Two robbers are tied up in Mack Alley off Twelfth Street". The caller hung up, leaving John puzzled and unsure of what to do next.

"All I need is some nut job with his prank calls," he thought. Still, if I don't send someone and it's real I'll catch hell for it."

He picked up the radio and began, "I need any black and white units to report to Mack Alley off twelfth. Possible citizen arrest; perps restrained. Acknowledge, over."

The radio crackled, " Car 48 responding. En route, two blocks away. Will advise asap. Over."

A minute later, the radio crackled again, "Officer Blake, reporting from Mack Alley. Two criminals tied with zip ties. Perps have some bruises and facial scrapes. They seem groggy. You ain't going to believe this. I'm taking a photo on my phone and sending to your cell if you give me your number."

John replied, "567-974-5431. What is it?"

"Just hold on. You should get it now."

He tapped his phone message icon and opened the incoming message. The image of a scrawled bat with spread wings appeared on the screen.

"Blake, is this some kind of joke?"

"No sir, there is a bat image pinned to the perps' clothes."

"That's all we need— some hero wannabe vigilante. Do these fellers require medical attention?"

"Probably just some first aid, but I'll take them to the hospital for evaluation."

John sighed, "Why do I get all the crazies on my shift? Must be a full moon."

He resumed his paperwork, anxiously awaiting Blake's bringing the criminals in. Two hours later, Blake escorted the two men to the front desk.

Michael asked, "So what's their story?"

Blake shrugged. "They say they were attacked by Batman — not a jerk in a suit but the real thing."

"Did they get a description?"

"All they say is they were attacked by Batman. Let me finish booking them."

After the men were processed and in the cells, Blake came to Michael's desk. "So, what do you think it was?"

"I guess we will have to go with Batman." They both laughed loudly.

Around one A.M. the next night, when Michael answered the phone, the same guttural voice responded, "Attempted rapist restrained on Market Street behind Kohl's."

Michael yelled into the phone, "Look, I don't know who you are but …" but before he could finish, the caller had hung up.

"Damn it! he thought. "Attention, I need a black and white to report to Market Street behind Kohl's. Possible rapist detained. Please acknowledge and advise."

"Car 67, Officer King reporting, I am en route."

In a few seconds, the officer reported. "King here. Man with hands zip tied; has bruise on jaw. And get this, some joker pinned a drawing of a bat to him."

Michael could feel his temper rising. "You gotta be kidding me. Take a picture of the man, the drawing and the area around him. Did he get a look at his attacker? What does he say?"

"He was scared to death but admitted he had tried to rape a woman. Said he was attacked by Batman."

"Any sign of his victim?"

"I found a makeup compact. No sign of the victim. On the way in with perp."

Michael decided to wait by the intake desk and met Officer King when he brought the felon in. "Okay, you piece of shit. Play time is over. Who assaulted you?"

The man replied in a tremulous voice, "I told you, Batman. He told me to confess or I would regret it. Scared the hell out of me."

"Can you describe him?"

"It happened so fast. He was big, six three or four. Bulked up. Maybe two thirty. Deep bass voice that I don't want to hear again."

Michaels stepped back and said to King. "Lock him up. Damn it. Any way to track his victim?"

"We are still canvassing the area, but it doesn't look good."

"Just a matter of time until this lunatic gets himself killed," Michael said.

The phone calls from the same basso voice continued to filter into the police station over the next week. The crimes ranged from muggings, rapes, assaults, burglaries, and drug pushers, but showed little differences in the reports and the sketchy descriptions never changed —nor did the roughly drawn bat images.

After ten days of this, Michaels reached his breaking point. He called the chief of detectives and briefed him on what was going on.

"Chief Robbins, we have some public hero nut case out there attacking people and turning them over to us. I had hoped this would blow over but it seems to be getting worse. We've gone from one report per night to as many as three. I think we're dealing with a real psychopath."

Robbins replied, "I had heard some chatter about this but I figured you were on it and didn't need me interfering. So, it's getting worse?"

"Yes, sir. So far, our only descriptions have come from the perps themselves and they are so rattled who knows what they saw?"

"Have any officers seen this man? Any clues?"

"None. CSI and forensics have combed through every crime scene and found nada. Just some perps zip tied with that bat signal thingy on them. Here's the weird thing. Every one of the perps has confessed to their crimes because whoever this is, he has scared them shitless."

The chief rubbed his hand over his mouth as he listened to the summary report. "Okay, let's keep this quiet. We do not need a bunch of copy cats out there trying to get their fifteen minutes of fame. Are these incidents reported from all over the city or are they concentrated in one area?"

"We have had a few scattered around but most are concentrated around Mercy Hospital and Long-Term Care Facility. Always between about midnight to four A.M."

"All right, double the police presence in that area during those times. He has to make a mistake some time."

Michaels replied, "We hope we catch him before he gets killed or kills someone. I'll keep you apprised."

"I want daily reports first thing in the mornings. Probably should call the FBI profiler or a shrink to get a psychological picture of what we are dealing with. I'll have them call you."

III

The reports continued unabated for the next week before a forensic psychiatrist, a lovely thirty-two-year-old brunette, showed up to talk to Michaels. She scanned the room and saw his nameplate on the desk.

"Officer Michaels? I'm Barbara Stein from the medical center. I hear we have a hero on our hands."

John rose to greet and shook her hand. "John Michaels. Pleasure to meet you. Apparently, we have our own Batman."

"May I see any reports you have?"

He nodded and handed her a thick stack of manila envelopes marked 'SENSITIVE'.

"Here you go. Not much to go on. I've gone over these things a thousand times, but maybe you can see something I missed. You can use that break room. Make yourself a cup of coffee. If you need anything, please let me know."

"Sure thing. So, it looks like what, thirty cases?"

"Thirty-two. We got lucky three days ago. The victim of an attempted rape caught a glimpse of whoever this thing is and her description is like the others. Six feet four, two forty or so. Seems to appear and disappear at will. Sounds like the Dark Knight, doesn't it?"

Stein nodded, "I guess, but let's see what I can find out. You say there's coffee in there?"

"Yeah, we bought one of them K cups…best thing since sliced bread. Sugar and creamers are by the machine. We have several kinds of flavored coffee and regular roasts. Help yourself."

She carried the files to the table in the break room and made herself a cup of coffee before she began poring over the files, jotting down details as she read. Three hours later, she returned to Michaels' desk.

He rose to greet her. "What did you find out?"

She sighed heavily. "Not much. Whoever this man is, he is good. He may as well be the comic book Batman based on what I am seeing. I would say, based on his physical traits, he is about thirty. Seems driven by anger and maybe a sense of revenge. He may have been the victim of a crime or knows someone who was."

She gave a soft chuckle, "I think your top suspect is Bruce Wayne."

Michaels laughed. "I'll send out a unit to arrest him…I guess Alfred is home. Thanks, Dr. Stein. If we get any more reports, I'll call you."

Two nights later, a new report came in. This time, the victim had actually snapped a picture on her phone which the attending officer had temporarily confiscated to download the image. Michaels transferred the image to the computer and enlarged it on the monitor. The low-quality image revealed a dark blurry shape on the right side of the screen. Michaels stared at the screen and walked away to see it from a distance. He caught his breath. "Well, I'll be damned." He exclaimed as his eyes made out what appeared to be the scalloped edge of a cape. Shaking with excitement, he phoned Dr. Stein and asked her to come by as soon as possible. She said she would be there in an hour.

When she arrived, Michaels turned the screen around to show her the image. "Tell me what you see."

After a couple of minutes of staring and squinting at the screen she said, "I don't believe it ——.it looks like Batman's cape. Jesus, what are we dealing with?"

"Beats the hell out of me, but at least we are both seeing the same thing. He left a mugger tied up with zip ties and the bat sign like always. She could not add any more details."

"I don't know what to tell you. I'm reluctant to release the information to the public. God knows we have enough looney tunes out there already. We just have to keep looking. Thanks for the call. Good night."

Michaels thanked her and returned to his seat, where he sat staring at the screen. A brief image crossed his mind, but try as he might, he could not focus on it enough to summon it to his consciousness. Finally, he turned the screen off and went home for the night.

IV

Despite the efforts of the police to keep a lid on these cases, word leaked out to the press who sent out feelers for information. The mysterious crime fighter continued his attacks, but police efforts to solve the mystery of "The Batman" were obfuscated by floods of calls claiming to have seen the man or a Batmobile or someone who looked like the Joker. One industrious young man built a bat-signal spotlight and shone it into the clouds of the night sky before the police confiscated it.

After dismissing most of the reports as fakes from wannabees, Michaels and Stein came to believe that at least one or two of the Batman sightings could have been genuine. One night after yet another perp was brought into the station, they sat comparing notes over coffee.

Michaels emptied the cold coffee from his cup and stood watching as a new cup was brewing. "You want to know the best part,

Barbara? We are actually seeing a decrease in crime in the area around St. Mary's Hospital."

"So, what are you saying, that one of the residents there is secretly Batman who beats the hell out of crooks, drives a souped-up Batmobile and escapes capture by the police?"

Michaels sat back down and carefully took the first sip of hot coffee. "I don't know what to think. But somewhere..."

"Yes? Somewhere what?"

"I have this nagging feeling that keeps popping into my head that I'm missing something."

"Maybe if you go over all of your old cases, something will click."

"I've been trying to do that, but so far nothing pops out."

They chatted a while longer before Stein left. Michaels returned to his desk and began sorting through his old files until he found the file labeled JEREMIAH KANE. He flipped through the file, looking at the photographs of the crime scene where the Kanes were murdered, trying to recreate the scene from his memories.

"What the hell. I'll deal with this tomorrow."

The next day, he drove over to St. Mary's Hospital and Long-Term Care Facility and went to the desk.

"I'm Detective John Michaels from the police. We are trying to solve this Batman thing you've heard about. A family was mugged about ten years ago. Parents were killed, but the son survived. As I recall, he was brought to this hospital. Name was Jeremiah Kane. Do you know what happened to him?"

The clerk shrugged, "He's still here, but I'm not sure why that matters. Would you like to speak to a physician about him?"

"That would be great."

Shortly a doctor in a white coat appeared and introduced himself. "Hello, Officer. I'm Dr. Janson. I understand you had questions about Jeremiah."

"Nice to meet you, Dr. Janson. Yes, what can you tell me about him."

"Please follow me."

The men walked down a corridor that led to Jeremiah's room. He lay quiescent staring into space.

"This is Jeremiah Kane. He has been here for fifteen years, but has been in a catatonic state pretty much since he came here. Are you familiar with catatonia, Officer?"

"A little."

"The patient is very much alive and is trapped in an unresponsive shell of a body. We monitor their vital signs and do routine checks and feed them on IV's, but we have no protocols in place to stop treatment when there is no next of kin, which is what we have here. Let me show you something."

Janson led Michaels to his office where he pulled several large files out of a cabinet. "Here is the complete history of Jeremiah Kane. But I want to point out some things. We have ten years of EEG's. All of them since he was brought here. Pretty unremarkable until about eight months ago when we started seeing abnormal activity in his amygdala and hypothalamus. Those centers are tied into emotion, fear, the endocrine system and we found surges of adrenaline. Here's the weird part. These eruptions always occur between midnight and five A.M. We taped him during those times and we saw violent spasms. I guess really *grand mal* seizures, but his flailing arms seemed to be fighting someone. He must hit the bedrails sometimes because once in a while we find bruises on his knuckles."

Janson whispered, "Don't take this the wrong way, but we call him our Batman. When he was first admitted, some of his friends came to visit and told us of his obsession with Batman. Occasionally, an old friend will come to visit but since none of them have medical power of attorney. Jeremiah is in limbo and we cannot withhold life sustaining treatments."

"Is there any higher brain function at all?"

"Once in a while, he shows some autonomic reflexes and rarely we hear some random verbal outbursts, completely unintelligible. Why, you don't think he is your Batman, do you? I can assure you that would be impossible in his perpetual catatonic state. Whatever he knows is locked away inside his mind and we have no way to access it. Whoever or whatever Jeremiah Kane is or whatever or whoever he was or hopes to be is trapped in this shell, slowly atrophying over time. Eventually, he will succumb to organ failure or infection, but until then he will only be Batman in the innermost recesses of his mind. I need to go, but you can stay here as long as you wish. Nothing will change."

Michaels left but returned around eleven pm. Softly, he pulled a chair over and sat down. He cupped his right hand over his chin and lower jaw, stroking them as he contemplated the inert form lying in the bed, staring blankly into space. The wall clock echoed hushed tick tock tick tock as he watched the hands of the clock align on top of the twelve. He gasped and watched in astonishment as the thin young man's arms began to flail about, fighting some imaginary foe over the next four hours before lapsing back into catatonia.

Michaels stood up and held Jeremiah's frail hand, stroking it lightly as a small purplish bruise appeared on his knuckles.

"Give'em hell, Batman, give'em hell," he whispered before leaving Jeremiah alone in the room.

ASK WHATEVER YOU WISH AND IT SHALL BE GIVEN

The last thing Jason Goldman remembered before he awoke face down in the sand clinging to a piece of an airplane wing on a remote Pacific Ocean island was asking the pretty stewardess for her phone number. An errant seagull flying too close to the plane was sucked into the engine, causing it to explode into hundreds of pieces raining down over a vast expanse of the ocean and its myriad of islands.

Raising himself up on his elbows, he turned over and tried to sit up. The sharp pain of a broken rib tearing into his intercostal muscles made him yelp in pain as he fell back into the sand. Regrouping, he crawled over to a piece of driftwood that might support his weight as a cane. With a loud scream of pain, he managed to grab the wood and rise to his knees; he paused before heaving himself more or less vertical. He saw a nasty gash on his right calf had bled rivulets of blood before the sea's salt has coagulated them into dark streaks. A throbbing headache made him dizzy until he shut his eyes and waited for the vertigo to pass.

After his blurred vision cleared, he scanned the shoreline and island. Flotsam from the explosion littered the sandy shore along with what appeared to be various parts of human bodies torn apart by the blast. The island itself supported abundant plant life as well as flocks of seabirds who used the island as a breeding ground.

Five minutes of yelling loudly in hopes of finding other survivors proved fruitless. He accepted the fact that he was alone and, grimacing with every step, he managed to make his way to the shade of some palm trees. Exhausted by his efforts, he lapsed back into unconsciousness.

A light rain awakened him and he quickly used concave pieces of debris to catch water for several gulps for his parched mouth. The leg had stopped bleeding, but his ribcage still ached as he started a slow search for food, water and shelter. Luckily, he found some seabird eggs which he greedily scarfed down. He found a nearby waterfall and noticed several kinds of flowers and fruits, including a breadfruit tree he recognized from a National Geographic show.

The next days, he scrounged any usable debris from the shore and shallows and found a small cave for shelter. After several unsuccessful attempts, he finally made some tackle he could use to catch fish. The ribs and leg slowly healed as he settled into his solitary life on the island. Despite intermittent spells of hopelessness, he grew more optimistic that he was still alive and would possibly be rescued eventually. He could survive on birds, and their eggs, fish, shellfish and the waterfall so he resigned himself to toughing it out until he was rescued.

Over the next few weeks, he collected bottles, a few scraps of paper and some pencils. He wrote some SOS messages that he stuffed into bottles that he sealed with corks of wood before throwing them into the surf. He chortled as he thought of the low probability of anyone finding them before he died. Still, he was alive and he resolved to persevere until some passing ships found him.

He found several pieces of luggage containing clothes, shoes, toiletries and toothbrushes. One briefcase had two novels so he could pass the time reading. Although he had food and water, he lost weight and conserved energy by sleeping much of each day.

Every day he patrolled the shoreline searching for anything that he might find useful. On one of these strolls, he noticed an odd bottle sticking out of the sand. Puzzled by its odd shape, he scooped away the sand to expose an ornate brightly colored bottle.

"What the hell is this?" he muttered as he turned it over in his hands to brush away the sand. "Almost looks like a bottle with a genie in it. Wouldn't that be a hoot? Maybe he could rescue me."

Amused by the silliness of his flight of fancy, he took the bottle back to his cave and laid it in a pile of other things he had collected over his months on the island and forgot about it.

One day after a lunch of crabs and fruit, he grew bored with reading the same books again and began to rummage through his cache. He grinned as he picked up the bottle, he pulled the stopper out of the bottle and intoned the magical phrase he remembered from an old Bullwinkle show, "Eenie, meenie, chili beanie, the spirits are about to speak."

A loud explosion knocked him back and blinded him. The cave filled with billows of white smoke and a spicy smell of incense. He flailed his arms to fan the smoke away, but passed out when he saw what appeared to be a Middle Eastern man with black hair and neatly trimmed goatee dressed in loosely flowing robes. After a few minutes, he stirred and sat up, thinking he had had a dream, but the man was still there, smiling broadly.

The man spoke in a guttural voice, "Ah, Master, you have awakened. I am Jinni, the spirit in the bottle. I am here to serve you. What are your commands?"

Startled by the turn of events and convinced that he was hallucinating, Jason passed out again and fell back. In a few minutes, he awoke to find the man still sitting there by his fire.

Jason shook his head before he said, "I must be out of my mind. Maybe I got poisoned by some bad crabs or fruit. This can't be real."

The man flashed a beaming smile. "No, master, you are not dreaming. I am Jinni. I am here to serve you. What are your wishes?'

"Wishes? Now I know I'm crazy. Where am I? In The Arabian Nights?"

"No, you are on a deserted island in the Pacific Ocean. You have been here for six months. As the servant of Allah, I must grant you three wishes."

"Three wishes? Now I know I'm nuts."

"Once again, Master, this is real. I will grant three wishes, but there are some rules. Life and Death belong to Allah alone, so I cannot kill for you nor can I resurrect the dead. Now what are your wishes?"

Jason, still unsure that he was awake and sane. "Now, as I recall from the fairy tales, I need to be careful or these wishes can backfire. So, enlighten me as to pitfalls I need to avoid."

Jinni, nodded. "Obviously, you will wish to be rescued and I can certainly do that. But you might want to think this through."

"Why? I've been here for months. Of course, I want to be rescued. What's the problem with that?"

Jinni made a face. "Well, if I just magically transport you to civilization, people are bound to wonder how you got there. You would still have two wishes left and anyone who suspects the truth might try to coerce you in some way. I have lived in the bottle for thousands of year, seen many masters come and go and I can offer some good advice. If I were you, I would make all of my wishes while I am still here and then bury the bottle where no one else can find it. Only you would enjoy the pleasure of my service."

Jason thought about the warnings and agreed. "Okay, let's start with something simple. I want to be fabulously wealthy. I wish for a billion dollars. So where is it?"

Jinni, shook his head. "Maybe I did not make myself clear. Suppose I just snap my fingers and a fortune appears. How are you going to explain it to anyone who rescues you? What's to keep them from killing you and stealing it?"

"I hadn't thought about that. Same thing if I asked you to put money in a bank for me."

Jinni said, "If I may be so bold, Master, I could conjure a treasure hidden in your cave so that no one will see it. Once you are rescued you can retrieve the treasure so that no one suspects anything odd. Behold!"

He motioned his arms and a bright flash illuminated the cave. When the smoke cleared, Jason saw piles of gold coins and precious gemstones in the back of the cave.

"You got to be kidding me. This can't be happening."

"Go see for yourself. It is very real."

Jason staggered over to the treasure to find that it was indeed real. After a few minutes of thought, he dug out a hole and stashed the treasure under a layer of sand.

"Ok, so I'm convinced and you are not a hallucination. Now about getting rescued…"

Jinni held up his hand and warned, "Once again, if I transport you out of the clear blue sky you are asking for trouble...and you will still have one wish left. Make that your last wish. I can see a small pleasure craft fifty miles way. I can interfere with their instruments just enough to divert them to this island and they will just figure a malfunction in the equipment caused them to go off course. You will be safe and can return for your treasure."

Jason agreed. He stood thinking about his last wish before he snapped his fingers, "I got it. I wish for more wishes!"

Jinni clicked his tongue against his palate. "No, Master, each master I serve is allotted only three wishes so asking for more wishes is not permitted. Perhaps you should think about this overnight. I have already disrupted the directional finders on the boat so it should be here by midmorning tomorrow. Get some rest and summon me in the morning." With that admonition, he reverted to a flume of white smoke and disappeared into the bottle.

Jason could not sleep as his mind feverishly went over possibilities for a safe third wish. Toward morning, he had an epiphany of inspiration. He picked up the bottle, "Okay, Jinni, I have my last wish. Come out and grant my last wish."

Jinni appeared in a flash. "Ah, master, before your wish, go to the shore. The boat is within sight of the island. You need only to signal them with smoke or a fire."

Jason ran out to the shore to see a small speck on the horizon. "Well, I'll be damned. I'm saved!!"

He quickly started a fire that belched a column of dark smoke that would make the boaters turn toward the island.

"Now, Jinni, here is my wish. I cannot wish for more wishes, but I wish for the ability to make wishes come true1"

Jinni smiled, nodded and made an upward sweeping motion with this muscular arms. In a flash, Jason disappeared and a tall thin Middle Eastern man appeared in his place.

The man laughed uproariously. He picked the bottle up from the sand and replaced the stopper. Still laughing, he tapped the bottle and said, "You know, that was the same thing I wished for over two thousand years ago and that is how I wound up in the bottle. At long last, I am free but you are bound to the bottle."

His voice trailed off. "Just to be sure, I think I'll bury the bottle somewhere. I guess I should thank you for all the treasure…and for setting me free. Good bye, Mr. Goldman. Enjoy your sleep."

After digging a hole, he placed the bottle inside and quickly covered it up before walking out to the shore to wave to the boat as it floated to the shore.

THE BEST LAID PLANS

The black limousine glided to a halt outside the front entrance to Broughton Hall and chauffeur Jack Wright got out of the driver's side, walked around and opened the rear door on the passenger side. Richard Langham stepped out and said, "Thank you, Jack. I think I should be ready to go in about two hours so if you want to take a break and come back, that'll be fine."

When Jack drove off, Richard rang the bell by the front door. A few seconds later, Reginald Broughton opened the door and greeted him, "Richard, I'm so glad you could make it. Come in, come in. Let me have your topcoat."

Richard handed him his coat and shook his hand, "I'm so happy to be able to spend a dinner and an evening with you. It has been a while since we had time to talk. I have to ask where your butler is since you answered the bell."

Reggie smiled and replied, "Actually, Ashford has not had a vacation for years so I gave him two weeks off. He will be back next week. We can have the entire evening to ourselves."

Richard smiled graciously, "That is very kind of you. Are we having our dinner delivered by Grub Hub?"

"Heavens, no. Over the last few years since Margaret and Junior passed, I have watched Ashford cook and I have become quite a chef. I hope you like beef Wellington, mashed potatoes, tossed salad, asparagus, and cherries jubilee for dessert."

"Wow, that is impressive. Their deaths shocked the whole community. I can only imagine what you have been going through. How are you holding up?"

"I have my days. I have traveled a bit and purchased some new pieces that I want to show you. One in particular will intrigue you, but let's hold all that until after dinner. Please have a seat while I bring the food in from the kitchen."

Richard nodded and took a seat at the table. With great aplomb, Reggie brought in the meal. "Please hand me your plate."

Richard handed it to him and remarked, "That looks delicious. You must have spent hours preparing it."

"What is time for old friends? By the way, how are Claire and Tyler?"

"Fine. Claire is in Europe and Tyler just returned to Brazil working on his doctoral research on amphibians. She will be back in two weeks so beside my assistant, Jack, I have the house to myself. What have you been buying?"

"Now, Richard, I told you we will see them after dinner. How is your food?"

"Outstanding. You may have to write a cookbook. Are you still involved with your shipping business?"

"Only nominally. I have a fine young protégé who has agreed to watch over my interests and cast my votes by proxy. I prefer my solitude these days."

Richard looked at him and sighed, "Now, Reggie, that is not healthy. I know it must be hard, but you need to get out. Maybe you can meet a new lady friend to occupy the time."

"I have no interest in other women since Margaret died. I do travel some to buy new works. I occasionally visit major exhibitions. With the internet and my own collection of references I have sharpened my acumen as an art expert."

"That is fantastic, but you already had a reputation as a connoisseur. Have you expanded your impressionist holdings?"

Reggie laid his fork down. "You seem determined to discuss my surprises. To answer your question, yes, I found a Cezanne and a Renoir for sale and I just could not pass them up."

"I know better than to ask what you paid for them. If I have to ask, I couldn't afford them."

"Precisely. How is your collection going?"

"I found a Monet at a reasonable price and have leads on a Degas and a Rembrandt. If those pan out, my collection should be worth as much as yours. This friendly rivalry of ours has led us both to acquire some excellent pieces."

"Yes, I have enjoyed the rivalry as well, but I have to admit that I was miffed a bit when you outbid me for that Van Gogh two years ago."

"That was an intense bidding war. The ironic thing is that I found a buyer last year and I sold that for a tidy profit."

"Really? If you don't mind me asking, to whom did you sell it?"

"A third party handled the whole transaction, so I never learned who the buyer was, but ten million dollars is ten million dollars."

Reggie smiled, "Quite true. Ten million dollars is still ten million dollars. But, as they say, it is only money. The most valuable things in life do not have price tags on them, do they?"

Richard swallowed nervously and shook his head before whispering, "No, they do not."

An awkward silence settled on the room as the men dined quietly. Reggie finished his last bite of asparagus and asked, "Do you keep in contact with the university?"

Richard nodded, "I contribute a lot of money to the art department to expand their holdings and I host exhibitions. Do you have any contact with the school?"

"Oh, yes. As a matter of fact, I attended the opening of your last exhibition. Very impressive. Since I have no one to inherit it, I have decided to donate my collection to the school."

Richard took a deep breath and said, "Okay, let's talk about the elephant in the room. Reggie, I am very sorry what happened to your son. I guess you still hold me responsible for his death."

Reggie's face darkened, "Why, Richard, why would I blame you for his death? Or for Margaret's?"

Richard leaned toward him. "Look, I might do something different if I had it to do over again I knowing what we know now. But maybe not."

Reggie clasped his hands. "Richard, you were well within your rights to handle it as you chose to. Junior was a drug addict who always needed money after I threatened to cut him off unless he entered rehab. But instead he turned to a life of crime."

Richard lowered his head. "Sadly, that was his choice."

Reggie rose from his chair. "Let's not dwell on the past. Why don't we go to the library? You know where it is. I will get us some coffee."

"That sounds good. Are your surprises in there?"

"Yes, but no peeking."

Reggie returned to the kitchen while Richard went to the library where an easel draped in cloth stood near the center of the room. Shortly, Reggie brought the coffee in and set it on a table. He filled both cups before taking a seat and taking a sip.

"Have you ever heard of Kopi Luwak coffee? Some people don't care for it although I have developed a taste for it."

"Isn't that the coffee made from beans that some civet cat pooped out? I have never tried it. It seemed very bizarre. Here goes."

He took a sip and frowned. "Reggie, I have to admit, I am not impressed. It just tastes bad. I think I will pass."

Reggie replied, "At five hundred dollars a pound, it is still an acquired taste. Give me your cup and I will bring you some Jamaican Blue Mountain. I have a Keurig so it will just take a minute. I need to bring in the dessert as well."

Richard passed the cup to him and Reggie went toward the kitchen. "The cherries are simmering, just need to flambee them there. Let me bring you your coffee first."

He brought a new cup of coffee to Richard. "Oh, I wanted to show you one thing I did buy. It's there on the end table by my recliner. Take a look while I get the dessert."

Richard walked over, sat down in the recliner, and picked up a copy of Godey's Lady's Book. It had a book mark inserted near the middle. He opened to the page where Edgar Allan Poe's short story, "The Cask of Amontillado" began.

Reggie beamed as he returned to the room carrying the flaming cherries jubilee. “That is an original copy of the journal that first published my favorite Poe story. I fell in love with that story when I first read it in high school. Let me set this down.”

He carefully placed the dessert onto the table beside the men’s coffee.

Richard replied, “Yes, I do recall that story. A very disturbing tale about revenge.”

Reggie walked over to the easel. “It was a cleverly devised revenge scheme. The weird thing is that Poe never tells us why his protagonist wanted revenge. What had the victim done to provoke such hatred?”

“I’ve often wondered the same thing, but I guess it doesn’t matter.”

Reggie sniffed. “If I were planning such an intricate plot, I think I would do things differently.”

“How so?”

“As I see it, the intended victim was already so drunk so he could not really appreciate what was happening to him. Don’t you think part of the pleasure of revenge is that the victim knows he is about to be called into account for his misdeeds?”

Richard shifted his seat uncomfortably and answered, “Yes, seeing your victim squirm would heighten the sense of pleasure.”

Reggie took another sip. “But there are so many ways to get revenge and merely killing someone seems too extravagant. If it were me, I would want the victim to, as you say, squirm a bit. How is your coffee?”

“Much better, and the dessert is heavenly. But back to the story. You mean to say that death is not the ultimate revenge?”

“Precisely. But I can contain myself no longer. Prepare to be awestruck.” Reggie walked over to the easel and with a great flourish flipped the cloth back over the easel to reveal Rembrandt's 'A Lady and Gentleman'.

Richard gasped. "Oh my God, Reggie, is that what I think it is?"

Reggie beamed triumphantly, "Yes, it is. This is one of the Rembrandts stolen in the Isabella Stewart Art Museum theft in 1990. What do you think?"

Richard sat stupefied and stammered, "How? Who? Is this the real thing?"

"Now Richard, why would I pay eighty million dollars for a copy? Of course this is the real thing. But before I tell you how I got it, let's chat a bit."

Richard sat agape. "How do you know it is real?"

"I told you that I had become an expert on art since thanks to you I am not distracted by family."

Richard felt his heart begin to beat more rapidly. "Reggie, what are you talking about?"

"Why Junior and Margaret of course. You callously took them from me with your lack of compassion."

Richard swallowed hard again. "Reggie, what did you expect me to do? Junior broke into my house and stole a very valuable Renoir painting worth millions of dollars."

"Yes, yes, he did. I managed to find the painting and buy it back for you in hopes that you would not press charges. But you, in your cold-heartedness, chose to proceed with the trial and he was sentenced to prison for five years."

"Reggie, he was a grown man who should have known better than to steal, especially from someone who was a close friend. He needed to be taught to face the consequences of his actions."

"And you chose to be the authority to whom he would answer. Somehow, seeing your son beaten, sodomized and brutalized in prison until he committed suicide seems more significant than some piece of art."

"That was not the point. You knew Junior had serious problems and yet you kept using your wealth to bail him out of one mess after another. I was horrified to hear of his death, but I really thought serving time in prison would make him reform."

"Did you think that maybe his death would in turn cause his mother to die of a broken heart? Or did you just not give a damn?"

"There was no way anyone could have foreseen any of this happening."

"You think? Did you even entertain the possibility that tragedy might follow your actions? I returned your painting intact and offered you a gift of fifty million dollars to drop the charges, but you refused."

"Reggie, I am truly sorry for your loss and I have spent many sleepless nights regretting what happened. But what's done is done and we must go on."

"Yes, we must. And that is why I bought this painting. I wanted you to know what it feels like to see something you cannot have."

"How did you find this painting?"

"There are hundreds of missing masterpieces in the art world and a large network of shady dealers and thieves who are willing to procure things for a price. It took some time, but I finally found a man who could get this piece for me. Sadly, shortly after I bought this masterpiece from him, he was a victim of a hit and run driver. Ashford does not know I have this. The only people who know I have it are you and me."

Reggie pulled a gun from a drawer under the table. "I'm sure you understand I cannot risk letting you tell anyone that I have this masterpiece."

Richard stood up and cried, "Reggie, do you mean to kill me?"

"Yes, now you can go to your grave for taking my son and wife from me, knowing that I finally have my revenge."

"But you forgot one thing. My driver will expect to pick me up soon."

"Oh, you mean the driver whose car they will find in a few days ten miles from here after he accidentally went over a cliff overlooking the river— you mean that driver?"

He picked up the gun and motioned for Richard to sit back down. "No, my friend, I have plotted this for a long time as I sat alone here feeding my pain and anger. Now I can savor watching you trying to save yourself from the justice you so richly deserve."

Richard nervously took a sip from his cup. "You know, Reginald, you really should have gotten out more over the last five years. Of course, I am all too familiar with the hidden world of stolen art. Where do you think I found that Monet? When I heard through the underground that someone had arranged to buy this stolen painting, I started wondering who it could be. Then, completely out of the blue, you invite me here for dinner when only you and I would be here. It seems that Ashford had told Jack that he was going on vacation, so I figured you were up to something."

Reggie laughed, "It really does not matter, because you will be dead very soon and your body will never be found. We're going to spend your last few minutes together. It is the least I can do."

Richard continued, "Like I said, you need to get out more. I believe I told you Tyler had come home from Brazil. He is researching a very interesting little frog called the golden poison arrow frog. It is a small beautiful little creature whose skin excretes a particularly nasty toxin called — I think I am pronouncing this correctly — batrachotoxin. The natives tip their poison blow darts with it. A fatal dose is less than a single grain of salt so it is completely undetectable in the body of the victim. And there is no antidote even if the victim knows he has eaten it. The paralyzing effects set in fairly quickly; possibly they already have. When you went to get more coffee for me, I put a drop in your coffee."

Reggie sat frozen in his chair. He could only watch helplessly as Ricard carefully rolled the stolen painting up and tied a string around it. Richard raised his cup of coffee to him as he took his last breath.

"Thank you, dear friend, for the delicious meal and this absolutely wonderful gift. You really shouldn't have."

Richard called Jack on his cell phone. Then he picked up the gun with a napkin and returned it to the desk drawer. While he waited, he loaded all the dirty dishes into the dishwasher and turned it on while he busied himself wiping finger prints from anything he had touched. By the time he had finished, he heard Jack blow the horn and he left the house to get into the car.

Jack opened the door for him. "I take it things went as planned, sir."

"Flawlessly, Jack, flawlessly. An autopsy will find nothing, especially since no one will find the body until Ashford returns. The cause of death will be natural causes."

Jack got back into the car and drove down the long entranceway where a dense fog had settled. When he reached the road, he strained to look for traffic before he pulled back onto the highway. He did not see the pickup truck whose driver had not turned on his headlights. The truck t-boned the limousine, killing Jack instantly and flipping the car upside down trapping an unconscious Richard inside.

EPILOGUE

Three weeks later, Richard slowly opened his eyes to see he was lying in a hospital bed with numerous tubes and wires connecting his body to machines. As he recovered his memory, he managed to summon a nurse to his room. In a few seconds, the nurse accompanied by a young man in a suit arrived at his bedside.

She patted his arm, "Take it easy. You have been in a coma for three weeks. It will take a few minutes for your head to clear. Do you feel up to talking?"

She handed him a cup of water. He took a sip and nodded. "Maybe a little. What happened?"

The young man stepped forward and said, "You were in a bad accident that killed your driver and left you barely alive. The man who hit you was driving without lights and did not see your car. I'm Detective Brian Walker. I know this is a bad time, but I do have a few questions to ask you."

He reached into his coat pocket and took out two photographs of the stolen Rembrandt. "We found the original of this painting rolled up in your car. It is one of the paintings stolen from the Isabella Stewart Museum in 1990. Needless to say, we have placed it in a secure location while we investigate. Coincidentally, we had some reason to believe that a reclusive billionaire art collector, Reginald Broughton, may have had something to do with the stolen painting, but he was found dead of natural causes a few days after your accident. As a detective, I am not supposed to believe in coincidences so maybe you can tell us how you happened to have this painting and why your car was involved in a fatal accident in front of his mansion."

GOOD BUSINESS IS WHERE YOU FIND IT

Scott Allen was a walking dead man, but he just did not know it yet. As a detective on the police force, he had been dealing with what appeared to be a serial killer who had committed six brutal murders within a ten square block area of Scott's apartment. The victims had been beaten with some kind of blunt instrument with an unusual shape. Scott and several other detectives had gone over the forensics of the cases with a fine-toothed comb, but no one could discern any pattern or motives.

Despite being advised not to get personally involved, he had become preoccupied with the cases and could not dissociate himself from them. For weeks, insomnia had made restful sleep impossible.

The effects of long term sleep deprivation were beginning to affect his work. In desperation, he consulted his doctor, Dr. Wayne Carter, who listened intently.

Scott said, "Doctor, I have not been able to sleep for weeks and that has affected my work and made me irritable as hell. I have tried various sleeping pills, but none of them have worked. What can I do?"

Carter replied, "Let's see what we can find out."

He spent five minutes examining Scott before sitting down and began writing out orders for tests. When he had finished, he asked, "Do you know much about your ancestry?"

"Not really much beyond my grandparents. I never got into that genealogy stuff."

Carter stroked his chin. "I am ordering a genetic profile to check for a very rare disease. It's so rare it's unlikely you have it, but let's not take chances."

Scott asked, "How long will that take?"

"The blood tests will be back tomorrow afternoon, but the genetic tests will take a couple of weeks. I'll call you when I get them."

Ten days later, Carter called him and told him to come in as soon as he could. Scott took a sick day the next day and went to the office.

Carter ushered him into the office and opened a manila folder. He took a deep breath. "I can't believe it, but the tests confirmed my suspicions. You have an extremely rare genetic disorder called sporadic fatal insomnia."

Scott leaned over. "Fatal insomnia? What the hell is that?"

"There are two kinds of this disease. One, familial fatal insomnia, is inherited, and the other one is sporadic fatal insomnia. Both are caused by a genetic mutation that allows prions to take control of your brain. My guess is that you have had a somatic mutation that gave rise to the problem."

"I don't understand. What's a prion?"

"A prion is a misfolded protein molecule that replaces the normal form of that protein. Bovine spongiform encephalopathy or mad cow disease, is caused by a prion; so is wasting disease in deer. These diseases are fatal, but a prognosis is difficult because they develop at different rates in people. But the end result is the same because there is no treatment or cure."

"How did I get this mutation?"

"Who knows? Maybe x-rays or some chemical caused it, but somatic mutations can arise during normal cell divisions. It doesn't matter."

Carter patted him on his arm. "I hate to be the bearer of bad news, but you need to get your affairs in order. You may have a few weeks or months. I think the average life expectancy is about eighteen months. I'm really sorry, but there is nothing I can do."

Scott could feel tears welling up in his eyes. "What can I expect as far as symptoms go?"

"Severe insomnia, panic attacks, hallucinations, paranoia, and dementia in the final stages. You might as well keep taking the sleeping pills as they may provide a brief respite, but they will not cure it."

Still in shocked disbelief, Scott left the office and returned to his car where he sat crying for several minutes. As he tried to process the maelstrom of emotions wracking his mind, he wondered if he should tell his girlfriend Charlotte or his precinct captain now or wait a few days to clear his head. He decided that he would not tell his boss, fearing he might remove him from the case of the serial murders that he wanted so desperately to solve. Likewise, with no definite timeline of life expectancy, he chose to not tell Charlotte just yet, but he would go about privately putting his affairs in order.

After clocking out of work, he stopped by a Texas Roadhouse for a steak dinner before going home. His dog Butch met him with his leash in his mouth expecting to go for his evening walk. He scratched Butch's head and strapped on his collar before taking him on a leisurely walk around the neighborhood. Being a good owner, he cleaned up Butch's poop and threw it into the dumpster when he got home around nine.

The warm July night sky was studded with a blanket of stars. His mind still in turmoil, he decided to take a meandering walk, hoping that it might tire him out enough that he could catch a short nap. He filled his water bottle and set out, trying to process the events of the day. Most of the traffic had died down. The stores had closed at nine and the only sounds were a distant train whistle and an occasional foghorn of a ship in the river. Remembering that he had not been to the harbor for a while, he changed course. He walked along the shore for three miles before turning south toward home.

After a few blocks, he heard the sound of metal on metal ringing through the night. He stopped, surprised that anyone would be working this late at night, and followed the sounds until he found a storefront bathed in a soft light. The sounds were coming from a small workshop that produced engraved headstones. He managed to see several shapes lying in the darkness surrounding the shop. After checking his watch and thinking about his inevitable end, he decided to inquire about the prices of headstones.

Rapping on the open door, he hailed the owner who was chiseling intently on a gray granite monument. "Hello? Are you still open?"

The man turned around and answered, "Well, I can be. I left the door open to let cool air in because I get pretty sweaty in here. Come on in. How can I help you?'

Scott walked over and introduced himself. "I'm Scott Allen."

The man laid his hammer and chisel down and shook his hand. "Arthur Bailey. Glad to meet you. I need a break. Have a seat."

Scott pulled a three-legged stool over and sat down. "I've never given much thought to how headstones are made. This looks fascinating, but I bet it's hard work."

Arthur wiped his forehead with a dusty rag. "It can be, depending on the kind of stone and how fancy the inscriptions are supposed to be. It's a lot easier than when my father taught me how to do it. When he started the business in nineteen forty, he had to do most of the carving using these tools. Nowadays, we use a masonry router to carve the letters very precisely and cleanly. I'm just chiseling away the base of this stone for esthetic purposes. I have already done the engraving. Would you like to see it?"

He motioned for Scott to walk around to see his handiwork.

"Wow, that's fantastic. How did you get the letters so perfectly well defined?

"Like I said, I use a masonry router with tungsten carbide bits. Sometimes, I have to use diamond-tipped bits, but they are expensive. I stick with the cheaper bits. What do you think?"

Scott ran his fingers over the engraving before stepping back to read the inscription carved into the black granite:

Maureen Stokely
May 20, 1982 – July 17, 2018
Gone to Be an Angel

He stepped back and straightened up before commenting, "Wow, she died just five days ago and you've already almost finished her stone? That's impressive."

"These high-powered routers can work quickly. In the old days, my father would probably have taken two or three weeks. What do you do, Mr. Allen?"

Scott resumed his seat. "I'm a detective with the police department."

"Really? I bet that's fascinating work. Can you tell me what cases you're working on or do you have to keep that secret?"

"I'd rather not say. We keep our cards close to our chests so we don't inadvertently provide crucial details that a suspect may reveal in interrogations."

"That makes sense. I love TV detective shows and that kind of thing pops up from time to time."

Scott surveyed the dusty shop where he could see several stones in various degrees of completion. He watched as Bailey wiped the dust off the headstone and blew the grit out of the channels that formed the letters.

"That looks beautiful. Just out of curiosity, what does a headstone cost these days?"

"It depends on the size, the kind of stone and the complexity of the inscriptions. Take this stone. It's two feet wide setting on a three foot base and is twenty inches high. This is high quality polished black granite with a simple inscription. I'll get a little over twenty five hundred dollars for it. I really try to keep my prices lower than the bigger operations to attract clients. The market is changing a lot these days."

Scott shifted his position and asked, "What's different? People are still dying, aren't they?"

Bailey laughed, "Of course, but more people are choosing cremation because it's much cheaper. With people more in tune with economic realities, people are questioning the need for an expensive coffin and concrete vault to lie in the ground and decompose."

"That makes sense, but I guess I'm still old-fashioned and would like to be buried."

Bailey replied, "I hear you. In fact, I've already made my marker, except for the date of death. A lot of people prepay funeral costs so their relatives don't get stuck with a bill."

Scott sucked in his breath. "I see those commercials and it does make sense."

His eyes teared up and he paused. Bailey could see him struggling to compose himself and whispered, "Are you okay?"

Scott wiped his eyes and nose with a handkerchief. "To be honest, I got some really bad news today. The doctor says I have a rare disease called fatal insomnia where I can't sleep. There is no cure, and I'll eventually die of it. Maybe sooner rather than later. I'm still single, but I hope to get married before too long so my girlfriend Charlotte can draw my pension. If I croak before we get married a single stone like this one would be fine."

Bailey patted him on the back to comfort him. "That's a hell of a note. I don't see how you're even able to walk around. I'd just go to bed. Hell, I might even kill myself to have control over my life and not have to deal with the uncertainty."

Scott blew his nose softly, "Honestly, I thought about that, but my strong Protestant religion takes a dim view of suicide. Besides, Charlotte might blame herself and I wouldn't want that."

"Absolutely. If you have the time, we can sketch out one of each and I can give you estimates. Do you have the time?"

"I'm not sleeping anyway, so I might as well do something constructive."

Bailey nodded and spread a large piece of paper out on a drafting table. Over the next fifteen minutes, he traced out the outline of a single headstone. "Would you like one about the size of that one?"

"For just me, that'd be fine. I like the black granite. Could you make the inscription in gold letters?"

"Sure. They make a special paint called Lithichrome that sticks to the porous stone like glue. That has to be done by hand. I'd have to charge a hundred dollars for that. I gotta say, I'd be glad to give you a ten percent discount considering your horrible situation. With your permission, I'd like to display it until you need it."

Scott smiled weakly, "That'd be fine. Can you figure out the cost of just this single stone while I wait?"

Bailey sat down at his desk and began to punch the buttons on his calculator while Scott walked around the workshop. The bulletin board had a map of the nearby area with colored stick pins randomly distributed over it. He stopped to read the headstone Bailey was working on.

Maureen Stokely
May 20, 1982 – July 17, 2018
Gone to Be an Angel

He stared at the stone and re-read it. Suddenly, he realized that this was the name of the most recent murder victim. Quietly, he returned to the bulletin board to see the locations of the pins. His heart raced as he walked over to the desk where Bailey was working.

He swallowed hard and asked, "Can you tell me anything about that Stokely woman? That name rings a bell."

"As a matter of fact, she was the latest victim of the serial killer who has been terrorizing this part of town. If you live nearby, perhaps you knew her."

Scott watched as Bailey's face darkened and lost all emotion. "No, that's not it. I'm a detective who is working on that case and I just remembered her name. And the pins on that map are where the other victims were found. How do you explain that?"

Bailey stood up and walked over to the headstone where he picked up his masonry hammer. "Well, this is very unfortunate, but like I said, business has been slow so I've had to do something to make ends meet. Too bad, you of all people would happen to stop by. But a man's got to do what a man's got to do."

Suddenly, he lunged at Scott, hit him on the head with the masonry hammer, knocking him to the floor. Scott felt the blood rushing into his eyes as he saw Bailey raising the hammer to strike him again.

NEITHER A BORROWER NOR A LENDER BE

Two years ago Gretchen Walker's husband, Mark, divorced her and moved from Mount Sterling, Kentucky, to New York City with his younger mistress. Mark had been an inveterate gambler whose habits had nearly bankrupted them, so the court was sympathetic to her predicament and awarded her sole possession of their house. She donated all of Mark's clothing and personal items to charities and homeless centers. To her horror, she discovered that Mark had stolen her jewelry, including a diamond and ruby necklace her grandmother had willed to her leaving her only a diamond brooch that she had worn to work the day he left. Anger soon replaced her horror, but realizing there was little she could do about it, she resolved to begin a new life and concentrate on earning promotions and better pay at Young and Sullivan Law Offices.

After the divorce, Gretchen had assumed more responsibilities at work and often did not get home until after six. The elderly couple who lived in the house next door had died in the last year and the house had sat empty for nearly a year. She seldom even gave the house any attention at all, until early one morning she saw a light come on in the rear of the house and surmised she had new neighbors. Curious, but cautious, she decided to watch for an opportune time to speak to her new neighbors when she saw them out in the yard. Since she never saw anyone enter or leave the house she thought maybe her friend, Matthew Patton, the mailman, might have gleaned some inklings from their mail.

One Saturday, she was working in her flowerbeds in the front of her house when Patton greeted her on his way to her mailbox.

"Good morning, Gretchen. How are you today? Those impatiens look mighty fine."

"Good morning to you, Matt. Yes, they always do well here because they don't get too much direct sunlight. Just put the mail in the box. My hands are dirty. Say, can I ask you a question?"

Matt dropped the envelopes into her mailbox. "Sure, what do you need?"

"What can you tell me about my new neighbors? I have never seen hide nor hair of them, but I thought you might know something from the mail they got."

"They've never got any mail. I assume they have a rented mailbox somewhere. I can't be sure, but I think they moved in about six weeks ago. One strange thing I did notice is that a few days after they had moved in, they put black film over all the windows so no one could see in. Didn't you see when they moved in?"

"No. I guess they moved in when I was at work or at night after I went to bed. Have you heard any scuttlebutt about them from anyone?"

"Not a word. Most people don't even know they moved in. It is peculiar. I guess you'll just have to find an excuse to introduce yourself to them. Have a good day."

Gretchen finished planting her flowers and took a quick shower. Afterwards, she made a cup of tea and sat at her kitchen table trying to think of a way to approach her new neighbors. Knowing that pineapples symbolized welcome and hospitality, she decided to buy some kitchen towels with pineapples on them and bake a pineapple cake to deliver to them.

A week later, she baked the cake and giftwrapped the towels before walking over to the house about twelve thirty on Saturday. She rang the doorbell and waited for someone to answer. In about a minute, a blond woman opened the door as wide as the security chain would allow.

The woman asked, "Can I help you?"

Gretchen smiled and held her gifts out for the woman to see. "I'm your next door neighbor, Gretchen Walker. I just want to welcome you to the neighborhood. I baked you a pineapple cake and bought some dishtowels for you."

The woman raised her eyebrows before answering, "That's very kind of you. We've been so busy with moving and working that we've not had time to meet our neighbors."

Gretchen smiled, "I can agree with that! Moving is hard work, especially if you're trying to hold down a fulltime job at the same time. Do you need any help settling in?"

The woman grimaced slightly, "Not yet, thank you. We both work third shifts so we've not had much free time. Please don't think I'm rude but I need to fix us something to eat before work and get dressed. Maybe next week we can chat more. Have a good day and thanks again."

Gretchen nodded, "You're welcome. I look forward to getting to know you."

Taken aback at the terse reception, Gretchen was nearly home before she realized that the woman had not introduced herself. She whispered to herself, "I guess she was too sleepy to think clearly," and forgot about the encounter.

Four days later, Gretchen was tending to a flower bed in her backyard when she saw the woman tossing a bag into the garbage can behind the house. She hailed her, "Good morning, how are you today?'

The woman looked at her suspiciously before walking over to the fence and saying, "Good morning to you. I don't think I introduced myself the other day. I'm Becky Martin. That cake was delicious and the towels are a godsend for the kitchen. Forgive me, but I have forgotten your name."

Gretchen replied, "Not to worry. Gretchen Walker. I'm glad you enjoyed the cake and towels. If you don't mind me asking, what is your husband's name?"

"James Martin. I guess you are wondering why you never see him."

"I had not given it much thought since you said he worked third shift."

"James has a very rare condition called solar urticaria. Basically, he is allergic to sunlight and has to limit his exposure. He breaks out into hives and nasty oozing sores so bad he was once hospitalized for it. That is why he took the third shift and I just managed to find a job then to accommodate his life. We had to put black film over the windows of the house and car to keep the light out."

"So sorry to hear that. I don't know what I would do if I had to give up working in my flower beds."

"You do have a beautiful garden. Maybe you can help me get some beds started. I have to go now, but maybe we can have lunch sometime."

Gretchen replied, "Sounds good. Have a good day."

Becky went back into the house, leaving Gretchen to resume working in the flower beds. When she had finished, she went inside to do her housework.

That night, she was up late reading a book when she heard a car motor from next door. She peeked out the window and saw an old Volkswagen and an old Chevrolet back out of the two car garage. The garage door closed and the cars drove off in opposite directions.

As she went to bed, she thought, *What a bizarre life that would be. Allergic to sunshine. Not sure I could live like that.*

Over the next few weeks, she managed to engage Becky in short conservations. Once she felt comfortable talking to Becky, Gretchen asked, "If you don't mind me asking, where are you folks from?"

Becky replied, "We are originally from Dearborn, Michigan, but we moved to New York about thirty years ago. James was involved with banking there and I worked as a travel agent."

"Do you have any children?"

"No. James was afraid his kids might inherit his condition and he didn't want to risk that. Besides, we were both so busy with our careers we didn't have time for a family. So what about you? Are you from here?"

"I was born in Hazard, but my ex-husband is from here. I moved so he could keep his good job. I'm a paralegal for a law firm."

"If you don't mind me asking, why did you get a divorce? It's really none of my business, but I don't want to risk saying something that might offend you."

"Well, where to begin. He had a bad gambling habit and nearly put us in the poorhouse. Last year, he started screwing around until he finally found a woman who would have him and they ran off to New York City. Son of a bitch emptied our bank accounts and stole most of my jewelry. The court gave me the house and car. I moved on and with any luck that bastard is out of my life once and for all. Good riddance."

Becky chuckled, "Men. You can't live with them but you can't shoot them either. Nice to chat, Gretchen, but I have to go. I have a day off next week. Maybe we can have lunch."

"That would be wonderful. Could your husband join us?"

"Oh no. His condition makes him feel conspicuous. His third shift has only one other man so he fits in nicely. Have a good afternoon."

Gretchen went back into the house and made a shopping list for the week's groceries. When she went to her car, she noticed a dark gray Plymouth slowly driving past her neighbors' house. The car paused for a few seconds before making a U-turn and driving past the house again before returning to the main road.

Gretchen sat in her car wondering why the driver was so interested in her neighbors, but soon forgot about it. Over the next three weeks, she noticed the car inspecting the house again. Although she was curious, she had an uneasy feeling and decided to not ask Becky about it.

She had still not seen James since they had moved in. One day, as she was trimming around the walkway, she saw Becky driving off to shop and gave some thought to seeing if she could meet James. As she wrestled with what to do, she snickered, "Maybe he is a vampire and that is why he can't be in the sunlight. That sounds like a Stephen King novel. I must be losing my mind."

Two weeks later, Becky agreed to meet her at a local diner Buona Sera for lunch. Gretchen arrived first and took a booth for them. When she saw Becky come in, she motioned for her to join her.

Becky said, "Hope I'm not late. We don't get out much. This is a quaint little place. Is the food here good?"

Gretchen replied, "It's not gourmet Italian food like you got in New York, but it's pretty good. The restaurant has been in the family for three generations. They make all the ingredients fresh every day."

Becky shrugged, "We do miss all the different cuisines of the Big Apple, but we were willing to make that sacrifice. So far, we've enjoyed the slower pace of life here."

A waiter walked over to greet them. "Good afternoon, ladies. Welcome to Buona Sera. Would you like a drink while you browse the menu?"

Gretchen nodded, "A glass of red wine for me, please."

Becky smiled, "Make it two. Thank you. Gretchen, what do you recommend?"

Gretchen answered, "It's all very good. I think I'll have the lasagna, but the pollo primavera is also excellent. They'll bring us wonderful homemade rolls."

Becky said, "I'll try that chicken dish. James and I seldom get a chance to eat out except for fast food."

"If you don't mind me asking, why did you leave New York to move to the boonies?"

Becky replied, "Well, it's not quite Hooterville. As I said, James worked in a bank that went belly up in the recession of 2008 and so did the travel agency I worked at. Luckily, James has a lot of sense about money matters and our investments were well diversified. We took a hit but didn't go completely under. One man at his bank committed suicide. Even though James had nothing to do with the collapse, some people who lost everything blamed him and started threatening to kill him. After a few months of that, we pulled up stakes and moved to France, but we missed America so we moved back. By then we had decided that we had had enough of the rat race and looked for a place like this to just live out our lives. We enjoy the peace and quiet."

"You look great and happy."

Becky smiled and nodded, "I admit I've had a little plastic surgery to remove the wrinkles and I dye my hair blonde regularly. James had a particularly bad episode of his disease a couple of years ago and had to have some major plastic surgery to repair the damage. But that is his new normal and we have to live with it. He still has to wear sunglasses any time he goes out of the house. The UV light is very dangerous to him."

"That's so awful to think about. I have to work in my garden to be happy after my asshole husband left me."

"You sound angry and bitter. Was it that bad?"

"At first, I was happy. He was drop-dead gorgeous, intelligent, outgoing, and very successful. Then he got addicted to gambling and started going to the casinos in Indiana and nearly bankrupted us. Then when he found some young bimbo to screw, that was the final straw. But the worst thing was that he stole my jewelry that had been in the family for three generations. After a while I figured I had to let it go and move on. I am now the office manager at Young and Sullivan and they are paying for me to get my law degree. So it worked out fine. Around here, people say when God closes a door, he opens a window."

"I suppose. We are backslidden Catholics and haven't been in church for twenty years. We may go back sometime but not for the foreseeable future. Say, this is pretty good wine."

"Yes, it is. The only time I drink alcohol is when I eat here. Our food should be here shortly."

As the women chatted small talk, Gretchen began to sense a subtle tension in the way Becky spoke and in her body language. Nonetheless, they had a wonderful lunch while Becky regaled her with stories of life in New York City. After an hour and half, they said good-bye and went home.

That afternoon, Gretchen replayed the lunch date while doing her housework. She thought about the strange car that had driven by the Martin house two months before, but since they had not been back for three months, she dismissed them as someone who had gotten lost. In six months, she had not seen even a glimpse of James and she began to wonder if she was missing something.

When she got to work the next day, she did a people search on the computer for Becky and James Martin. The search turned up several pages of people with last name Martin, but only one couple named Becky and James Martin. When she clicked on that name to see where else they had lived, she found the listing that they had lived in New York City between 2009 and 2012. They had lived in France from 2012 to 2013, Shreveport, Louisiana, from 2013 to 2015, then in Scottsdale, Arizona, from 2015 to 2017 before moving to Mount Sterling. As she sat staring at the screen, she thought to herself, *For someone who is allergic to sunlight, they seemed to have lived in some places that get more than their share. Why didn't they just find a good place where the sun was not so intense?*

Richard Sullivan stopped by to ask her a question and teased, "Gretchen, did you get the Lindsay will filed? Now Gretchen, are you doing personal stuff on company time? What are you looking for?"

"Yes, I finished the will and it is ready for probate court. Ok, I admit it, I was doing a little research on my new neighbors. I have noticed some peculiar things."

"Really? Like what?"

Gretchen pushed her chair back from her desk. "Well, for one thing, that house sat empty for over a year with not even a nibble of an interest in buying it, even though it is a nice house in a good neighborhood. I'm not sure when they moved in. I finally decided to take the bull by the horns and introduce myself to welcome them to the neighborhood with a cake and towels. When I rang, a woman answered the door but she was not very friendly. She said they both worked third shift and spent the daylight hours sleeping."

"That does not sound very odd. A lot of people do that. Humans have evolved to be diurnal and it is very hard to shift your body rhythms against your internal clock."

"I finally got a chance to talk to her again. She told me they are James and Becky Martin from New York City. He was a banker and she was a travel agent until the 2008 recession hit. He is a night watchman and she works third shift as a telephone operator. Then she told me that her husband has a very rare condition that makes him allergic to sunlight which is why he works third shift."

"Makes perfect sense to me."

"They have covered all the windows with black film so no one can see inside. Same thing for their cars."

"Again, if he is allergic to sunlight, all that makes sense."

"Agreed, but when Becky and I had lunch last week, I got some uncomfortable vibes — nothing I can put my finger on. I decided to see what I could find out. Look here. If he is allergic to sunlight, why did they move to all these places where there was a lot of sunlight? Wouldn't you expect them to move where there was less sunlight?"

"I guess but maybe they just liked those places."

"And a few days after I noticed they had moved in, a strange car drove by the house as if they were looking for something, but they have not been back."

Richard chuckled, "Ok, Nancy Drew, enough detective work. Start finalizing the Hargood divorce papers."

Gretchen nodded, "I promise not to dig around on company time, but if you have any brainstorms about this, please let me know. I'll have those papers ready in an hour or so."

"My advice is mind your own business. You are sounding like Gladys Kravitz, the nosy neighbor on Bewitched. Oh wait, maybe your neighbor is a vampire and can't take the sun....oooooohh. By the way, how are your classes going?"

"Very funny. My classes are fine. I should be able to apply for the bar exam by spring. I can't thank you enough for paying my way."

"We see it as a good investment. You're a hard worker and very bright. When you get your law degree we can expand our practice. Back to the salt mines. "

Gretchen finished her work a little after five and stopped by Arby's for dinner. As she ate, she decided Richard was probably right: that she should forget her neighbors and focus on her classes and getting ready to take the bar exam.

Over the next few months, Gretchen managed to chat with Becky sporadically, but she never really learned much new about her or James. Becky would sometimes ask about the best dry cleaner or car mechanic in town, but she only rarely revealed anything about their life in New York.

One day, Gretchen inquired if Becky knew if the mail had been delivered. Becky shrugged and replied, "We don't get mail here. We have a mailbox at the post office."

"Really? Why?"

"Remember I told you we had gotten death threats after the recession? One guy was downright violent about it. Someone shot through a window in the house when we lived in Arizona and we thought he may have found us by searching through mail addresses. He can't track P.O. boxes so we've used them instead of addresses. It seems to have worked. How are your classes going?"

"Great. I finished all my coursework and got my degree. Now I have to pass the bar exam. My bosses have been wonderful about supporting me financially and plan to hire me as an attorney once I have passed the bar."

The women continued to build a not-too-close friendship, a relationship that frustrated Gretchen who wanted a closer bond. After she passed the bar exam, she was so excited she went to Becky's house to share the good news. She rang the bell and waited until a middle-aged man wearing sunglasses answered.

He asked gruffly, "Can I help you? Becky is not here."

Gretchen replied, "Ok, I hope I didn't wake you. You must be James. Please tell Becky I passed the bar exam. She had asked me to tell her."

The man nodded, "Ok, I'll tell her. I need to go back to sleep before work."

Gretchen smiled, "Nice to meet you. Thank you."

When Becky came home, she walked over to Gretchen's house and rang the bell. When Gretchen answered, she said, "James told me the good news. Congratulations. I have heard a lot of people do not pass the bar exam the first time they take it."

Gretchen giggled, "I can't tell you how much I studied for it. If you have time, I need an opinion. Can you please come in for a minute?"

Becky hesitated, but said as she walked in, "Sure. What do you need?"

Gretchen answered, "The office is having a party to celebrate my passing the exam and to formally announce my joining the firm this Saturday night. Let me show you what I plan on wearing."

The women went into the bedroom where Gretchen had hung a new long black gown on the closet door. "What do you think?"

Becky eyed the gown. "You can't go wrong with black at a semi-formal gathering."

"The problem is I don't have any jewelry to go with it since my asshole hubby stole mine. I was wondering if you had any I could borrow just for the party."

Becky nodded, "Sure. I think a simple pearl necklace would be perfect. I have one in mind that would highlight the dress. Come back to the house and I can get it for you."

"Thank you so much. I will guard it with my life."

Becky laughed, "To be honest, they aren't real pearls but they look real. You can return it next week."

They went back to Becky's house where Becky said, "Wait here. James is still asleep and he gets grouchy if I wake him up."

"I'm the same way if someone wakes me up."

Becky went inside and returned with a long strand of beautiful pearls she handed to Gretchen. "I think these will be fine."

"Oh Becky, those are beautiful. I will owe you big time."

'Not to worry. Enjoy your party."

On Saturday, Gretchen went to her salon to get her hair styled and a manicure with pearl-colored nails. When she got home, she tried on the dress and pearls and admired herself in the mirror. Around five thirty, she got dressed and went to the party.

Most of the guests were punctual and arrived by seven-thirty. Richard tapped a spoon on his wineglass to get people's attention.

"Okay, everybody, we're here to welcome Gretchen into our practice and celebrate her passing the bar. Congratulations, Gretchen, and welcome."

The small crowd clapped and cheered and began to mingle to chat. Richard's wife, Diane, greeted Gretchen. "Congratulations, girl. You look fantastic in that dress and those pearls are gorgeous. Where did you get them?"

Gretchen whispered, "Thank you. Don't tell anyone, but I borrowed them from my neighbor and they're not real."

Diane reached out, "Really? They look real. May I see them?"

Gretchen released the clasp and handed the necklace to Diane. She examined it and said, "The best way to tell if pearls are real is to rub them across your teeth. Real pearls have a subtle gritty feel to them. May I?"

"Sure."

Diane gently rubbed the pearls against her front teeth. She looked puzzled as she handed the necklace back to Gretchen. "This is odd. Those are very real pearls and expensive ones at that. I wonder why she told you they're not real."

Gretchen's gasped, "I don't know why she said that. I wonder what they are worth."

Diane replied, "I have a string that is very similar that Richard paid two thousand dollars for. Good pearls are not cheap."

Gretchen put the pearls back on. "I do have to be careful. Do you think I should ask her about them?"

"I wouldn't. She must have had a reason for doing it and she obviously does not want to share it. Just thank her graciously when you return them."

"Of course. I need to talk to other people. Thanks for the advice."

The party dispersed around ten thirty and Gretchen went home and changed into her negligee. She turned on the television to wind down from the excitement, all the while thinking about the necklace. Feeling the effects of the wine, she grew drowsy and went to bed.

The next day, she thanked Richard for the party and asked him, "Thank you for the incredible welcome. I would like to treat you to lunch and pick your brain."

Richard laughed, "That's not necessary, but I never turn down free food. Is twelve thirty okay?"

"Yes, where would you like to go? Is Ruby Jean's Café okay or Buono Sera? Your choice."

"Ruby Jean's is fine. I'll pick you up and drive us there."

Gretchen was just finishing her work by the time Richard stopped by.

He asked, "Are you ready to go?"

"Absolutely. Thanks for driving."

They went to the parking lot, got into Richard's Mercedes and drove to the café and parked the car. After the hostess seated them, they ordered some wine while they waited on lunch.

Gretchen lowered her voice, "Now don't get mad, but I need to ask you some questions about my neighbors."

Richard laughed softly and shook his head, "Why am I not surprised? Diane told me about the pearl necklace."

"I was flabbergasted when she told me they're real. Last night I got to thinking. Do you think it's possible they're in the witness protection program?"

A stern look crossed Richard's face. "I suppose it's possible. If that's the case you might as well forget it because you will never find out for sure."

"What do you know about it?"

"A few years ago, we represented a hitman for the mob in Chicago. He ratted out some big time Mafia bosses who were sentenced to long terms in jail. The US marshals constructed a whole new identity and backstory complete with new social security numbers, fake work history, addresses — everything to make him seem legit. They even did the same for his wife and even paid for plastic surgery to change their faces. We met with the marshals who told them the rules. They cannot have any contact with family and friends without first checking with the marshal's office. Basically, once they enter into their new lives, their old lives are gone."

"Really?"

"Really. When the client's mother died, the marshals told them, but warned them to think twice about attending the funeral because doing so could expose them and free their office of responsibility. The Mafia has a very long and vindictive memory. Sometimes they can take ten years to find where an informant lives so they can kill him. The client elected not to risk going to the funeral. His testimony shut down one whole mafia family in Chicago so you can imagine how pissed off they were. Now I have to tell you, the witness protection program has been one hundred percent effective. No one in the program has ever been killed as long as they have followed the rules. The marshals told us about two people who did something incredibly innocuous that led the mob back to them and they were murdered in a week. This is serious business. They cannot contact their parents, their children, anyone from their old life. Even if these are in the program, you will never be able to find out and, frankly, you don't want to know. If the mob thinks you have any knowledge of it, they will come looking for you — and you could wind up dead. My advice is to put this out of your mind once and for all. You have a bright future with us and I don't want to have to go to your funeral."

Gretchen grabbed her head and ran her fingers through her hair. "Oh, Jesus, I had no idea. This is scary as hell."

"You don't know how scary. Please let this go. You really can't cut them off altogether because they might get suspicious. Just maintain a casual relationship and stop asking questions. Promise me."

"I absolutely promise. I was thinking about taking them out for dinner to thank Becky for loaning me the pearls. Would that be okay?"

"That would probably be appropriate and not raise suspicion. Just avoid anything in conversation beyond idle chit chat. Under no circumstances do you ask any more questions about their past. NONE!"

She agreed and they returned to work after they had eaten.

When she got home, she saw Becky putting trash into the garbage can behind the house. "Hey, Becky, could you wait for a minute so I can return your necklace?"

Becky replied, "Sure. How did it go?"

"Wonderful. I got so many compliments. Wait here."

She ran into the house and returned with the necklace. "I can't thank you enough, but I would like to try. Would you let me treat you to dinner on your birthday or anniversary?"

"You don't have to do that, but sure, we can do that. Our anniversary is next Saturday and James is off then. Would that work for you?"

"Yes. Is Buona Sera okay?"

"Fine, James loves Italian food. Is seven a good time for you? Should we just meet you there?"

"That would be great. I get my hair and nails done Saturday morning. Thanks again for the necklace."

Gretchen was on pins and needles for the next week and did not sleep well. She laid awake, trying to think of safe topics for dinner conversation. The morning of the dinner she went to the salon and got her hair and nails done before going to the restaurant.

She was a little early but asked to be seated immediately where she could see Becky and James arrive. They arrived promptly at seven and joined her at the table.

Gretchen welcomed them, "Happy anniversary. May I ask which one it is?"

Becky stroked James' arm, "We have had twenty-five wonderful years together, haven't we, honey?"

James nodded and whispered, "Yes, twenty-five wonderful years and hope to have twenty-five more."

Gretchen tried to relax as they looked over the menu. Becky looked at James and said, "The food here is very good."

The waiter came over to take their drink orders. He brought them their drinks and suggested the specials of the day. James kept his sunglasses on while he read the menu. "I think I will have the chicken al fredo. Does that include salad and soup?"

The waiter replied, "Yes, it does, and lots of our famous homemade rolls. Be sure to leave room for the tiramisu or cannoli."

Gretchen ordered rigatoni and Becky ordered the lasagna for herself and James. The waiter took their orders to the kitchen. James smiled at Becky, "I do have an anniversary gift for you, honey. Would you like it now or later?"

Becky laughed, "Definitely now. You always find the best gifts to surprise me. Should I shut my eyes?"

James chuckled, "Of course, it's a surprise."

Becky closed her eyes and he laid a neatly wrapped rectangular box in front of her. "Okay, open your eyes."

Becky opened her eyes, quickly tore off the paper and opened the box.

"Oh, sweetheart, this is beyond marvelous. Please help me put it on."

He rose and stepped behind her when she handed him the necklace. After he had placed it around her neck, he returned to his chair, and smiled at her.

"Oh, Gretchen how do you like it?"

Gretchen felt a chill run over her that caused her to drop her wine glass when she recognized her grandmother's ruby and diamond necklace around Becky's neck.

"Oh goodness, I'm so sorry for being such a klutz. You'll have to pardon me, but that's the most beautiful necklace I've ever seen. I wish I had one like that, but I bet it's a one of a kind."

James smiled and replied, "Yes, it is, and you don't know what I had to go through to get it."

A MAN OF CONSTANT SORROWS

Phillip Rockwell rapped softly on the open door to Lowell Maxwell's office at the United Pacific Railroad Company in Omaha, Nebraska. Maxwell looked up from his work and peered at Rockwell over his wire-rimmed glasses. "Good morning, Phil. Come in. What's on your mind?"

Phil took a seat in the leather arm chair in front of Lowell's desk and handed him an email. "Looks like our friend is back."

"By our friend, I assume you mean the Gray Ghost. Where was he this time?"

"I got this email from the police in Goldsboro, Georgia. A deputy was rousting a hobo camp and saw a man matching his description running away."

"Of course, he didn't catch him. What the hell was he doing there?"

"I have no idea. I called the other railroad companies to see if they had seen him. Union Pacific had reports of a man matching his description. They called him the 'King of the Road' after that old Roger Miller song. The Kansas City Southern called him Freddy the Freeloader after the Red Skelton character. Canadian National called him Mr. Bojangles and the Genessee and Wyoming named him Glen Campbell after his song 'Gentle on My Mind.' They have received reports from all over the areas they serve and asked the railroad police to find him, but so far no luck. They all share our concerns."

Lowell frowned, "It's not like we've not had railroad bums before, but this one troubles me. Not many hoboes can pass for a college professor with a three-hundred dollar Coach briefcase. Add to that the fact that he is popping up everywhere around the country instead of staying in a small area and I see a red flag. My biggest concern is that he is a terrorist who is studying the railroads to plot a disruption."

Phil nodded, "He does stand out. Let me show you something."

He laid a map of the United States mounted on a foam core board on the desk. Colored stick pins marked several cities on the map.

Phil continued, "I thought if I mapped where he had been, I might be able to see a pattern. We are the red pins, Norfolk is blue, Kansas City is green, Canadian National is black and Genesee is white. As you can see, he has been spotted somewhere along every railroad, but not always in a terminal of the railroad. Sometimes he is reported in a town or city nearby the railroad."

He stood up and pointed to various pins: "Sardis, Mississippi; Glendale, Arizona; Dorcester, Massachusetts. I cannot find any rhyme or reason to his movements. The first sighting appears to be Madison, Alabama in 2010. Then he pops up in Columbus, Ohio.

He randomly jumps between railroads as well. It's not like he just uses one line all the time. He has been spotted from Washington State to New England and Florida. We really have no idea of how long he stays in these cities or what else he does there."

Lowell studied the map intently.

"And everyone gives the same general description?"

"Yes, sir. A slender salt-and-pepper haired man about early sixties, carrying an expensive briefcase, a guitar, a lunchbox and a Thermos bottle. He wears a worn gray jacket. Sometimes he is clean-shaven, at others he sports a scraggly beard."

Lowell rested his head on his hands before looking at Phillip. "Has he interfered with day-to-day operations or sabotaged any lines? Does he carry a gun? Hurt anybody?"

"Nope, but there are reports that he has been in scrapes and disturbances in some of the hobo camps, but nothing serious. My guess is that someone tries to steal his fancy briefcase. One would think that he would carry a gun to protect the case, but so far he has never been seen with a gun."

"Does he have a name?"

Phillip sighed. "We have lists from other railroads but the lists have different names. Daniel Miller appears on most lists, so there is a general belief that is his name."

"Anything else?"

"Just some anecdotal stuff. Sometimes, he seems destitute, but occasionally he has a wad of bills. He guards that high-end briefcase with his life and has even been seen with it handcuffed to his wrist. We think he may have had medical training because on some occasions he has treated other hobos who are injured or sick and has even taken some of them to the hospital."

"Where does he get the money?"

"We're not sure. Someone suggested that he may have a bank account he can access at an ATM. Using an ATM in a larger city like Houston or Los Angeles makes it harder to track him. Having money in the case would explain handcuffing it to his wrist. There are quite a few men named Daniel Miller in the country, but we have not identified anyone as our man. But remember: we are not even one hundred percent sure that is his real name."

He paused before adding, "We did find a copy of the hobo code that he may have dropped by accident. I pinned it to the back of the board."

Lowell flipped the board over to see the chart.

"Hmm. I remember in history class we talked about the hobos of the Great Depression and the teacher showed us one of their codes. Does anyone have a clue as to this guy's motivation?"

Phillip shrugged. "We're not sure, but a few people think he is running away from something or someone. Maybe on the lam from the law. One railroad engineer found a torn envelope with a child's valentine with the name Susie on it on the tracks a mile outside of Aztec, Texas, about the time he was reported there. But there is one more thing. He's a good guitar player. Other vagrants say he plays and sings songs like: 'You Are My Sunshine', 'Hush Little Baby', or 'Twinkle, Twinkle Little Star.'"

Lowell leaned back in his chair. "I've thought about offering a reward for any useful information, but then I realized that some wing-nut might think the reward was for 'Dead or Alive'. Some of the other railroad bums might kill him or someone who bears a passing resemblance to him for the reward. Then we would really catch hell."

He handed the board back to Phillip. "Thanks for the update. I guess all we can do is keep on it. Stay in touch with the other railroads."

II

Daniel Miller arose early from his bedroll in the railyard in Omaha, Nebraska and checked his watch. After relieving himself behind an empty box car, he joined a small group of early-risers who were making coffee over a campfire.

He greeted them, “Good morning, fellers. Mind if I join you for some coffee?”

A disheveled man in a red flannel shirt nodded, “Nope, that’s fine if you contribute to the coffee fund. When did you get here?”

Daniel fished a dollar out of his pocket and handed it to the man and extended his hand. “I got here about ten last night. I’m Daniel Miller.”

The man replied, “Freddy Bosch. Nice to meet you. That there is George Asher and Newt Goff. Do you have a cup?”

Daniel unscrewed the cap of his thermos bottle and handed it to Freddy. “Freddy, huh? I had a grandson named Freddy. Nice to meet you fellers. Thank you kindly for the coffee.”

As he poured the coffee Freddy said, “I hope you like it black. We used the last bit of Coffeemate and sugar last night.”

“Black is fine — that’s the way the Lord made it. The fire takes the chill off. Are you all passing through or do you stay around here?”

Freddy replied, “I’ve have been here about a week, but Newt and George are only passing through. Where are you from?”

“Came here from Chicago last night. Thought I’d rest a while before heading out west to Seattle.”

Daniel asked, “Is it safe here or do the railroad bulls harass you?”

Freddy replied, “I met a rail officer when I arrived and he told me that if I laid low I could stay for a few days. There’s a homeless shelter up the line that will feed you if you don't abuse their kindness. So you're going to Seattle?"

"That's the plan, but I will have a few stops along the way. Where are you headed?"

"No place in particular. Just go where I want."

"How long have you been riding the rails?"

Freddy sat back down and sipped his coffee. "I was an investment banker in Cincinnati until about eight months ago. Some son of a bitch embezzled half a million dollars and framed me for it. I finally managed to clear my name, but by then I had spent all my money on lawyer fees and I had a nervous breakdown. After all my hard work and fifteen years of outstanding evaluations, they were ready to kick me to the curb so I said screw it. I was tired of the rat race and decided to see the country. My grandpa had told me that he had ridden the rails in the depression and had fond memories of the experience so I just said to hell with it. Didn't take long to learn he had seriously overstated the romance of being a hobo. Once I get my head clear again, I'll find a new job somewhere."

Daniel drank the last bit of coffee and handed the cup to Freddy. "May I have another, please?"

Freddy nodded, "See this scar on my arm? Got that in Memphis when some lunatic attacked me with a knife. But I've been pretty lucky. Most of us are okay fellers who are just down on our luck."

Daniel looked at the other men. "What about you guys?"

Newt sipped his coffee. "Lost my job in Kokomo and had no reason to stay there. I just tour the country doing day labor to make a few bucks. I am too old for this cold weather up north so I am heading south for the winter. Maybe Florida."

George smiled, "The coal mine in Kentucky went bankrupt a year ago. The old lady and my daughter moved back in with her folks who would take care of them, but I hit the road rather than mooching off the in-laws. Let me show you something."

He unbuttoned his shirt to expose a ragged scar on his left shoulder. "A farmer shot me one night when I was relieving one of his hens of a few eggs. Lucky he didn't kill me. 'Course, I shouldn't have been stealing eggs, but a hungry man will get desperate. Now I just do odd jobs when I can find them. I'm heading south, too."

Freddy took a deep breath. "I don't judge people as long as they treat me right. We all have our private demons. What's your story, Daniel?"

Daniel's mouth twisted into a wry smile. "I just needed a change of scenery. Been riding the rails for over a year."

Newt asked, "What did you do for a living before you hit the road?"

"I worked in a hospital for a while, but the pressure got to me. So far I've not had to steal anything to survive, knock on wood. I did get mugged and robbed in Salinas, California, a few weeks ago. Taught me to be more careful. What say we go try to get breakfast somewhere? How far is that homeless center?"

Freddy motioned, "About a quarter mile that way. You need help carrying stuff?"

"No, thank you. Mind if I fill up my thermos before we leave?"

"Help yourself. Goodness, must be something valuable in that brief case you got handcuffed to your wrist."

Daniel laughed, "Just some personal stuff with a lot of sentimental value. Nothing that would mean much to anyone else. Thanks for the coffee. Shall we go?"

The men laughed as Freddy pissed on the fire to put it out. Each man picked up his bindle staff and bedroll and they set out. Newt walked beside Daniel and tapped his guitar. "Are you a pretty good picker?"

"I get by. Passes the time when I get lonely or depressed. Do you play anything?"

He pulled a harmonica out of his pants. "I blow this harmonica tolerably well. Done some gigs as a street musician in a few towns. Maybe we can do a song or two after breakfast."

Daniel grinned, "Sing for our breakfast, I guess. Why not? I bet they would all like 'Amazing Grace'."

The men laughed and joked as they walked along. They joined the short line of men who had assembled outside the homeless center working their way through the serving line. The server put two eggs and bacon strips with biscuits and gravy on their trays and pointed to a large coffee urn. After they took their seats, the men began to talk among themselves.

George asked, "So what's the weather like in Seattle?"

Daniel answered, "Pacific Northwest gets a lot of rain but the temperatures in winter are not that bad because of the ocean. Don't get much snow. I hear there are a lot of runaway children there. Runaway children. How sad is that?"

Freddy nodded, "Yeah, that is bad. You gotta wonder why they run away. I can't imagine how they think being a runaway is better than being at home."

Newt said, "Hell, maybe they were being abused. Pretty damned sick bastard to abuse a kid."

The men finished eating and Freddy stood up and asked, "Would anyone like to hear some music?"

The people applauded approval, so Daniel and Newt played the first and last verses of Amazing Grace. Three of the cafeteria workers handed them a little change before they took seats on the benches outside the center.

The morning sun had warmed the air and a few fluffy cumulus clouds drifted over the countryside. Freddy hummed a few bars of "The Old Rugged Cross" as he picked his teeth with his pocket knife.

He turned to face Daniel and said, "How long are you planning on staying in Seattle, Daniel?"

"Not too long. Why — do you want to come along?"

"Maybe. Never been out west. Where are you other guys heading?'

Suddenly, George and Newt stepped in front of Daniel and Freddy. George pulled a snub-nosed 38 revolver out of his coat pocket and thrust it toward them.

"Ain't nobody going anywhere until we see what is in that case. You, Freddy, take it off his wrist. Daniel, give him the key."

Freddy and Daniel froze in their tracks. Freddy snarled, "You lowlife thieving sons of bitches. I ain't helping you do any damned thing. Go to hell."

George stuck the gun in Daniel's face. "I'm warning you, I don't have time for no heroes. Newt, search him for the key."

When Newt stepped toward him, Daniel swung the briefcase at him and knocked him backwards into George, who dropped the gun. Quick as a cat, Freddy dived for the gun as he and George fell to the ground wrestling for it. The gun fired off with a loud BANG! and the bullet tore into Freddy's upper arm. With his adrenaline levels pumping, Freddy recovered enough to snatch the gun away.

"Goddamn you, you bastard, you shot me! I ought to kill you where you stand!"

Daniel shushed him and gently took the gun away from Freddy. "Calm down, Freddy. How's your arm?"

"Hurting like hell, but I'll live. Got to stop the bleeding."

Daniel glanced at the wound and motioned to Newt with the gun. "Newt, take off your coat and your shirt."

Newt was shaking as he removed the coat and shirt. "Be cool, man, I'm doing it. Be cool."

Daniel snapped, "Tear that shirt up into strips. Then use the strips to tie off the arm to stop the bleeding. If you try anything, I'll blow your goddamned brains out."

Still trembling with fear, Newt made a tourniquet for the arm while George snarled at Daniel, "I should have just shot you and cut your arm off."

"Yeah, well, you didn't. Freddy, is that helping?"

Freddy examined the arm and nodded. "Seems to be working."

Daniel pointed the gun at Newt. "Put your coat on. Then the two of you get the hell out of here before I do something we will all regret."

He fired the gun into the air to get their attention. The men backed away, muttering threats. Daniel fired again. "I'm counting to five and if you are still in range I'm going to shoot both of you in the ass. ONE! TWO!..."

The terrified would-be robbers bolted away, yelling back threats as they fled. They were out of range by the time he had counted to five.

"Freddy, we need to get you to a doctor. The wound is not fatal, but you need treatment and painkillers. Are you okay to walk with me?"

Freddy was shaking, but nodded weakly. "Yeah, I'll be okay. Wonder where the closest doctor or hospital is?"

"I saw a convenient store when I hopped off the train last night. About a half a mile. We can call for help. Wait a minute."

He knelt down and opened the briefcase to reveal a few small stacks of bills lying on top of several envelopes with names written on them and some small white candles.

Freddy whistled, "Shit! So you do have money in there! Damn!"

Daniel closed the case and stood up and the men started toward the store. "Yeah, there's a little, but not enough to get killed over. Here's three hundred dollars. That should pay for some drugs and a couple of meals. The ER will have to treat you and bill you later. They will have to report any bullet wounds. Just tell them the truth: some crooks tried to rob you, but you fought them off and they ran away. Please keep me out of it. Deal?"

Freddy's face was starting to blanch a little. "Sure. Might be hard to bill me with no permanent address. I hate doing it, but I guess they will get stuck for the bill. Damn. What about the gun?"

"You won't be the first man who stuck an ER with a bill. I'll throw the gun into the Missouri River outside the city. No one will ever find it."

Freddy smiled, "Maybe you should keep it to protect yourself."

Daniel took a deep breath. "No, I really don't like guns. You just saw the problems they can cause. I just want to be shed of it."

"Are you still heading west?"

"Not immediately, I have to visit a church before I leave. If you want, I can hide out for a while until this is all resolved so you can come with me if you like."

Freddy laughed, "Well, after what we have just been through, I think it will be interesting to see what happens next. There's the store. I'll call for help. Can we meet at the campsite tomorrow afternoon and catch the next train heading west?"

Daniel grinned, "Sounds like the start of a road trip movie. Take care and I'll see you tomorrow."

III

The store owner called the police who took Freddy to the hospital for treatment. A detective came to interview him and wrote up a perfunctory report that did not probe the incident too deeply. The bullet had passed through the flesh of his right arm so with a couple of stitches and antibiotics, he was allowed to leave the hospital.

He stopped by a diner to have a hamburger and fries before returning to the campsite. After putting a pot of coffee on the fire, he took a pain pill and dozed off in the morning sun. A little after noon, Daniel nudged him to wake up.

"Freddy, are you okay? Did you get your arm looked at?"

Freddy roused from his nap and stood up.

"Yeah, a couple of stitches and some pain pills. Damn it, the coffee pot has almost boiled dry. I was going to find a train heading west, but fell asleep."

Daniel shrugged, "No problem. I'm not on a schedule. I found a train with an open boxcar we can ride in. I haven't eaten so let's stop somewhere and grab a bite on the way."

The men spied a Burger King near the railyard. After getting their orders to go, they hurried to the boxcar. Daniel settled into a corner where he leaned his guitar and briefcase against the wall. He stretched out and used his bedroll as a pillow. In a few minutes, he pulled a worn Bible from his bedroll and sat up to read.

Freddy watched from the opposite wall. "I lost my Bible a few weeks ago. Don't have an extra one, do you?"

"No, but I'll share this one. I like to stop at some churches as I travel. I bet someone would give you a new one."

"You're probably right. Wonder where this train is headed."

"I think Salt Lake City. I know the Mormons will give you a Bible. Do you read it a lot?"

"It passes the time on the rails. I ain't been to church for years. I like some of the stories in it but a lot of it makes no sense to me."

"I can agree with that. A lot of people just cherry pick the verses they like and ignore the rest. You ever hear of bibliomancy?"

"Can't say I have. I assume it has to do with books."

"Yeah, some people try to gain insights and comfort by opening the Bible to a random page that God selects for them. My wife used to do that. I always thought it was nonsense."

"So you were married? You get a divorce?"

Daniel paused and wiped some tears out of his eyes. "No, she was killed. That was one reason I decided to become a hobo. Leaving bad memories behind."

"Sorry to upset you. What are you reading?"

"I read the twenty-third Psalm a lot. A lot of the rest of it disturbs me."

"Like what?"

Daniel flipped through the Bible before stopping near the front.

"Take the story of Noah. I can't understand why God drowned all those babies because of the sins of their parents."

"Collateral damage, I guess."

"But then why did he kill the first born son of the Egyptians? He specifically targeted those kids and people think that is just fine."

"So?"

"In Matthew, when Herod ordered the slaughter of all of the boys under age two, people thought that was truly evil. Have you noticed that God kills children to punish the adults? What kind of God is that?"

"I guess God can do whatever he wants to do."

Daniel stood up and stretched. "Have you ever really thought about all this? God creates the universe and people knowing full well they would sin and eat the forbidden fruit. Why put that temptation in front of them if he knew they were going fail the test and risk eternal damnation? Why not just let them be innocent and happy in the Garden of Eden?"

"One preacher told me that God gave us free will to do as we want and he wanted us to make the conscious decision to obey him."

Daniel was growing visibly agitated. "And how sick is that? How insecure is God that he cooks up this hare-brained scheme to have people worship him?"

Freddy stood up and patted him on the back.

"Hey, man, you're getting too deep for me. I just read the words."

Daniel replied, "That's the problem. People don't really think about it. Take Judas."

"The apostle who betrayed Jesus?"

"Yeah, him. People vilify him for betraying Jesus, but if you think about it, if he had not betrayed Jesus, there would have been no blood sacrifice and hence no salvation. So did Judas have free will to betray Christ? Somebody had to do it."

"Never thought about it that way, but you have a point."

"Here's the kicker. He repented the betrayal and tried to return the money but the powers that be would not accept it because it was blood money. Judas hanged himself out of a guilty conscience. So was his sin so great he could not get forgiveness?"

Freddy sat down and leaned against the wall and studied Daniel for a few seconds. "Why are you so interested in all this?"

Daniel joined him on the floor. "Look at it this way. Suppose you are a cruel son of a bitch who gets a new puppy. Now after a few days of loving the puppy and feeding it, you turn mean and start physically abusing it. What's the puppy supposed to do? It'll put up with the abuse to get its meals and water. What else can it do? Run away? Most dogs won't do that."

Freddy stroked his chin. "So what are you saying? God sends evil on us and then expects us to still worship him?"

"That's exactly what I am saying. And since God is everywhere, we cannot run away. We're stuck."

Daniel walked over to the side of the car and looked out the open door to see a spattering of rain drops beginning to fall. He took a deep breath to inhale the warm, sweet aroma of fresh rainfall on dry dust.

He smiled as he watched the countryside speed by. "Man, I love the smell of the air when it first starts to rain. I read somewhere that people all around the world like that particular smell. There is a word for it. Petrichor. Some animals are so sensitive to it they can smell the rain coming before it gets here."

Freddy joined him to enjoy the rain. "Yeah, that brings back a lot of memories. Funny how sometimes you smell something and your mind thinks back to something that happened years ago. You ever have that happen to you?"

Daniel smiled. "Oh, sure. I used to wonder if Noah smelled the rain coming or did it catch him by surprise."

Freddy chortled, "Seems like some preacher told me that the Bible says that it had never rained before Noah built the ark. He said the water rose out of the ground to water the Garden of Eden. Who really gives a damn anyway? One good thing about being a hobo is that you don't have to give a damn about anything."

Daniel cleared his throat and spat out the door. "Freddy, if you think about it, if there had been railroads then, Jesus and his disciples would have been hoboes. Seems like all they did was roam around and have adventures healing people and so on."

Freddy slapped him on the back and laughed, "You're right. They just rambled over the countryside putting the touch on people. I imagine people gave them money or free food. I bet they got tired of them damned fishes and loaves."

Daniel bit his lower lip and guffawed. "I bet they did, too."

Freddy twisted his mouth into a moue. "Still, people gotta eat and when I get tired of soup kitchens, I panhandle for money for fast food. Damn, with all that money do you ever panhandle much?"

Daniel sighed, "From time to time, but I have a little money as a backup."

"What about wandering around? Don't that get old?"

"There is a saying 'Not all those who wander are lost.'"

Freddy raised his eyebrows, "Wow, that is deep."

Daniel walked back to the corner of the boxcar where his guitar leaned against the wall and sat down. He motioned for Freddy to join him."

After Freddy settled in, Daniel said, "Sometimes people who seem to be drifting around aimlessly have a goal in mind. Take Jesus wandering in the wilderness for forty days. Remember the Devil tempted him three times, but he refused to yield to the temptation. What was Jesus looking for during those forty days? Clearly, he had something in mind because his eyes were set on loftier goals."

"So you're saying he was wandering, but was not lost."

"Yep, that's what I'm saying."

The train had passed through the rainstorm and the men fell silent reflecting on their conversation.

Daniel resumed talking. "I used to do a lot of reading when I was young. From time to time, I would run across something that was really so weird it boggled my imagination. Have you ever heard of the Loretto Chapel of Santa Fe, New Mexico?"

"Can't say that I have. Should I have heard of it?"

Daniel's eyes twinkled, "It's a great hobo story. The Catholic Church sanctioned the construction of a chapel there around 1873. The chapel was so small there was no room for a staircase to the choir loft."

"That sounds pretty stupid to me. Didn't they see the problem as they were building it?"

"Who knows? The nuns were so distraught that they could not use the choir loft so they begged God for help. One day, a wayward carpenter appeared at the chapel and offered to solve their problem under certain conditions. They could not watch what he was doing nor could he take payment. The sisters agreed and gave the man free rein over the building. After a few weeks, the nuns' curiosity got the best of them and they went to inspect the project. The carpenter was gone, but he had built a miraculous double-spiraled helical stairwell on one side of the chapel so anyone could reach the choir loft easily. The amazing thing was there was no visible means of support for the staircase. Most of these designs had a central pole called a newel that supported the stairs, but this one did not. Even today, carpenters are impressed with its design. The man never used nails or metal rods. Apparently, he understood how he could use the forces of tension and compression with wooden dowels to hold it together. It's still considered an inspired masterpiece of woodcraft."

Freddy was astonished. "Have you ever seen it first hand?"

Daniel replied, "Yes, I was in Santa Fe a few months ago and went to the chapel to light a candle for someone. It's awe-inspiring to see the craftsmanship. Some things are so beautiful they are indelibly etched into your mind. This is one of them."

"And no one ever learned who the man was or how he did it?"

"No, but it was not lost on the nuns that he was a traveling carpenter. Where have we heard that before?"

Freddy smiled. "I guess they thought it more than just a coincidence."

Daniel rubbed his hands. "Oh, I'm sure. But back to my point. Here was this hobo wandering around the countryside until he found a place to do something worthwhile or even miraculous. Was he lost because he was wandering around or was he fulfilling a higher purpose?"

He sat back down, picked up the guitar and began to strum it softly. "One reason I like to ride the rails is that it gives me time to think about all this. God knows I need absolution."

Freddy shifted his weight. "Well, I guess we're all in the same boat. We all need forgiveness."

Daniel fished a faded photograph of him and a woman holding a child on her lap from his billfold. "I was a family doctor in Kentucky a few years ago. This is my wife Laura and my grandson Freddy. They died two years ago."

"What happened to them?"

Daniel choked up, "Can we change the subject? Let's just say I blame myself for their deaths and leave it at that."

Freddy smiled weakly. "I understand, but you should not be too hard on yourself. "

"That's why I'm traveling across the country trying to find forgiveness, but I won't find it until my journey is complete. Hey, the train is slowing down. I need to get some fresh air."

The train pulled alongside a weathered station and Daniel saw the engineer leave the cabin. He grabbed the briefcase and hopped out of the box car and Freddy joined him. After walking around for a few minutes, they resumed their seats in the boxcar.

Freddy decided to change the subject. "You are a pretty good guitar player. Why don't you play something?"

Daniel took a seat on an empty crate and began to pick the strings. "My grandson liked 'Hush, Little Baby.' Is that okay?"

Freddy sat down as he answered, "Mom used to sing that to me when I was a kid."

Daniel cleared his throat and began.

Hush little baby, don't say a word
Mama's gonna buy you a mockin' bird
And if that mockin' bird won't sing
Mama's gonna buy you a diamond ring
And if that diamond ring is brass
Mama's gonna buy you a lookin' glass
And if that lookin' glass gets broke
Mama's gonna buy you a billy goat
And if that billy goat won't pull
Mama's gonna buy you a cart and bull
And if that cart and bull turn over
Mama's gonna buy you a dog named Rover
And if that dog named Rover won't bark
Mama's gonna buy you a horse and cart
And if that horse and cart fall down
You'll still be the sweetest little baby in town
Sleep child, and when you do
Dream a dream to drift you through the night
That lingers through the day
Tonight

If dreams are few
I'll sing this lullaby for you
Sleep child, for dreams always come true
Lullaby and goodnight, may sleep softly surround you
While your dreams fill your eyes with a melody of love
May the moonlight embrace you
The starlight caress you
May the sunlight still sing you this lullaby of love
Ladada ladada ladaladadalada

After he finished, he wiped away the tears from his eyes and quietly composed himself.

Freddy was so moved by the dulcet tones he, too, had teared up. "That was one of the prettiest things I've ever heard. Where did you learn to sing and play so well?"

"I used to sing to Freddy when he was little. Singing it brings back a lot of fond memories that ease the pain. He was such a sweet, beautiful child until some kids at school bullied him. Singing that song gives me hope that someday I can sing that song to him again. Do you mind if I take a nap? I'm tired."

Freddy smiled and said, "Me, too. Maybe we can get a bite to eat at the next stop."

Both of them fell asleep and did not wake up until the train had reached Centennial, Colorado. When they saw the engineers leave the train to eat lunch, they decided to do the same. They passed a small chapel on the way to a café and Daniel asked, "Would you mind waiting here for a minute?"

"That's fine. I'll order for you. What do you want?"

Daniel retrieved a small white candle out of his briefcase and replied, "A BLT would be great. I'll just be a minute."

Freddy hurried to the café and bought some sandwiches before returning to the chapel. He slipped inside quietly where he watched Daniel place the candle on the altar, light it, lay a small envelope beside it, and say a short prayer. After he had finished, Daniel walked to the door where he saw Freddy watching him.

Freddy stammered, "Hey, man, I'm sorry, I didn't mean to pry. I was just seeing if you were still here."

Daniel nodded silently and they wolfed down the sandwiches before returning to the boxcar. After they had got back on the train, Daniel picked up his belongings and shook Freddy's hand.

"Freddy, I need to seek my absolution alone. I hope you understand. I owe you big time for saving my life in Omaha, but I must bid you good-bye. Maybe we'll run across each other again."

Blindsided by the good-bye, Freddy said, "Hey, man, I hope I didn't piss you off. I enjoy your company. Are you sure you can't stay?"

Daniel shook his head ruefully.

Freddy felt emotion bubbling up. "I wish there was something I could do to help. How much longer do you plan on riding the rails?"

"I still have quite a few candles to light before I can rest. Take care of yourself, Freddy. Godspeed till we meet again."

He picked up his belongings, leapt out of the boxcar and disappeared as the train pulled out of the station.

EPILOGUE

Three days before Christmas, Phillip Rockwell knocked on the office door of Lowell Maxwell. He asked quietly, "Lowell, you got a minute?"

"Sure, what's up?"

"I think I may have solved the mystery of our transient railroad hobo."

"Really? How did you do that?"

"Last week, he showed up in Newtown, Connecticut. You know, the town where all those kids were murdered at the Sandy Hook School?"

"Yeah, so?"

"I did some checking and apparently he is going to every city where kids have been killed by school shooters. With a little digging I discovered in every place, someone had placed a candle on the altar of a church near the railroad. These were small towns with no claim to fame so we had no reason to see any connection. I think he was randomly choosing the towns to visit so we can't predict where he will be next."

Lowell frowned slightly, "Do we know where he started?"

"As best we can tell, he started in Hazard, Kentucky, where he had given his grandson a rifle for his Christmas present when he was fourteen. Two years ago, on Valentine's Day, the grandson, Freddy Miller, killed his grandmother and then killed four kids at his high school, before turning the gun on himself. After the funeral, the grandfather disappeared from town and began to ride the rails. We think he is doing penance for giving his grandson the gun he used to kill people. He's lighting a candle and saying a prayer in the towns and cities where children were killed and leaves valentines addressed to the children who were killed in that town. We surmise that he carries those valentines in his briefcase and that is why he is so protective of it. My hope is that when he has visited all those places, he will stop and find a place to live out his life. Of course, now that we know more about him, we have a better chance of catching and getting him the help he needs. He's not really a threat."

Lowell sighed heavily and walked over to the window where he could see snow quietly filling the streets. He said softly, "Phil, I think we need to just let him go. He's not harming anyone and God knows the demons that plague him at night. He's seeking absolution — making amends for his sin of giving his beloved grandson a gun that he used to kill people."

Lowell motioned for Phil to join him at the window. "I don't know about you, Phil, but I love to just sit and watch the snow slowly filling up the world. So soft, so white, so pure — it seems to change our mean little world into a little piece of heaven."

They stood watching the snow as it began to blanket the parking lot and neighborhood. Lowell whispered, "Have you ever read that poem by Robert Frost, 'Stopping by Woods on a Snowy Evening?'"

Phil took a deep breath. "I read it in high school English classes. It's very peaceful and soothing."

Lowell continued in a hushed tone, "Every time I see the snow falling I think of that poem and how it ends."

He wiped some errant tears trickling down his cheek. "Merry Christmas, Phil, and to you Daniel, wherever you are. How many more miles do you have to go before you can sleep?"

ALL OUR YESTERDAYS

Sheriff Danny Piercy was surprised to see a silver and black Monte Carlo with its driver's side door opened parked near the lake at Twyford's Point. Many local fishermen used the ramp to put in their boats on Lake Cumberland, but they used trucks to tow the boats. This car piqued his curiosity so he pulled his cruiser alongside the car. He scanned the shoreline to see if anyone was around, and seeing no one, got out of the car to inspect the abandoned vehicle.

As he walked around the car, he noticed there was no trailer hitch and no license plate. He found some clothing folded neatly lying by the open door and he deduced that it was damp from the rain that had fallen the previous evening. He carefully searched the clothes for any identification, but found none. Slowly, he walked around the car and took several pictures on his cell phone.

Puzzled by the unattended car, he returned to his cruiser and called his headquarters.

"Carl, if you're there, please pick up."

His radio crackled when Carl answered from headquarters. "I'm here, Danny. What's up?"

"I'm here at Twyford's Point and got a mystery. There's an abandoned car parked here with its door open. Late model silver and black Monte Carlo. Has a broken tail light on the right side. Doesn't have a license plate but I did find a pile of clothes by the driver's door. Has anyone reported a stolen car?"

"No, not here, but it may be from another county. There's no identification on it?"

"None. Might be hard to track it down. Wait. Give me a minute. Maybe I can read the VIN number on it."

He returned to the car to look for the VIN, but he did not find it on the windshield or the door post. Stroking his chin, he stood eyeing the car wondering how he might identify it before calling Carl on the radio.

"No dice. VIN numbers are missing. What concerns me is the pile of clothes. They're damp from the rain last night. I'm afraid we may be looking at a suicide here. Call the dock office and see if there is anyone who has a boat to search for a body. I'll wait here until you call back."

While he waited, he made his way along the shoreline about two hundred yards in both directions around the car. By the time he returned to his cruiser, he heard Carl hailing him.

"Danny, the game warden was at the dock and he's on his way. Said it was probably a good idea to have the rescue squad come out. He should be there in fifteen minutes."

"Okay, I'll just wait here and take more pictures of the scene. Already searched the shore but found nothing."

Carl replied, "This is weird. Bobby Feltner is on his way, so hang loose."

While he waited for the game warden, Danny hiked through the woods near the car, but found nothing. By the time he returned to his cruiser, Bobby had pulled his boat onto the concrete ramp sloping to the water.

"Hey, Danny, have you found anything yet?" he asked as he strode toward the car.

"No, I did not want to search until I had a witness here to verify that anything I found was legit and not planted. Is the rescue squad on the way?"

"Yeah, they should be here any minute. So let's see what we can find."

Danny slid into the driver's seat of the car and scanned the dashboard and front seat. He found a slender white feather in the glove compartment. When he flipped down the sun visor, he saw that a paper bearing a message written in calligraphy.

IT IS A TALE TOLD BY AN IDIOT,
FULL OF SOUND AND FURY,
SIGNIFYING NOTHING.

"What the hell…?" He handed the note to Bobby. "I always hated them high-faluting words. I cannot make heads or tails of it. What does it mean?"

Bobby replied, "It seems sort of familiar. Let's call the high school English department and see if they can recognize it. From the looks of it, I would say that feather is a writing quill. See, the tip is stained black. Good, here comes the rescue wagon."

The head of the rescue squad, Gerald McFarland, got out of the wagon and joined Bobby and Danny.

"Hey, fellers, so this is the mystery car. Any idea whose it is?"

Bobby handed him the note, "All we found was this note and feather. Maybe you know it."

Gerald read the note. "Oh, yeah, this is from Shakespeare. Macbeth, I think. Faulkner used part of it for the title of one of his novels. You hear the phrase 'Sound and fury' a lot but most people don't know where it came from. We read it in high school senior English a long time ago and I guess it sort of stuck with me."

Danny shrugged, "I guess you're smarter than me. What does it mean?"

Gerald knitted his brow. "I don't know the context since I don't recall the whole play. You might call Karen Daniels at the high school and see if she can interpret it for us. In the meantime, I'll call for the boats to come out and drag the water around here, but I doubt we'll find anything. If he jumped into the water before the rain, his body would have washed downstream. But we may get lucky."

Gerald phoned the boat crew and told them where they were. The men bantered idly, whiling away the time until the rescue boats began to drag the lake hoping to find a body. After an hour of futile efforts, the rescue team gave up. Once Danny was satisfied they had taken enough pictures and done an exhaustive search of the car, he called the towing company to move the car to police headquarters.

II

No one at the Poets Coffee Shop in Cookeville, Tennessee paid much attention when a black and silver Monte Carlo pulled into a parking place in front of the coffee shop. A middle-aged man with salt and pepper hair got out, removed a book bag got from the car and came into the shop. He laid the bookbag on a table near the back of the shop and ordered a large cup of Earl Grey tea at the counter. The three customers who were working the crossword puzzle or reading the morning newspaper ignored him as he pulled a stack of papers out of his bag. After straightening the sheaf of papers, he removed a tapered white feather quill and bottle of ink from a side pocket on the bag. He sat staring into space, in deep thought before dipping the quill in the ink bottle and beginning to write.

After writing a page, he drank his tea and went to the counter to get more hot water for a second cup. The barista greeted him, "Good morning, sir. May I help you?"

He replied nervously, "Good morning to you. How much is a refill of tea?"

"We allow folks to have one refill of hot water with no charge if they use the same teabag. After that, we have to charge you for a new cup."

"Wonderful. Could I please get a refill? Would you mind if I sat in your shop and worked a while? If I try to work at the hotel, I get distracted."

"No problem. Most of our regulars are students who are gone over the summer months. If you don't mind telling me, where did you get that quill?"

The man nodded, "I am a rabid fan of Shakespeare and was browsing through some bookstores and shops in London a couple of years ago. I found this in a dusty little antique shop whose owner swore to me that it is really a goose feather quill that was used by the Bard himself. I figured he was just giving a sales pitch but thought what the hell."

"Wow. That's a neat story, but I think you were sold a bill of goods. If that were really Shakespeare's quill, it would be over 400 years old and I doubt a feather would last that long."

"I had the same misgivings, but I found that there are some taxidermized dodo birds that date back to the time period and they are still in good shape. I am amazed at how well it writes the exact words of Shakespeare. Let me show you what I have written this morning."

He retrieved two pages of his work and handed them to her as he asked, "What's your name? People call me Will."

The barista smiled, "I'm Beth Michaels. Taxidermy birds are one thing, but don't you think that the tip of the quill will wear away the more it is used?"

Will took a deep breath and sighed, "I thought the same thing but I have used the quill for several months and can't tell any difference in the tip. It is what it is. Here is a sample of what the quill can do."

He handed her the paper he was writing on. She raised her eyebrows as she read over the hand scripted page.

Friends, Romans, countrymen, lend me your ears;

I come to bury Caesar, not to praise him.
The evil that men do lives after them;
The good is oft interred with their bones;
So let it be with Caesar. The noble Brutus
Hath told you Caesar was ambitious:
If it were so, it was a grievous fault,
And grievously hath Caesar answer'd it.

Here, under leave of Brutus and the rest–
For Brutus is an honourable man;
So are they all, all honourable men–
Come I to speak in Caesar's funeral.

Beth looked up from the papers and said, "Okay, it's from Julius Caesar. We read it in one of my English classes. I'm sorry, but everyone will recognize this. It's one of the most famous passages in English so how could you have just written it?"

A sly grin crossed Will's face. "But I didn't write it the quill did."

Beth replied, "Huh? What do you mean the quill wrote it?"

"That's what has convinced me that the quill really was Shakespeare's because no matter how hard I try, the only thing that appears on the page are lines from Shakespeare."

"Get out of here. Will it work for me?" Beth reached out her hand to get the quill, but Will pulled it back. "I'm sorry, but I don't let anyone else touch the quill. It might jinx the quill."

Beth returned his papers and thought, *This man is obviously a lunatic, but he seems harmless so I will just let him work until he decides to leave.*

"Okay, I can see that. I'll let you get back to work. Thanks for sharing. Enjoy your tea, Will."

He returned to his seat and resumed writing for another hour before placing the teacup on the counter and hailing Beth.

"Beth, I like your shop. Would you mind if I came back tomorrow?"

"Of course not. You can come as often as you like. Have you just moved here?"

"No, since I retired I decided to just tour the country for several months just to see the country scenery. I'm staying at the Holiday

Inn. I don't really have a schedule to be anywhere. I'll see you tomorrow," he said as he left the shop.

True to his word, Will appeared again the next day around ten o'clock. "Good morning, fair maiden Beth. How goes it with you?"

Beth replied, "Well, fair sir. How goes it with you? Doing more writing today?"

"Yes, I'm anxious to see what the pen has in store."

"Okay, Will. Are you telling me that you have no control over what the quill writes?"

"Sometimes it does seem to have a mind of its own. May I have my cup of Earl Grey tea?"

"Sure. I'll be curious as to what the quill writes today. Do you keep all the pages the quill writes?"

"Yea, I have quite a collection of them at the hotel that I have checked for accuracy."

"If you don't mind me asking, what do you do for a living that you have all this free time?"

"I was an English teacher, but I took early retirement. Now I'm a playwright as you can see," he replied. "Is it still $2.25?"

"Yes. Here you go. Be careful. I overfilled it a bit."

Will handed her the money and carefully took the tea back to his chair where he began writing again. Beth began to wipe off the tables and sauntered by to see what he was writing.

"Will, do you want to share what you have written?"

Will nodded and handed her the paper that read:

All the world's a stage,
And all the men and women merely players;
They have their exits and their entrances,
And one man in his time plays many parts,
His acts being seven ages. At first, the infant,

Hugging and loving in the nurse's arms.
Then the whining schoolboy, with his satchel
And shining morning face, creeping like snail
Unwillingly to school.

She knitted her brow as she tried to recall the passage.

"I know it's Shakespeare but I can't recall where it's from. Want to refresh my memory?"

"It's from *As You Like It.* Jacques is giving his monologue about the seven ages of man from infancy to old age where he has become like a child again: toothless and feeble in his senses."

Beth replied, "I've never read that play but I have heard it. Ready for your second cup?"

Will drank the last bit of tea and handed her the cup, "Thank you, fair maiden."

She smiled back and brought him more tea and left him alone to continue his writing. After an hour, he said, "Have a good day. I'll see you tomorrow."

He returned the next day, bought his tea, took up his seat again and started writing. Beth watched him as she washed some cups and thought, *He seems harmless, but I think I need to tell someone that he is coming here every day.*

After an hour and half, Will got his second cup of tea. Beth asked, "What has the pen written today?"

Will handed her the new pages that contained the passage.

Double, double toil and trouble;
Fire burn and caldron bubble.
Fillet of a fenny snake,
In the caldron boil and bake;
Eye of newt and toe of frog,

Wool of bat and tongue of dog,
Adder's fork and blind-worm's sting,
Lizard's leg and owlet's wing,
For a charm of powerful trouble,
Like a hell-broth boil and bubble.
Double double, toil and trouble;
Fire burn and caldron bubble.
Cool it with a baboon's blood,
Then the charm is firm and good.

Beth read the pages and handed them back. "Now that I know. It's from the witches scene in Macbeth. Macbeth has consulted witches to cast a spell that will make him king."

"Yes, that's correct. It's another well-known passage. It imparts a great sense of evil that is really scary."

Noticing that his cup was empty, she offered to refill it while he continued to write. When she returned, she said, "I'm beginning to enjoy seeing you because it's making me remember some of the plays. I have a friend who would love to meet you. Would you mind if I introduced you to her?"

Will replied, "That would be okay. I think I need to leave early today so let me finish that tea."

After he left, Beth called her therapist friend Jenny Sharp. "Hello, Jenny, can you come by the shop tomorrow about ten? I've had this man come in who writes passages from Shakespeare because he thinks he really has the quill that Shakespeare himself used. I don't think he's dangerous, but I need to see what kind of vibes you get from him."

Jenny replied, "I have a client appointment at eleven thirty tomorrow but I can chat for a few minutes around ten. What in particular has you concerned?"

"He says his name is Will. I think he thinks he is Shakespeare. He knows a lot of passages from the plays by heart. I think he's nuts."

"I thought I had heard it all. I'll stop by tomorrow morning."

Jenny arrived the next day a few minutes before ten and greeted Beth. "I came a little early to settle in. Where does this fellow sit?"

Beth pointed to the seat that Will always used. "That seat in the back. He gets Earl Grey tea while he writes. You have more experience dealing with people who are a little off. Just sit over there where you can watch him without being noticed. Is he eccentric or genuinely crazy?"

Jenny ordered a cup of coffee and sat where she could see the seat Beth had pointed to. Will came into the shop at ten and greeted Beth.

He said, "Good morning, Beth. I hope all is well with you today. My usual tea, please."

Beth nodded, "Good morning, Will. Yes, it's a good day. Here's your tea. What are you writing today?"

Will shrugged, "As I said before, sometimes the quill seems to have a mind of its own. Thank you for the tea."

A few minutes after he took his seat, he began to write. Jenny observed him carefully. She watched as he wrote as she went to the counter for a refill and leaned over to whisper to Beth. "He seems perfectly normal, but he is highly focused on what he is doing. Why don't you introduce me? Just don't tell him I am a counselor."

Beth led her to the table where Will sat working. "Excuse me, Will, I want you to meet a friend of mine who loves Shakespeare. Would that be okay?"

Will stood up and extended his hand to Jenny. "Of course, Beth. My name is Will."

Jenny shook his hand, "I am Jenny Sharp, an old friend of Beth. Nice to meet you. Beth tells me you are quite a scholar of The Bard."

"Yes, I used to teach English but retired early. I found this quill in a little shop in London. The owner told me it once belonged to Shakespeare himself. I thought, what the hell, I'll play along."

"What makes you think it belonged to Shakespeare?"

Will shifted his position and replied, "The only things I can get it to write are lines from Shakespeare's works. You can see it, but I can't let you touch it. It seems to have a mind of its own and I don't want to jinx it."

"I understand. What has it written today?"

Will sat back down and handed his paper to Jenny. "This is what it has written today."

Jenny took the paper and studied the writing.

> We are such stuff as dreams are made on, and our little life
> Is rounded with a sleep. Sir, I am vex'd;
> Bear with my weakness; my brain is troubled:
> Be not disturb'd with my infirmity:
> If you be pleased, retire into my cell
> And there repose: a turn or two I'll walk,
> To still my beating mind.

After reading the passage, she handed it back to Will. "Wow, that's impressive that you can remember that passage from The Tempest perfectly. I didn't catch your last name, Will."

"Just call me Will. I taught Shakespeare plays and sonnets in English classes for years, so naturally I memorized some of the better known passages, but the quill knows them perfectly. It is amazing, isn't it?"

Jenny agreed. "Yes, it is. You were very lucky to have found it. I'll let you get back to work. Would you mind if I stop by tomorrow to see how things are going?"

"That would be fine. It's always good to speak with a fan of the Swan of Avon. Nice to meet you, Jenny."

Jenny returned to the counter where Beth was washing some cups. Beth whispered, "Well, what do you think?"

"It's interesting that he would not tell us his last name. He was an English teacher so I'm not surprised he could write that whole passage from memory. It is a very well-known passage. He seems harmless. Gotta run, but I'll stop by tomorrow."

After Jenny left, Beth returned to washing the cups and silverware, pausing to give Will a refill. After he drank the tea, he waved bye and left her to her work.

The next day, Jenny returned to the shop a few minutes before ten. She greeted Beth and said, "I thought I would try to talk to Will a bit to see if I can glean any more about him."

"Good. He should be here soon. He's very punctual."

Jenny sat on a stool at the counter to chat until Will came in at ten.

"Good morning, fair ladies. I trust you are both well. My usual tea, please Beth."

Beth prepared his tea and handed it to him. He settled in and began to write. After a few minutes, Jenny went to his table.

"Hi, Will. Remember me? Jenny? What have you written today?"

"Yes, we met yesterday. Like I said, it is the pen that writes. Today it has written from Hamlet again."

He handed her the pages and she read it silently.

> To be, or not to be: that is the question:
> Whether 'tis nobler in the mind to suffer
> The slings and arrows of outrageous fortune,
> Or to take arms against a sea of troubles,
> And by opposing end them? To die: to sleep;
> No more; and by a sleep to say we end
> The heart-ache and the thousand natural shocks
> That flesh is heir to, 'tis a consummation
> Devoutly to be wish'd. To die, to sleep;
> To sleep: perchance to dream: ay, there's the rub;
> For in that sleep of death what dreams may come
> When we have shuffled off this mortal coil,

Will sat drinking his tea while she read. After she finished reading, she handed him the pages.

"I have to say, that I'm impressed, Will. Sure, that's probably the most famous passage from any of Shakespeare's works, but most people can only recite the first few lines. I notice that you have written from famous passages. So do you have any inkling what it will write beforehand?"

"Sometimes, but I just let it do what it wants."

"Do you find any special meanings in what it writes?"

"Not really. I have a whole folio of writings at home. The quill writes passages from many different plays and even some sonnets."

Jenny replied, "I'm curious. Suppose I ask you to reproduce some lines from lesser known works. Could the quill reproduce those passages?"

Will shrugged, "The quill writes what it writes. Remember that stanza from The Rubaiyiat of Omar Khayyam?"

> 'The Moving Finger writes; and, having writ,
> Moves on: nor all thy Piety nor Wit
> Shall lure it back to cancel half a Line,
> Nor all thy Tears wash out a Word of it.'

Jenny replied, "You do have a remarkable memory, Will. Have you ever wondered what it means?"

Will grimaced, "Sure. There is no way to change anything in the past so you just have to let it go and move on."

She nodded. "I have to go. I'm really enjoying talking with you. Can we meet tomorrow and see if the quill can write some more obscure passages?"

"Sure. Looking forward to it."

The next day, Jenny chatted with Beth until Will had finished writing. She took her cup of coffee and joined him.

"Good morning, Will. What does the pen have in store for us today?"

Will replied, "Macbeth." He handed her the pages he had written. She read the first page.

> Out, damned spot! out, I say!
> One; two: why, then, 'tis time to do 't. Hell is murky!

> Fie, my lord, fie! a soldier, and afeard?
> What need we fear who knows it, when none can call our power to account?
> Yet who would have thought the old man to have had so much blood in him?

She nodded approval before reading the second page.

> To-morrow, and to-morrow, and to-morrow,
> Creeps in this petty pace from day to day,
> To the last syllable of recorded time;
> And all our yesterdays have lighted fools
> The way to dusty death. Out, out, brief candle!
> Life's but a walking shadow, a poor player,
> That struts and frets his hour upon the stage,
> And then is heard no more. It is a tale
> Told by an idiot, full of sound and fury,
> Signifying nothing.

"Two passages from MacBeth. Very nice, but let's try my test."

She unfolded a paper containing several lines of script and asked him, "Let's try The Merchant of Venice. Could the quill write the opening speech by Shylock Act 2, Scene 5?"

Will smiled and accepted the challenge. He dipped the quill in the ink bottle and began to write.

> Well, thou shalt see, thy eyes shall be thy judge,
> The difference of old Shylock and Bassanio:--
> What, Jessica!--thou shalt not gormandise,
> As thou hast done with me:--What, Jessica!--

And sleep and snore, and rend apparel out;--
Why, Jessica, I say!

He handed the paper to Jenny who compared the text with her paper.

She chuckled, "Wow, amazing. Can we try another?"

Will grinned, "Sure."

Jenny scanned her paper before saying, Try Twelfth Night. Valentino's speech at the opening of Act one, scene four."

Will flashed a mischievous smile and began to write. When he finished, the handed his paper to Jenny.

If the duke continue these favours towards you,
Cesario, you are like to be much advanced: he hath
known you but three days, and already you are no stranger.

Jenny's countenance grew more pensive as she confirmed the accuracy of his text. She sat in deep thought looking at him incredulously.

"Does the quill write only plays or can it also write sonnets?"

Will shrugged, "Yes, as near as I can tell it can reproduce anything attributed to the Bard."

Jenny nodded as she did a search on her smartphone for a sonnet. "Can the quill write sonnet one hundred sixteen in its entirety?"

Will finished his tea and took a deep breath before starting to write. He hummed quietly as he wrote for about five minutes.

"Here you go. How did it do?"

Let me not to the marriage of true minds
Admit impediments. Love is not love
Which alters when it alteration finds,

Or bends with the remover to remove:
O no; it is an ever-fixed mark,
That looks on tempests, and is never shaken;
It is the star to every wandering bark,
Whose worth's unknown, although his height be taken.
Love's not Time's fool, though rosy lips and cheeks
Within his bending sickle's compass come;
Love alters not with his brief hours and weeks,
But bears it out even to the edge of doom.
If this be error and upon me proved,
I never writ, nor no man ever loved.

Jenny shook her head in amazement. "I don't know what to say. This is incredible. But let's do one more test. Let me look up something."

After a quick internet search, she said, "Here's a tough one. Shakespeare wrote some poems including one titled A Fairy's Song. Can the quill reproduce it?"

Will held the ink bottle up to the light. "I think I have enough ink left. Here we go."

He scratched the quill over the paper and handed the paper to her.

Over hill, over dale,
Thorough bush, thorough brier,
Over park, over pale,
Thorough flood, thorough fire!
I do wander everywhere,
Swifter than the moon's sphere;
And I serve the Fairy Queen,

To dew her orbs upon the green;
The cowslips tall her pensioners be;
In their gold coats spots you see;
Those be rubies, fairy favours;
In those freckles live their savours;
I must go seek some dewdrops here,
And hang a pearl in every cowslip's ear.

Jenny compared the phone screen with his text and sat stupefied after confirming its accuracy.

"Will, I have to say I don't know what to say. I have never seen or heard of anything like it. But you cannot really believe this is Shakespeare's quill."

Will collected his papers and put them in his bag with the pen and ink bottle. "It does not matter what I believe. It is what it is. This has been fun. I had never really tried to explore lesser known works. I am more convinced now than ever."

She walked with him to the front of the store where Beth was wiping down the counter. Beth asked, "How did it go?"

Jenny replied, "He's intriguing to say the least. There is no way in hell that is Shakespeare's quill as it would have worn out long ago. But it's hard to believe that he can remember all those passages. If only we knew more about his backstory."

Beth grimaced. "He's never mentioned anything about his past other than being an English teacher. Do you think he would be willing to tell us much more?"

"I have to admit it might be hard to get him to let his guard down. Maybe we could use his obsession with Shakespeare to tell us more about himself. I wonder if he would be willing to have other people challenge him."

Beth took a deep breath, "I guess we can ask."

The next day, the women joined Will at his table. Jenny said, "Good morning, Will. I'm still amazed at that magical quill of yours. Would you be willing to let other people challenge you to write out Shakespearean passages?"

Will laughed softly, "Why not? It might be fun. Who would these people be?"

Jenny leaned over, "How about some high school kids? They would get a charge out of it. Might inspire them to read more."

Will looked out the window as if he were trying to remember something or someone.

He looked at Beth, "That would be fun. Sometimes I do miss my teaching days. Some students stick with you. When do you want to start?"

Jenny answered, "Give me a couple of days to line up some students from the high school. I will tell them to find some passages from any of Shakespeare's works they like and copy them verbatim along with the complete reference to the passage. Today is Monday. Does Thursday sound good to you?"

Will chuckled, "Let the games begin. If this inspires kids to read more it'll be worth it. I will stick to my daily schedule so have the students meet me here at ten o'clock. One more cup of tea and I have to go."

Jenny waved goodbye as she left and Beth filled his cup again and asked, "Would you mind if I get a picture of you before you leave town? You are a very interesting man, and it would be a great memento of your time here."

Will demurred, "Beth, I'm flattered, but I don't like being photographed. I must have some Amish blood in me."

He finished his tea and handed the cup to Beth who took it to the counter. When she returned, he handed her a folded note as he left the shop.

A little surprised at his quick exit, Beth read the note

> Good night, good night! Parting is such sweet sorrow,
> That I shall say good night till it be morrow.

Will never returned to the shop again.

IV

After he had supervised placing the car into the compound garage behind the sheriff's office, Danny called the high school. A cheery voice answered, "Good afternoon, Wayne County High School. May I help you?"

Danny replied, "Yes, this is Sheriff Piercy. Is this you, Linda?"

"Yes, it's me. How are you, Danny? What can I do you for?"

"I'm fine. Can you please have Karen Daniels call me when she gets a chance? I have a mystery she can probably help me solve."

"Sure thing. I'll have her call you after school. Take care."

Danny busied himself in the office until Karen called.

"Hello, Karen? Yeah, this is Danny. I have a mystery on my hands. Do you have a minute?"

Karen answered, "Of course, anything to help out boys in blue, or are you wearing khakis these days?"

Danny chuckled, "Yes. Khakis. I found an abandoned car out at the lake and a pile of wet clothes. I never found any kind of identification anywhere but we found this note and a feather quill. It says 'It is a tale told by an idiot, full of sound and fury, signifying nothing.'

Written in some fancy script. Bobby Feltner said he thought it was Shakespeare, but not much else. I was wondering if you had time to look at it."

"Yes, it's from Shakespeare's Macbeth. Say, do you have time to meet for coffee at Burger King? I bet you would like to hear more about this play. As they say, thereby hangs a tale."

"Sure. I can meet you there at four."

"See you there. Bring the note."

Danny and Karen arrived at the Burger King at the same time. After ordering coffee, they took up seats in the rear of the restaurant. Danny handed Karen the note and the quill.

She examined them closely. "So this is it. Interesting that someone took the time to write the message in calligraphy. It looks like he used this quill to write it. Do you know much about the play?"

"Not really. All those Shakespeare plays bored the hell out of me.... excuse my French."

Karen laid the paper and quill down and sipped her coffee. "You might change your opinion after you hear about this particular play. According to stage folklore, the play is cursed."

"Get out of here. Really? Cursed?"

Karen smiled, "You'll find this interesting. When I took a class on Shakespeare in college, the professor spent a whole lecture discussing the stories around the curse."

"Okay, I'm in. Tell me about the curse."

"Macbeth tells the story of a Scottish lord and his wife who lust for the power of being a king. Macbeth killed the King and took the throne, but then it really hits the fan."

"So why the curse?"

"In the play, Macbeth consults three witches to guide his quest for power. You may have heard the phrase, 'Double, double, toil and trouble.' That was the opening of a spell the witches were casting. Supposedly, Shakespeare quoted a real curse used by real witches. They were so pissed off they put the curse on the play."

Seeing that Danny's curiosity was clearly piqued, she paused to sip her coffee as she pulled some papers from her bookbag and laid them on the table.

"I still have the notes from that class and I use them when we read the play in senior English. We usually alternate it with Hamlet. Anyway, the belief in the curse is so widespread and intense it is considered to be extremely bad luck to even mention it by name when it is being performed. People refer to it as The Scottish Play. Some people call it The Bard's Play. Just saying the name Macbeth outside its mentioning in the play will bring disastrous consequences. Are you ready to be freaked out?"

Danny laughed, "Go for it."

"The history of performances of the play is full of weird stuff happening, starting with the first performance in 1606. The actor playing Lady Macbeth died suddenly, so Shakespeare himself had to take the part. There are tales that real daggers were used by mistake and killed the man playing King Duncan."

She flipped to the next page as she drained her cup. "I need a refill. You want one?"

"Sure. Let me get it."

Danny brought the coffee to the table and resumed his seat. "So tell me more about this curse."

Karen replied, "There's quite a bit to tell, but some of it may be apocryphal. Here are some of the more famous incidents."

Danny began to read the papers.

In 1672, the actor playing Macbeth in an Amsterdam production used a real dagger and killed the actor playing Duncan in front of the horrified audience.

When the play opened in London in1703, the city was hit by the worst thunderstorm in decades.

In 1721, a mob angry about an interruption during the play burned the theater to the ground.

Many of the actors in the play have been viciously attacked for one reason or another.

Abraham Lincoln said that Macbeth was his favorite play and was supposedly reading it just before going to Ford's Theater the night he was assassinated.

In 1937, a large counterweight crashed to the stage, narrowly missing Sir Laurence Olivier.

In a 1942 performance starring Sir John Gielgud as Macbeth, two of the actors playing witches and the one playing Duncan died during the play's run and a crew member committed suicide.

Charlton Heston suffered severe burns to his groin and legs during a production in Bermuda.

Karen said, "You can keep those copies. There are many more cases of actors, accidents, deaths, muggings and so on."

Danny laid the papers down. "So do you believe in the curse?"

She shrugged. "Not really, but actors are very superstitious. You may know that saying 'Break a leg' is a way to say good luck to an actor before he goes on stage. My guess is that many people do believe in it. Most likely, the accidents are self-fulfilling prophecies where people do things that cause problems. Much of the play involves very dark lighting that may contribute to accidents."

Danny sat looking at the paper he had found in the car. "So what does this passage mean?"

Karen finished her coffee and set the cup on the table as she leaned back. "In the play, Macbeth had just found out that his wife who had helped him murder Duncan has died. After seeing all the bloodshed and realizing that he was facing a hard battle with MacDuff, he had decided that life is meaningless. Life has no rhyme or reason and all of existence is absurd. All of his scheming to become King had unraveled and he himself would die."

She paused. "Whoever wrote this was in a lot of pain and had given up on life. My guess is this was a prelude to a suicide — or a cry for meaning in a life that had lost all meaning."

Danny rested his chin on his hand before replying, "I guess what you're saying is that whoever wrote this committed suicide."

Karen made a face. "Or gone completely bonkers. You may never know."

V

After his meeting with Karen, Danny went back to the office where he sat musing over what he had just heard. Karen's ominous suggestion that the owner of the car had indeed committed suicide gnawed at him. He went out to the impound garage where the car was parked and stood thinking if maybe he had missed something. The car was completely out of gas when he found it as if someone had driven it until he ran out of gas and then drowned himself in the lake. Danny searched the car again but found no new clues. Ordinarily, the car would have been sold at auction or junked after a year, but he felt that there would be no harm in keeping it stored in the nearly empty garage.

Over the next several months, he posted pictures of the car with a short synopsis of its history on the internet hoping that someone would recognize it.

His efforts were in vain until fifteen months after the car was found, a middle-aged bald man came into his office. Danny looked up from his paperwork and greeted the man.

"May I help you?"

The man walked over to the desk and put out his hand. "Yes. My name is Chase Hunt. I'm a private detective from Cincinnati. I'm working on a case of missing persons for a family in Lexington."

Danny shook his hand and motioned for him to have a seat. Hunt sat down and said, "I was surfing the net and saw you had an abandoned car in your impound lot. Do you still have it?"

"Yes. We found it by the lake over a year ago along with a pile of clothes. Figured it was a possible suicide, so I decided to keep it for a while. Do you know anything about it?"

"Maybe. Can we go look at it?"

"Sure. Follow me."

Danny led him out the back door to the garage where the car was parked. "Here it is. It had no gas in it when we found it and we have not put any in. Do you know something about it?"

Hunt pulled a photograph from his shirt pocket and held it up to compare it with the car. Satisfied that this was indeed the same car, he said, "Yes, I think I may have some answers for you. Isn't this the same car?"

He handed the photo to Danny who agreed that it matched the car.

"I have to say they are the same. What can you tell me about it?"

Hunt returned the photo to his pocket. "This may take a while to explain. Is there some place to get something to eat close by? I'm starving."

"Jeanette's Diner is very good. I'll drive us in the cruiser."

"That'll be great. I'm so sick of McDonald's and Arby's. I have been working on this case for over a year. It has been a real slog."

The men got into the car and Danny drove them to the restaurant. Rita, the waitress, greeted them, "Well, howdy, Danny. Two for lunch?"

"Yes. This is a detective working on the abandoned car case. Rita meet Chase Hunt."

"Nice to meet you. What do you folks want?"

Danny replied, "You still have the best chicken around. Mr. Hunt, you'll love it."

They both ordered the fried chicken plate and coffee. Hunt stirred sugar and cream in his cup and said, "This may take a while. If I'm correct, the car belongs to a man named Garrett Moore. He was a teacher in Lexington who disappeared almost two years ago. This is pretty complicated so it will take some time to explain. The family hired me to investigate his disappearance. They gave me a photograph of him and his car."

Danny rested his chin on his right hand. "Didn't they report him as missing?"

"Yes, but nothing turned up. After a couple of months, I told them that I was at a loss and saw no point in continuing to take their money, but I would keep an eye out for him. Here's his picture."

He handed Danny a photo of a handsome man in a suit and tie. Danny asked, "So what's his story? Why would be kill himself?"

Hunt clasped his hands in front of himself. "Moore was a popular English teacher at Dinsmore High School in Lexington. Originally, he was hired to teach at Morgan Junior High School. As I understand it, there was a special education unit there that taught mentally disabled kids. There were several kids with Down's Syndrome in it. If you are familiar with the disorder, you know there is a particular set of characteristics associated with it. Almond shaped eyes. Wide flat faces. Short hands. A lot of them smile a lot."

Danny nodded as Hunt continued, "For some reason, Moore took a special interest in one of these kids named Rodney Perkins. Little black kid about fourteen or so. Poor family. Father had died when the kid was two. Alene was a single mom trying to raise a special needs kid by herself."

The waitress brought their food over. She said, "Here's your dinners, Danny. Hope you enjoy them. Holler if you need anything."

As they began to eat lunch, Hunt occasionally interrupted his lunch to tell the story. "Now, Moore was a single man. And before you ask, he was not gay or a child abuser. He just seemed to be dedicated to his work. Anyway, he sorta took Rodney under his wing. Bought him birthday gifts and Christmas gifts. Basketball, football, things the kid could enjoy. This is delicious chicken and great mashed potatoes."

"Best food for miles. I guess he saw the kid as a charity case."

"Probably. When Rodney turned sixteen, he had to transfer to the high school. As luck would have it, Moore was also transferred there so he could keep an eye on the kid. Moore was a Shakespeare aficionado who sometimes dressed in costumes to engage his students. The kids loved him."

He paused to take a drink before continuing, "Things were fine until Rodney turned twenty-one and aged out of school. There were some good-hearted people who hired him as a busboy or dishwasher so he could earn a little money. His mom was on food stamps and worked at a local shirt factory so the extra money came in handy. Anyway, once he left school, Moore couldn't keep up with him as much."

"Understandable. So what happened?"

Hunt finished eating. "Damn fine meal. I need more coffee."

Danny motioned for Rita to bring the coffee pot.

She came over and asked, "How was your lunch?"

Hunt gave her a thumbs up. "Great. Best meal I've had in a long time. Good coffee."

"Leave room for dessert? Apple pie a la mode."

"Not yet, I'm stuffed."

Rita left and after a sip of coffee, Hunt said. "Where was I? Oh, yeah. Senior English classes at the high school were required to study one of Shakespeare's tragedies and present the play. For years, the classes had chosen Hamlet but once in a while they had done King Lear or Romeo and Juliet. No one had ever staged Macbeth."

Danny interjected, "Because of the curse?"

"Oh, you know about that curse. About three years ago, Moore discussed the story of the curse and all the weird crap that happened and the kids were sold. They decided it was all a bunch of hooey and they would prove it by performing the play. They fell in love with the idea of the cursed play you know how kids are. They figured they could use the curse as a promotion to attract larger audiences."

"Yeah, I can see kids doing that. Teenagers. What can you say?"

"When word leaked out about the kids performing the play, Moore caught some pressure to not do it I guess because some other teachers spread the word about the curse. But Moore argued that this was the students' idea and he did not want to curb their enthusiasm."

Danny stroked his chin. "Why do I get the feeling this is not going to end well?"

Hunt leaned back and turned both palms up. "Finally, the opposition gave in. The kids and their parents built all the sets and made most of the costumes themselves. One of them went online and found an inexpensive crown that looked like the real thing. Moore paid for it himself. The kids were through the roof and volunteered to have extra practices to make it as good as they could."

"So what happened? Someone forget their lines or get hurt?"

"On the contrary. Opening night was a huge success and the actors got a standing ovation. After the play, some parents wanted to take the whole cast out to dinner and asked them to stay in costume."

Danny raised his eyebrows. "I bet that was interesting."

"Oh, very. As it turns out, the cast chose to go to a fancy restaurant that had hired Rodney as a busboy. Needless to say, he was fascinated with all the costumes and rowdy behavior. Some people were so moved to see him enjoying the night they took selfies with him. When the kid playing Macbeth made his selfie, he put his crown on Rodney's head. You can imagine how absolutely delighted Rodney was. Moore took a picture of them and agreed to send a copy to Rodney."

"So where was the curse?"

"Good question. The play was such a smashing success they added two performances and got television and newspaper coverage. Some people made substantial donations to the school drama department. Moore won teacher of the year. Hey, I think I will have some pie and more coffee. Where's our waitress?"

Danny answered, "Rita." He motioned for her to come over. "Mr. Hunt wants some pie after all and we need more coffee."

Rita replied, "Sure. Be right back."

She returned with the coffee pot and a piece of pie for Hunt. He took a bite and rolled his eyes. "That is good pie. Thank you."

Rita smiled and nodded as she left the table.

Danny sipped his coffee. "So I guess the kids were right. The whole curse thing was just superstitious bullshit."

Hunt's countenance and demeanor changed to a more somber state.

"Well, as far as the play and the kids went, yeah, it was malarkey. But sometimes weird shit happens. The play ended just before Thanksgiving. Some of the kids believed Rodney had been a good luck charm for them. They told Moore they wanted to give the crown to Rodney because he had enjoyed it so much. Kids, right? Moore agreed that would be a great idea. The cast had a Christmas party the last day before holiday break and invited Rodney to attend. Of course, no alcohol — just plain eggnog punch —usual stuff. Rodney just went ballistic when they gave him the crown. Like a kid in a candy store."

Danny stared at him intensely. "I guess the other shoe is about to drop."

"That would be putting it mildly. Alene wanted to spend Christmas with some family members in Nashville. As she was driving along interstate sixty-five, Rodney began to choke. She knew that she had to clear his throat but there was no place to pull over so she tried to slap him on the back while driving. But she lost control of the car and it ran off the road and exploded. Threw Rodney out and broke his neck. Guess he was not wearing a seat belt. No matter. His mother catches fire and is staggering along the road dripping flesh trying to find her son. Some good Samaritans saw what happened and pulled off to get her out of the road. Luckily, there was a cop driving by who could stop and divert traffic. By the time the ambulance got there, they had found Rodney's body but his Mom was in shock with third degree burns over half of her body. Excuse me — I have a hard time with this."

Hunt wiped his nose and eyes with some napkins and took a minute to collect himself. Danny sat stunned at the story he had just heard, shaking his head in disbelief. "My God. This is beyond incredible."

Hunt took a deep breath. "It's a hell of a way to remember Christmas the day your only child whom you have spent your life raising and protecting is killed. And you will relive it every Christmas."

The men sat in silence contemplating the horrors of the moment.

Hunt continued to wipe tears and blow his nose softly. "The mother was in the suicide ward at Vanderbilt under heavy sedation when they brought Rodney's body back home. He had some aunts and uncles who took care of the funeral and put the obituary in the paper."

He paused. "That is how Moore found out about it from the obituary column in the newspaper while he was having coffee and a doughnut on the way to work. So traumatized he missed a week of work. After he learned the funeral details, he had a friend go with him to the visitation. Rodney's mother was still in the suicide ward so she could not come to the funeral. Moore asked another friend to go with him to the funeral where the crowd was so big he could not get into the building until the final viewing."

Danny sat staring at his cup. "Why do I get the feeling I know where this is going? He loses his mind?"

Hunt nodded. "Eventually, but it took some time. For the first few weeks after he returned to work, he was morose and withdrawn. Then his teaching lectures became disorganized, then nonsensical. There were reports people saw him talking to himself. When the students began to complain, the administration insisted that he take a medical leave of absence and see a shrink if he wanted to keep his job. Got time for one more cup of coffee?"

Danny motioned for Rita to bring the pot. When she got to the table, she teased, "You fellers have drunk enough of this to float a battleship. You'll be awake all night."

The men chuckled before Hunt continued, "The shrink diagnosed him as having a psychic break brought on by a traumatic event Rodney's death. He admitted Moore to the psych ward and began treating him with drugs. Once the doctor was sure the drugs were working, he sent Moore home and cleared him to go back to work."

Hunt saw the quizzical look on Danny's face. "But things are not always what they seem. When he came back to work, he was carrying the feather and a bottle of ink. He told people that during his time off he had gone to England and found the feather in a dusty little shop. As a matter of fact, he did go to England where he bought the feather. The shopkeeper convinced him that it was Shakespeare's quill."

He sipped his coffee and poked at the last bit of pie. "I got it in my head that maybe the quill had some special meaning so I started researching quills. Here is something I bet you didn't know. Twenty goose quill pens are placed at the tables every day the Supreme Court is in session. You can't just lop off the end of a feather to make a quill. The tip has to be cured and sharpened. They have to be re-sharpened as they age, but they can last a long time. But not four hundred years. Moore had been taken. But he was convinced that he had the real McCoy. When he returned to work, he showed everybody and demonstrated that the quill could write passages from the plays by some kind of automatic writing all that paranormal bullshit."

Danny asked, "But it was really just him. How did he remember all that?"

"Moore was not stupid. Have you ever heard of hyperthymesia?"

"No. What is it?"

"Perfect memory. There are some people who remember almost every day of their lives, right down to the weather on a particular day. One Japanese man has memorized nearly one hundred twelve thousands digits of pi. Some chess grand masters can recall every game they have played and can reproduce them move by move years later. Moore had taught Shakespeare so much I guess he had memorized a lot of it. At first the kids thought his story of the enchanted quill was a hoot, but the administration had to let him go. Out of pure compassion, they paid his salary for the rest of the year. Two months, I think. So Moore collected his pay and disappeared."

Hunt paused before adding, "Now it gets weird."

"You mean this was not weird?"

"Ok, weirder. He is a public high school English teacher in a poor school district. Where did he get the money to go to England?"

Danny suggested, "Maybe he just saved it up."

"That's what people thought. A few of his fellow teachers tried to keep an eye on him, but one day they found his apartment emptied out with no forwarding address. After a few weeks, they put out a missing person bulletin and placed his photo in newspapers and flyers for post offices. Now are you ready for the shocker?"

"I'm already pretty damned shocked, but go ahead."

"Garrett Moore was not his real name. His real name was Alexander Burns and his family was extremely wealthy. Made millions in the oil industry in Oklahoma."

"You gotta be shitting me."

"Nope. When one of the family saw his picture, they called the school for information. But the school could tell them nothing."

"So why the fake name?"

"Apparently, the family became wealthy because they had cheated some of the Indians in the Oklahoma reservations out of their oil rights. There is some evidence that one of the family killed Indians to get their land. When Alexander found that out, he repudiated his whole family and chose to make his own way as a teacher. Legally changed his name to Garrett Moore and became an English teacher and cut off all contact with the family except for his grandmother Melissa Burns. Melissa doted on him and gave him three million dollars under the table."

"But why go looking for him now?"

"When his rich grandfather Chandler Burns died, he left an estate of twenty million dollars to be divided among his three grandchildren Alexander, Sterling, and Joseph. Now, his two brothers had overextended themselves and were in dire financial straits. They desperately needed the money. But the will is held up in probate court because they cannot find Alexander and they cannot have him declared legally dead for seven years."

"So did you ever find him I mean before now."

"That is when they called me. But it was like looking for a needle in a haystack."

Hunt sipped his coffee and poked at the last bit of pie. "Apparently, after he lost his job, he drifted aimlessly around the country. No rhyme or reason to his travels, but then I got really lucky. Someone had posted a story on Facebook about a man spending time in a coffee shop in Cookeville, Tennessee, where he would just sit and write out passages from Shakespeare. I drove to Cookeville and showed the waitresses at the coffee shop a picture of Burns. One of them recognized him and the car she had seen him driving. She told me everything she knew about him right up to his sudden disappearance about fifteen months ago."

He paused. "I posted a picture of the car on Facebook. Someone around here name of Parker Hollars recalled you had been looking for the owner of the car and called me. I came here hoping to find him, but all I have found is his abandoned car."

Danny grinned, "And since we have not found the body, the family can still not have him declared legally dead for seven years so all the money they paid you was wasted."

"They have paid me a fortune, but they were expecting to inherit their shares of twenty million dollars. Both brothers declared bankruptcy six months ago so they are desperately trying to track him down to get their share of the money. But nothing has changed. I still do not have a body so the will cannot clear probate for seven years or until Burns turns up. I did some background checks and found out that the family did indeed cheat and kill the Indians to get their land and oil rights. So I just said to hell with them. Seven years of good investments of twenty million dollars would generate a lot of compound interest. Karma is a bitch with a long memory and a voracious appetite."

"But why did he use that particular passage? I don't know too much about Shakespeare."

"As I said, when Rodney was killed, Burns had a psychic break. The world did not make sense anymore. Here he was, born to a wealthy family and blessed with high intelligence and a good job — had the world by the tail. Then he finds out that his family's wealth was based on theft and murder. Then the only retarded son of a poor mother was killed on Christmas, well, that was just too much to fathom. He blamed himself for inflicting the curse of Macbeth on the poor innocent child by giving him the Macbeth's crown from the play and could not live with that guilt. He withdrew into the world he knew best the world of Shakespeare where there was a sense of order or causality or maybe justice. Eventually, he found no balm in Gilead to ease his guilt so I guess he just got into his car and drove around at random until he arrived here where he drowned himself."

Hunt laid his napkin and fork on his plate, downed the last swig of coffee and looked at Danny. "But I tried to make sense of all this, I found the perfect passage from Shakespeare's Hamlet:

> 'There are more things in heaven and earth, Horatio,
> Than are dreamt of in your philosophy.'

EPILOGUE

The silver and black Monte Carlo glided to a stop as the last bit of gasoline sputtered out in its engine. The summer sun was sinking below the line of the mountain when Alexander Burns got out of his car and laid a new set of clothes and shoes on the hood of the car. After he had stripped himself naked, he put on the new clothes, and folded his old clothes into a neat pile that he laid by the car. He stuck the MacBeth passage behind the visor and placed the quill in the glove compartment. Satisfied that there were no identifying marks in the car, he walked around the car and opened the trunk of the car where he lifted a new bicycle and a large knapsack stuffed with camping supplies. Realizing that bicycle tracks might queer his plans, he slipped his arms through the straps of the knapsack and carried the bicycle over to the pavement. He mounted the bicycle, took one last look at the car and pedaled away into the dying light.

Made in the USA
Monee, IL
18 October 2021

80295080R00164